Vivian Conroy is a
25+ contracted titles.
crafting and spending ━━━━━━━━━━ on Twitter where
readers can connect with her under @VivWrites.

Also by Vivian Conroy

Cornish Castle Mysteries

Rubies in the Roses

Death Plays a Part

Country Gift Shop Mysteries

Written into the Grave

Grand Prize: Murder!

Dead to Begin With

Lady Alkmene Callender Mysteries

Fatal Masquerade

Deadly Treasures

Diamonds of Death

A Proposal to Die For

Merriweather and Royston Mysteries

Death Comes to Dartmoor

The Butterfly Conspiracy

Murder Will Follow Mysteries

An Exhibition of Murder

Under the Guise of Death

Honeymoon With Death

A Testament to Murder

MYSTERY IN PROVENCE

Miss Ashford Investigates

VIVIAN CONROY

One More Chapter
a division of HarperCollins*Publishers*
1 London Bridge Street
London SE1 9GF
www.harpercollins.co.uk
HarperCollins*Publishers*
1st Floor, Watermarque Building, Ringsend Road
Dublin 4, Ireland

This paperback edition 2022

First published in Great Britain in ebook format
by HarperCollins*Publishers* 2022
Copyright © Vivian Conroy 2022
Vivian Conroy asserts the moral right to be identified
as the author of this work

A catalogue record of this book is available from the British Library

ISBN: 978-0-00-854925-1

Chapter One

June 1930

When the news that would change her life forever reached Miss Atalanta Ashford, she was climbing the rocky path to the ruins of an old Swiss burg, fantasizing those tattered grey remains were the white marble columns of the Parthenon.

Her vivid imagination filtered out the tinkling of bells attached to the sheep grazing on the grassy slopes of the surrounding mountains and replaced them with the murmur of tourists' voices, speaking all the languages of the world. Beside her she pictured eager young people whom she was telling everything about Greek mythology, and a few feet away walked a handsome man with intriguing deep brown eyes who had cast interested looks in her direction as she explained about the Hydra of Lerna.

He might invite her later to try baklava at a table under

a large old tree in a shaded courtyard while a sole musician lured melancholy notes from his mandolin. 'I've rarely heard,' her male admirer would say, 'someone speak about a multi-headed monster with such passion, Miss Ashford.'

'Miss Ashford!' A voice echoed the words from her imaginings but it was not male or admiring. It was female, young, and decidedly impatient.

Atalanta halted her upwards movement and slowly turned to look over her shoulder. At the bottom of the steep path, one of her younger pupils stood waving a white item in her hand. 'Miss Ashford! A letter for you. It looks awfully important.'

Atalanta sighed as she gave up on the glittering vision of the Parthenon behind her back and made her way, precariously, down the path to her real life. She had done this many times before, always with a sharp stab of regret that the fantasies that made her so happy were just that: daydreams.

But she also renewed her determination with every step she took that she would one day see Athens or Crete or Istanbul. Now that she had at last paid off her father's debts, she was finally in a position to save money for her travel plans.

If only the letter wasn't from another debtor, who had found his way to her via the others who had been paid. It had taken her years to settle things and finally be her own woman. She wanted to enjoy that freedom. Admittedly, her vacation this year would just be a small trip to a nearby valley, but it would be the first money she could spend on herself since she had stood at her father's grave, knowing she was now all alone in the world, faced with two choices: running away from responsibility or paying the debts, no matter how long it took, and making a fresh start of it. The idea that that money might be snatched away by yet another debtor made her heart sink.

'It looks like a crest on the envelope,' the girl called, studying the item in her hand. 'Perhaps it comes from a duke or an earl.'

Atalanta smiled involuntarily. She liked it when people expected the winds of change to blow through the cobwebs of their daily treadmill existence. Still, it was extremely unlikely that a duke or earl would write to her. Her father had come from an aristocratic family but he had broken off all ties with them, forging his own path in life. He had so wanted to achieve something, make a name for himself, away from his birthright. He had longed to prove to his father that he could be more than merely an heir to a title, a man waiting in the wings to take his place in the row of ancestors who were commemorated in the family tree.

Sadness washed through her. Her father had died feeling that he had failed. Not failed himself, but failed her, his only child.

I wish he could know how well everything turned out for me.

Swallowing quickly, she forced her attention back to her pupil. A frown furrowed her brow. 'Why are you still here, Dotty? Shouldn't your father's driver have picked you up already?'

Dorothy Claybourne-Smythe was the daughter of an

3

English diplomat who had a house in Basel. She was supposed to spend the summer vacation there, if the family didn't decide to go to their Tuscan villa. If Atalanta was lucky, Dorothy would send her a postcard that could further feed her fantasies about travel abroad. She had entire albums full of postcards and pictures cut from newspapers with an invisible promise written beside them: *one day I will see these sights for myself.* The albums were her lifeline when things got hard.

Dorothy's expression set. 'I don't want to go home.'

It didn't sound rebellious, just achingly sad.

Poor girl. Atalanta jumped down the last few feet across a large boulder and landed beside her pupil, putting an arm around her narrow shoulders for a moment. 'It won't be that bad.'

'But it will. Father never has time for me and I hate my stepmother. She will comment on everything from my wardrobe to my freckles. I want my mother.'

Atalanta's gut clenched. How could she say something uplifting to his girl whose situation was similar to her own? Like Dorothy, Atalanta had never known her mother. From her untimely death onwards it had been just her father and her, rocked on the tides of his spending, with times when money was abundant and they could afford books and clothes and desserts, and months when they had absolutely nothing and Atalanta was sent to the door when the debt collectors came because they might take pity on a little girl in a tattered dress.

She had learned quickly how to read their posture, the

4

look in their eyes, and to determine whether she could bargain with them to give her father a little more time or whether she should offer right away that they could take something from the house by way of payment.

She had kept her face composed while her mother's jewellery was taken. Only after the door closed had she sobbed like a baby. Nothing left of her mother but memories, and the photograph beside her bed.

'At least you have family, a place to call home,' Atalanta said softly to Dorothy. A stable home instead of constantly changing addresses and an existence walking a tightrope between hope that their circumstances would this time really change for the better and fear that it would never turn out the way her father projected. In his enthusiasm he often overlooked risks.

'Home?' Dorothy grimaced. 'Often I feel like my presence is too much. It's just about the boys.'

The boys were the rambunctious twins her stepmother had borne. Especially the elder, and heir to the estate, who never got corrected or punished for anything he did, Dorothy had often explained to her.

Atalanta couldn't deny that male descendants—heirs—mattered, a lot, in any well-to-do family. Still, she couldn't stand to see her pupil so dejected. Being able to adapt, constantly, to new circumstances was a great asset in life, as well as understanding that you could not always have your way. And that unpleasant situations could be made better if you changed your outlook on them.

'You'll have to devise a plan then.' Atalanta pressed

5

Dorothy's shoulder. 'Whenever your stepmother isn't nice to you, just imagine yourself someplace else.'

'Where?' the girl asked, rather perplexed.

'Anywhere you'd like. A place you've read about, a place you've been to. A place you made up, all to your liking,' Atalanta enthused. 'It can be your secret castle where you hide away when the world feels like a lonely place. In there you have everything you need. Friends, even. That's the beauty of imagination. It has no limits.'

Dorothy looked doubtful. 'Does that really work? My friends are here and they can't come with me. I'm not allowed to bring even one friend. My stepmother says we get too loud and it gives her headaches. But when the boys scream all day, it doesn't hurt her ears at all. It's so unfair.' She sighed and pressed her head against Atalanta. 'I wish I could stay here with you.'

The simple gesture and words raised a lump in Atalanta's throat. To have a younger sister like this, to feel an unbreakable bond... But the boarding school director was very strict. The pupils shouldn't form too close a connection with the teachers. Emotion was discouraged, empathy disapproved of. She had to keep her distance even though she didn't want to.

'But I'm not staying here.' Atalanta smiled down on her warmly to soften this blow. 'I've found a little village in a remote valley where I can climb and explore to my heart's delight.'

'So I can't write to you either,' Dorothy said, her

expression setting. 'I so wanted to write to you whenever I feel sad or the boys tease me.'

'Then write it all down and pretend you send it to me.' As a girl she had written countless letters to her mother, telling her what she had learned to play on the piano or how gorgeous the park looked with the budding blossoms. She had never written about her father's business transactions, or when the jewellery had been taken. That would only have made her mama sad.

Dorothy didn't seem to have heard her. 'But I couldn't have written anything meaningful anyway,' she said, pursing her lips. 'Miss Collins would have read it. She steams open the envelopes and glues them shut again, you know.'

'It's not polite to say such things about other people.' *Even if they were true*, Atalanta added to herself. Miss Collins was their housekeeper, postmistress, and much more. She was kind to the girls and an ally when Atalanta had a more unusual educational plan, but she was also insatiably curious.

Now, Atalanta took the envelope from Dorothy's hand and studied the flap to see if it had been opened, but the sender had taken the precaution of sealing it with an old-fashioned red wax seal. He had even pressed his ring into it. It wasn't a crest, though, as Dorothy had suggested. Rather, initials: an I and an S entwined like vines on an old tree. Whose initials could they be?

She turned the envelope over and studied the front with the neat name and address directing it to her at the

7

International Boarding School for Young Ladies of Good Repute.

No sender address though. Mysterious.

'Dorothy Claybourne-Smythe.' The name should have been pronounced with indignation but the speaker's lack of breath made it sound rather like an engine that had run out of steam. Miss Collins stood beside them, putting her fleshy hands on her hips. 'Your father's chauffeur has arrived and is waiting for you. Why are you not packed and ready? Where is your hat? It does not do to run around bareheaded.' She cast a half-reproving, half-amused look at Atalanta. 'That goes for you too, Miss Ashford.'

Atalanta reached up with her free hand to feel across her head as she became suddenly conscious she wasn't wearing a hat. 'Yes, Miss Collins,' she murmured obediently, noting to herself that if, by some miracle, she did ever get to the Parthenon, a stylish sunhat would be an essential.

Dorothy said, 'Bye, Miss Ashford. Thank you for what you said,' and ran off down the broad paved footpath leading back to the school.

Atalanta felt the emptiness where the girl's head had rested against her. Her pupils trusted her and confided in her, but those wonderful moments reminded her sharply that she herself had no one to turn to. That she had to fend for herself.

Miss Collins stayed in position, glancing curiously at the letter in Atalanta's hand. 'I didn't know the mailman had come.'

Apparently, Dorothy, skulking about to avoid her

father's chauffeur for as long as she possibly could, had managed to lay her hands on the letter before the postmistress had even noticed its arrival.

'It reached me without problems, *merci*.' Atalanta smiled. 'I will now continue what I was doing. *Au revoir*.' And she retraced her steps up to the burgh ruins. She knew Miss Collins thought it very unladylike to 'scramble up paths', as she called it and would not follow her, giving her the privacy she craved to look inside her mysterious letter. If it was bad news, she would have time to compose herself before returning to the school.

And if it was good news... But what good news could it possibly be?

After a few minutes of climbing, she stood on the top of the small hill amongst the cracked stones and mossed formations of what once had been a burg overlooking the village below.

Pink and white wildflowers bloomed between the stones, bees buzzed, and overhead the red kite let out its eerie high cry as it circled against the blue sky, its wings spread wide to catch as much rising hot air as it could to stay soaring.

She pulled a pin from her hair to use to slit open the letter and then dropped the pin carelessly in her jacket pocket to look inside as soon as she could.

Extracting a leaf of fine, high-quality paper, she unfolded it and read the opening lines, written in a strong— probably male—hand with expensive blue ink.

Dear Miss Ashford,

I trust this letter finds you well and in good health. It pains me to write to you expressing my condolences at the death of your grandfather, Clarence Ashford, Esq.

Atalanta gasped, pushing her heels hard against the cracked stones under her feet to maintain balance. She had only seen her grandfather once. She had been about ten and he had come to their house to offer her father his help in paying off his debts. Atalanta had believed the arrival of a fine coach and a well-dressed man was the answer to their prayers but her father had only fought with their visitor, throwing terrible accusations and insults at him, and sent him off with a sharp order never to call on them again.

Later, as their situation got increasingly desperate and her father's health began to suffer, she had been tempted to pick up a pen and write to her grandfather, begging him for assistance. But she never had. It would have been too painful to receive a cool reply stating that he was too mortified by the earlier treatment to look kindly upon her request, or something of that nature. Her father had treated him horribly, and such a response would be natural.

Besides, she hadn't known how the revelation that she had contacted his family would affect her father. What if he became so angry with her that he suffered a heart attack or a stroke? She couldn't risk it. The chances of a happy outcome were simply too slight.

And now it was too late.

Her grandfather had gone.

The breeze felt suddenly cold on her neck and she blinked against the burn behind her eyes. She steeled herself to read on.

Your grandfather left very specific instructions concerning his last will, which I must convey to you in person. I have taken up residence in Hotel Bären across from the station. I will await you there at your earliest convenience so you may learn something to your benefit.

Yours faithfully,

I. Stone, lawyer.

She read and reread the short message. Her heart pounded painfully in her chest. On top of the shock that her grandfather had died without her ever having properly known him, she was now informed she had something to do with his last will.

And the letter said she could learn something that would benefit her. But how was that possible? Surely, after her father's terrible behaviour, her grandfather wouldn't have been open to supporting her in any way?

What could it mean?

Pushing a hand against her hot cheek, Atalanta forced herself to think, to ignore the turmoil inside her about the death, and the memories of that one time she had seen the imposing man with his grey hair and walking cane, and the baritone voice that exuded natural authority. He had smiled at her with a sudden kindness.

Before Father had said all those hurtful things.

11

She bit her lip. She shouldn't judge what had happened between them before she had been born, and couldn't fathom what bitterness of past injury had driven her father to react in that manner.

She looked at the letter again. *At your earliest convenience*, it said. And she was leaving for her remote valley the next morning. So the only opportunity to do it was today.

She checked her watch. Three in the afternoon was a perfectly suitable time, she assumed. All she had to do was dress for the occasion.

Meeting an unknown lawyer about a will was something very special. Despite her sadness over her grandfather's death, and confusion as to how she might be involved, she should try and enjoy this unique experience. It would probably never again happen to her.

Chapter Two

Fifteen minutes later, dressed in her carefully conserved best satin dress with her favourite soft-blue purse and matching gloves, Atalanta made her way down the street leading from the boarding school on the top of the hill to the train station below.

Red geraniums filled the pots decorating the wooden balconies of the authentic wooden houses, and an old man led a donkey by the bridle, firewood for cooking piled up on its back. A few branches fell off as he passed her and Atalanta bent down to retrieve them for him. '*Danke*,' he said with surprise in his features that a finely dressed lady would bother to lend a hand. Atalanta waved off his repeated thanks and hurried on.

The river wound like a shimmery silver ribbon to her right, and a sharp call rang out from the steam train traveling the track beside the foaming water, taking tourists to Lauterbrunnen where famous waterfalls dropped hundreds of feet along a steep rock face.

Atalanta could almost feel the chill of the water's spray on her face as she recalled her visit when she had first come to work at the school. Having lived in simple conditions in the busy city of London, she had never seen anything so beautiful and imposing. Working in these gorgeous surroundings had been a gift, even though it was one that hardly came for free. She spent long hours teaching both French and music, settling quarrels amongst staff, and drying tears from the eyes of pupils who were sure they'd never master the subjunctive. Her relationships with the other teachers were amiable but distant; they were colleagues foremost, not friends. The strict school rules prevented them from spending time with each other in their rooms at night, and when they were allowed to have an outing every now and then, those trips were organized by the school and usually had the same formal feeling as class outings that served an educational purpose. 'They are not meant for pleasure,' the director had once told Atalanta, and coming from his mouth *pleasure* had almost sounded like a dirty word.

Hotel Bären sat across from the station and was flying the regional yellow and red flag. A boy was sweeping the steps in front and withdrew his twig broom a moment so he didn't swish it across her neat shoes. She stepped from the blinding sunshine into the dimness of the lobby and halted a moment to allow her eyes to adjust.

Behind the reception desk, the daughter of the middle-aged owners was writing in a thick leatherbound book. Atalanta stepped up to her and addressed her in the German she had picked up easily while living here. '*Gutentag.* Is Herr Stone present?'

The woman looked up and smiled. '*Gutentag.* Yes, he's here. I will call for him.'

She gestured for the boy to come inside and instructed him in quick sentences. Atalanta looked around her, from the deer antlers on the wall to the cuckoo clock and the portrait of a stern man in local costume. Perhaps some ancestor who had run the hotel before them?

The boy came back through a door with a tall man in a dark suit who was carrying a briefcase. He reached out his hand to her. 'Miss Ashford? You are prompt.'

Or did he think her greedy, having rushed out here to see what she could get?

Atalanta flushed at the idea. She had never expected anyone to support her as she had worked hard to set straight her father's mistakes. To be considered a scavenger now, swooping in as fast as she could, would be a blow indeed.

But she couldn't be sure he actually thought that. He could appreciate her promptness as it helped him to conclude his business here swiftly. She had to expect the best—of him and the whole strange situation.

She pressed his hand. 'I like to get things done. Besides, I'm leaving tomorrow for a holiday in the Kiental.'

'You might want to change those plans,' the lawyer said drily.

'Why would I?' Atalanta queried, astonished. 'Do you need my involvement in paperwork of some kind?'

Mr Stone glanced at the woman and the boy, who were both gawking at them, and gestured for her to follow him. 'We will speak in private. You'll soon see what I mean.'

With a pounding heart she walked after him. His paces were short and sharp, underlining everything about him that was absolutely correct, as it should be.

He took her through a dining room where the tables had been cleared from breakfast, through open doors into the back garden with a wonderful view of the region's world-famous mountain range of Eiger, Monch, and Jungfrau. Even in high summer there was snow on their summits.

Atalanta smiled at them, the familiar sight calming her nerves. She was on her own territory here. Whatever was expected of her she'd face it with dignity.

The lawyer halted near a pond. Something jumped away into the water—a frog perhaps.

He turned to her and spoke slowly. 'My condolences, again, on the loss of your grandfather. Although I got the impression that you were not... personally acquainted with him.'

'No. My father was estranged from his family.' Atalanta put it quietly and without flinching. If this lawyer took care of all the family business, he would know about the unfortunate events that had shadowed her life for so long. Her grandfather might have discussed with him, at some prior occasion, what a disappointment his only son had been to him and how he had to guard the family fortune against someone who would not hesitate to waste it away.

But if Mr Stone didn't know, she wasn't keen on enlightening him.

He nodded. 'My client, your grandfather, has been very concerned for a long time that the estate built by the careful foresight of his ancestors would...'

Atalanta cringed inwardly, waiting for the word the lawyer would bestow.

The lawyer seemed to think it best if he was most prudent and said, 'Would be lost for future generations. He strongly believed in tradition and in passing on a lasting legacy. Therefore, he was pleased to learn that his granddaughter had developed into a young woman with integrity and a level head on her shoulders.'

The compliment took her by surprise. She had never imagined he would look into her situation, let alone approve of her behaviour.

Mr Stone obviously took her silence as encouragement to continue and said, 'Your grandfather informed himself thoroughly of how you handled yourself through life, both when his son was still alive and after his untimely death, and he believed he could entrust you with something special.'

Atalanta's mind whirled at the idea that the grandfather she had only known as the imposing figure from a one-time meeting had known everything about her. Why had he watched from the shadows, so to speak? Why had he not reached out to her when he was still alive? She would have given so much to get to know him.

'But I... don't deserve to get anything,' she protested. 'I never met him properly. I haven't been the granddaughter he might have liked to have.'

'On the contrary. You are exactly the granddaughter he wanted to have.'

Atalanta blinked. 'I don't understand.'

'This letter explains.' The lawyer extracted an envelope from his pocket and handed it to her. 'Your grandfather entrusted it to me with his will. I was to hand it to you personally and have you read it before I explain what his will entails.'

'I see.' Atalanta stared at the envelope in her hand. Her grandfather had written to her. She had sometimes imagined what it would be like if he did, if he had contacted her, instead of her having to reach out to him. *Now the moment has come.*

She opened the envelope carefully. It bought her time to steel herself against the possibly hurtful words in this letter. Would he refer to that terrible argument when her father had turned him out of their house? Would he explain how he had reached out a helping hand to them and her father had coldly rejected to take it, preferring to plunge himself—and her—into more trouble than to accept assistance?

Dear Atalanta,

18

He used the word 'dear'. A breath of relief wafted through her, and her eyes raced to learn more.

When this letter reaches you, I will no longer be alive. I never planned for it to be this way. When my son died, your father...

Here the handwriting became less assured, as if he had been moved.

...I thought about writing to you. But I wasn't certain you would welcome my approach after I had left the both of you to manage on your own. I should never have been so stubborn as to retreat after that one offer. But my relationship with your father was always extremely difficult and fraught with so many emotions. We could not be in the same room without feeling such pressure, as if the entire house was going to come down around us, burying us both under the rubble.

Atalanta's throat tightened. She could well remember those highly charged moments when the two had faced each other. Even as a child of only ten she had sensed the emotions brewing and the unsaid words hovering in the air. She could not blame him for having felt slighted after the way in which he had been turned away from their door.

He had thought about writing to her, reaching out, like she had thought about doing. Perhaps he had, like her, sat at his desk with a pen in hand to write and then refrained, casting the pen aside with a frustrated sigh.

She swallowed hard as she read on.

I shouldn't have left in blind anger like I did that day. You were there to consider. My granddaughter, the little girl I had never seen before. I thought your father would be open to my offer, for your sake. It was obvious he could not raise you properly on his own. But your father was a proud man and I should have phrased my offer differently. Instead of pointing out how ill-suited his situation was for a child, I should have reminded him that I was getting older and needed him at the estate. Appealing to his pity for me might have brought me further. Although I sometimes think he would have seen right through it as he knew me well.

Those little words touched Atalanta to her core. These two men, estranged as they might have been, had known each other like no one else in the world did.

I assume you yourself have experience of his temper, but also of his kindness and generosity. He always followed his feelings, whether those were beneficial to him and his loved ones, or whether they led him astray. He stayed true to himself, always. As I stayed true to what I believed in.

When I heard of his death, I wanted to write to you and offer my support, but I didn't want to force you to make a painful choice. You might have felt like accepting my outreached hand was a betrayal of your father, of everything he had stood for. So soon after his passing I felt it was inappropriate and unkind. I had once...

20

Again, the handwriting wavered as if it had cost him trouble to keep going.

...believed your mother could be my ally in bringing about a reconciliation between your father and myself. It was shortly before their marriage that I spoke with her. I was very impressed with her and I believed we had a chance of succeeding, but your father was extremely angry when he found out and blamed her. It almost came to a breach between them. Your mother was devastated. I have never seen anyone so heartbroken. That convinced me it was better to leave things be, at that time, and also later when you were born. I didn't want to spoil their happiness. Remembering your mother's hurt, I couldn't write to you after your father's passing and ask you to make the most difficult choice: to respond to my letter or ignore it. I was worried you might feel obliged to reply, while deep inside sensing that it went against anything your father would have wanted. I couldn't tear you up like that.

Atalanta swallowed. Her grandfather had considered it well. He had not acted from anger and pride, but from a genuine concern for her situation. And beneath it all reverberated his love for a son who had never wanted to be near him but whom he had never been able to let go.

Still, I asked my lawyers to keep an eye on you and inform me as soon as you were in trouble. I felt ashamed when they informed me you had found a position at a prestigious Swiss school and were a respected teacher there. I should have known you would make something marvellous of yourself, without me.

The words blurred a moment before her eyes and she had to blink to clear her vision.

I thought you had started a new life, far away from England and all your difficulties. Only later did I learn how you sent all your pay to England to satisfy his debtors. You must have loved him dearly for what you did, paying off all his debts and ensuring his name wasn't blemished. When Stone told me about it, I felt it confirmed the plan I was already considering.

You see, Atalanta, I have much to leave behind, and I can only leave it to someone I trust.

Atalanta sucked in a breath as the weight of this moment became clear to her. She was holding a letter from a man she barely knew who was entrusting a legacy to her.

'I do not deserve this,' she said to Mr Stone.

He regarded her pensively. 'Your father's debtors all spoke very highly of you. They assured me that your behaviour stemmed from a choice you yourself had made, not outward force. You could have washed your hands of it. You had no reason to protect your father, they said. He treated you badly, like he did everyone else in his life.'

Still, I loved him.

Atalanta stood up straighter and led the conversation back to the letter. 'Even if you informed my grandfather of what I did, I don't see why it would lead him to feel he could entrust anything to me. I'm but a simple teacher here. I've never been used to wealth.' Her head spun. 'I certainly can't manage an estate, if that's what he has in mind. Is that why you said I'd want to change my travel plans? Because I have to come to England with you to manage my late grandfather's affairs?'

'England, France, Corfu.' Now a smile flickered around his lips. 'You will certainly not need to hide in the Kiental when you have the money to take you around the world.'

Around the world... Imagine that.

An hour ago she had been alone, playing her game of wishing herself away to the places she dreamed of, and now she could actually go?

In a flash, the hotel garden around her changed to the grand remains of the Colosseum. Could she actually travel to the eternal city? From there on to Florence, Venice, Vienna?

Copenhagen?

Moscow?

Her mind whirled that it would actually be possible, closer to hand than she had ever imagined.

'There is one condition.' The lawyer's dry voice broke through her reverie. 'I don't know if it's in the letter? Or do I have to explain?'

A condition? What could that be?

She eyed him suspiciously.

'Do I have to marry someone?' Could she marry someone she didn't love or even care for to get the money and the lifestyle she had craved for so long? It seemed

23

unromantic and it felt like a lie. 'My grandfather might have felt I would benefit from a male protector...'

'Oh no, your grandfather wasn't like that at all. He valued independent women.'

'Really? I wish I had got to know him.'

'Perhaps I'm misphrasing it by calling it a condition,' Mr Stone said with a frown. 'It is more like... a vocation. Something he wished for you to do as he himself would no longer be here to do it. To continue the good work he has always done. Please read the letter to see what he himself writes about it. If it leaves any questions in your mind, I can further clarify.'

Vocation sounded quite interesting. Like a mission in life. A grand purpose.

She found the place where she had stopped reading.

I hope you will forgive me for checking on you behind your back, but I had to. It always hurt me that your father was such an unpractical man. He dove headlong into situations without thinking them through. I wasn't certain if you were the same as I only met you briefly when you were but a child. What I learned about your behaviour after his death suggested to me that you are very different. That you are level-headed and not afraid to take a difficult task upon you. You seem to think in solutions sooner than in problems.

Atalanta smiled and whispered, 'I had to learn how to in order to survive.'

I need someone who knows what commitment means, to handle my inheritance wisely. There is money, yes, and wealth involved, but those things should not blind you. They are merely things that can make life very pleasant. What matters is our purpose. I believe we all have a purpose, a role to play. My role was allotted to me, entrusted, so to speak, by the people who confided in me.

Atalanta thought of the many times a knock had resounded at her door at night and a pupil had come in to confess some minor transgression or ask advice to settle a quarrel with a friend. Even a younger teacher had taken her aside in the garden one day, whispering low and urgently, blushing as she wanted to know how to handle a sudden romantic interest from a life-long friend.

After their conversation, Atalanta had asked her why she had come to her. They had never before shared anything personal, just small talk. The other teacher had considered her question for a moment and then said, 'I think it's because you seem to enjoy problems. I mean, other people avoid them and ignore them but you face them head on. You actually like to look at the various angles of the situation and find the best solution.'

It was as if her grandfather had known. Because he himself had been the same? Was it a trait they shared, a connection across the generations?

Discretion guaranteed. Those are the words I used, sometimes, referring to what I did. I solved sensitive matters for people in the highest circles. They confided in me and I investigated.

Atalanta gasped. 'Was my grandfather a private detective?' she asked Stone. 'How incredibly exciting. My father gifted me a volume of Sherlock Holmes stories when I turned twelve and I devoured them all in a few short days.'

She had looked for those streets in London mentioned in the stories and stood there wishing the figure of the great detective would walk around the corner and she could shadow him to see where he went and what he did... although it might be impossible to follow someone that observant without being noticed. She had reread the stories many times after that, and the well-worn volume was amongst her dearest possessions. She didn't have much, but that book, and the one her mother had left her about Greek mythology, were things she'd never part with.

'A private investigator?' Mr Stone seemed to ponder her designation. 'In a sense, perhaps, but he never advertised his services, nor did people around him know. Somehow, he told me, the clients always knew how to find him.'

The lawyer frowned as if he wasn't quite sure how this worked but had accepted his client's word for it. 'He told me that once his death was widely known and the heiress following in his footsteps appeared on the scene, people might come to you.'

'To me? Surely that is a misunderstanding?'

Atalanta cast her eyes back to the letter in her hand.

I leave it all to you on the condition that when someone approaches you to ask for help, you must try to help them, the

26

best way you can. I can't tell you here and now what kind of help they will need. Sometimes you will have to find information. Sometimes you have to go amongst people to see how they behave. You have to be observant, loyal, and determined. You have to protect your client's interests, but you also have to follow your own path, as the investigation directs you. Most of all, you must never be afraid to do the hard thing and stand alone. I know you're capable of the latter; you've proven it. I trust you will also have the other capacities needed to make this work.

But I'm but a schoolteacher.

Atalanta felt again like she had as a four-year-old, sitting in a carriage pulled by horses that began to run faster and faster towards an unknown destination. The landscape outside the window was just a blur and she felt dazed and scared, wanting to get out of this. 'But will anyone even want to engage me?' she blurted. 'They don't know me like they knew him so why would they come to me at all?'

'He wasn't sure that they would,' Mr Stone said. 'But he wanted you to know that they might. If they do come, you can listen to the problem and see how you might contribute to a solution. You should consider it a great honour that your grandfather had such faith in you.'

A great honour and a huge responsibility. Her grandfather had written about how her father used to dive into things headlong without thinking through the consequences. She wasn't like that. She wasn't sure she wanted to take this risk.

Her gaze returned to the letter and the closing lines.

I realise I am thrusting quite something onto you. But it occurred to me while I thought it over that a woman can have advantages in this business; that she might sooner win the confidence of other women, much more than a man ever can. Women often know secrets of a household. And their instincts are second to none. I believe you can become better at this than I have ever been. And I will guide you.

Atalanta reread those simple words. 'He says here he will guide me,' she said, running her finger across the line. 'How?'

'He didn't tell me the details. But you are to live in his houses, and drive in his cars, and visit the parties he did, and then you will come into contact with the people he knew and discover what he meant.'

'Houses? Cars? Parties?' Disbelief filled her at the almost casual mention of all these things that had been far away from her, in another world, just this morning, and were now suddenly within reach.

But more than that, living his life could show her who he had been. It could connect her with a man she had never known but whom she had wanted to know. She could ask his servants questions about him. There might be letters, photo albums, clues to explain the troubled relationship between her father and his family.

In accepting this assignment to become an investigator of other people's troubles, she would also get a unique chance to learn more about her own past and about the family she had never had.

How could she pass up such an opportunity? 'I do want to try...' she said to Stone, her voice shaking with nervous energy.

'That's all settled then. I need your signature on some paperwork and after that I'll hand you the key to your Parisian home. You must go there first.'

My Parisian home.

Atalanta caressed the words in her mind, picturing herself dropping them casually to someone she knew. Miss Collins, for instance. What eyes she'd make!

'Your grandfather's manservant is there. He has the keys to the other homes and cars and he knows about all the arrangements. He will instruct you further.' The lawyer looked her over. 'Congratulations, you are now a very wealthy woman. I would advise you not to share this widely as it may attract the wrong kind of people.'

'I won't tell a soul,' Atalanta assured him. 'I'll leave in the morning just as I would have for the Kiental but I'll go to Paris instead.'

Excitement rushed through her veins and she felt like throwing up her arms and shouting for joy. Soon she would have her own house to live in, instead of having but a room in a boarding school where even the furniture wasn't hers. She'd have her own bed and her own bookcase to house her beloved Sherlock Holmes and Greek mythology books.

She need not work to a schedule of lessons but could instead make her own plans for the day. She'd stand at the foot of the Eiffel Tower, eat fresh croissants, visit the gardens of Versailles. Her head was full of images of everything she would see and do and try.

Try foremost. Life was rather dull when you could never try something new.

And every step of the way Grandfather will be with me because he made all of this possible. He will guide me. I will walk in his footsteps, finally feeling connected to a family member, to the past. No longer adrift and alone, but connected.

Thank you, Grandfather.

You have changed my life.

Chapter Three

'R ue de Canclère'.

Atalanta stood and looked up at the street name plaque with a sense of disbelief. This was it. Here on this fashionable Parisian street was *her* house.

She had just walked past the windows of dress shops and hat shops, of restaurants and coffee houses, and seen the silhouette of the Arc de Triomphe. Every few steps she wanted to halt and pinch herself to ascertain she was really here and not dreaming this up while walking in the Kiental where she was supposed to have been now. It was all a dream from which she feared to wake up all too soon, realizing that everything, especially the connection with her grandfather, was but a figment of her imagination; something she could only wish for because it would never truly be hers.

Someone bumped into her and she caught a flash of red and blue as the telegram boy sped past. He muttered some curses he probably thought she didn't understand. '*Pardonnez-moi*,' she called after him but the busy traffic drowned out her apology. Finally she was speaking the language to people who had known it all their lives.

She cast the street sign one more loving look and then turned into the street itself, walking slowly, relishing every footfall past the stone steps of imposing houses with lace curtains and polished brass doorbells. At one of them a lady appeared, dressed in an elegant coat over a silk dress that fell just below the knee. Her heels were so high Atalanta wondered how she could walk on them. She descended the steps of her home with an easy grace, flinging an end of her thin scarf over her shoulder, and stepped into a waiting gleaming motorcar. A car like that might be Atalanta's. A Mercedes Benz or a Rolls. She didn't need fancy cars per se, but the idea that she suddenly owned them was grand and she intended to enjoy every moment of it.

Number eight, number ten... Hers was fourteen. She craned her neck to see it, to drink in the glow of the soft beige façade in the morning light, the elegant shapes of the high windows, the gleam of gold on the stone lilies worked into the edge just under the high roof. Everything about it was perfection.

And behind its windows lay rooms that would tell her about the man who had lived here, who had taken her under his wing, a man she desperately wanted to know more about.

She had a key but knew that house owners rarely used it,

instead ringing the bell to have the staff let them in. In her case this seemed especially appropriate as she was new here and had not even met any of her employees. To simply walk in and surprise them with her presence seemed impolite.

She put her gloved hand on the railing of her very own front entrance, walked up the three steps and rang the bell. She could not hear it sound. She imagined that it was attached to a board somewhere in the depths of the house where servants worked behind the scenes to keep everything prim and proper. There was not a speck of mud on the steps or the door, although it had rained overnight and violent downpours always threw up sand and dirt. Someone had done their best to make it look impeccable for the new owner.

The door opened softly and a man stood before her, wearing a uniform. He had thin grey hair combed back across his skull and a narrow face with deep-set blue eyes. He studied her dispassionately.

'I'm Miss Atalanta Ashford. I am...' She suddenly felt a bit awkward appropriating what had been his territory under her grandfather. How much did he know about the troubled family relations, and her father's disgraceful behaviour? Did he have his own thoughts about her new position as heiress to it all?

Putting strength she was hardly feeling into her voice, she said, 'I am your late master's granddaughter. I'm so sorry that he died.'

'So am I, mademoiselle. He was a very good master. Do

come in. I'm glad you arrived so promptly. We have a situation.'

'A situation?' Atalanta repeated as she stepped inside. The curious word choice distracted her from her worried thoughts about his opinion of her.

The house smelled of wax and polish. Ahead of her were broad carpeted stairs leading up, with portraits in heavy gilded frames guiding the visitor. To the right were doors and in the back a corridor led away to what she assumed would be kitchens and servants' quarters.

To the left were more doors that had to give access to a delightfully light drawing room. She had worked out quickly that the house faced the north, which provided excellent light for painting and drawing. The back then was to the south, which was warm and pleasant. She wagered her grandfather had a conservatory there with rare plants.

If not, she could have one added. The first thing she'd buy for it was a snow-white orchid. Her mother had grown them, and after her death the plants had died as well, missing the loving care put into them. But here she would grow new ones. *Also pink and yellow ones, Mama. I can start shaping my own home. It's unbelievable.*

'A situation with a client, mademoiselle,' the manservant said. He leaned over slightly. 'She rang the bell this morning asking for the master. I informed her of his passing but explained that a successor was on the way. She insisted she'd wait.'

'For me?' Atalanta queried, surprised. 'But you had no idea that I would be coming today, did you?' He seemed to suppress a smile. 'I assumed you would want to see your new property. I was aware that the season had ended at the boarding school where you worked and I can imagine it must be dull and empty when all the pupils have left.'

'Indeed it is. Good thinking.' Naturally, her grandfather had employed a man as observant and quick to draw conclusions as he himself had been. 'Then we will see to this situation promptly.'

She had taken off her gloves and coat and handed these to the manservant with her purse. In front of the tall hall mirror she removed the small hat from her curls and gave herself a critical assessment. Her cheeks were full of colour from her vigorous walk and her hair was neat. Her clothes weren't very elegant perhaps, but it would do well not to outshine her visitor. Better to look professional, she supposed. She had no idea what this client would expect of her, but she was determined to tackle the 'situation' head on.

'You haven't told me your name yet,' she said to the manservant.

'Excuse me, mademoiselle. You may call me Renard.'

'Renard? Fox?' she queried. 'Are you French?'

'Half-French, half-English, mademoiselle.' He didn't blink under her questions, and though she was entitled to them it did feel odd to interrogate a man who was twice as old as she was, or older. There was something about butlers and manservants that was kind of impersonal and ageless, she had observed before. Still, they had feelings too, and she didn't want to treat him callously. In fact, she might

35

even learn something useful by tapping into his knowledge. Servants were the eyes and ears around a house.

'Can you tell me anything about the client? Do you know her?'

'Everyone in Paris knows her, mademoiselle.' It sounded like a matter-of-fact statement but still Atalanta felt a bit chastised. Should she have bought a few papers and read up on the news, perhaps? What matters currently excited the Parisian public? What whispers echoed in the halls of theatres and opera houses?

'So she is famous?' she asked carefully, feeling her way to more information.

'She comes from a very well-to-do family here in the city. Her father owns several factories and her mother was a concert pianist before she married. She still performs regularly at soirées. The client is the youngest of three daughters but the first to get married. A few months ago her parents suddenly announced her engagement to the Comte de Surmonne. The two of them have been in all the social columns since then, attending parties and exhibitions. You can hardly open a newspaper without the pretty face of Eugénie Frontenac smiling back at you.'

'I see.' Atalanta tried to commit the essentials to memory as best she could. 'And Eugénie Frontenac is now here? With a problem?'

'A situation, we like to call it. My master... he was very discreet.' Renard smiled. 'Rich people don't have problems, he used to say. They are too important and too self-sufficient for that. Instead they get into situations, which careful consideration might solve.'

It sounded like her grandfather hadn't just been discreet but also discerning. Indeed, the affluent families of her pupils had considered themselves above the daily cares of the other people in the world. They didn't want to hear from the school that their daughters missed home or failed tests. The school was supposed to take care of that.

She would have to learn how to phrase things in a circumspect manner, something she feared would be quite contrary to her inclinations. But as a teacher she had often not been in a position to talk back and had learned how to deliver the truth without offending anyone. That might come in useful here.

'We must then see this young lady,' she told Renard. 'And find out how we may assist her.'

'How do you know she is young?'

'You mentioned her being the youngest of three daughters and the first to marry. Girls from well-to-do families often marry young. So her sisters won't be forty.' She realized too late that it had been a less than subtle test and gave him a probing look. He didn't show any sign of being satisfied or slightly put in place.

Had her grandfather given this man instructions to test her? His enigmatic words in the letter that he would guide her still occupied her thoughts. *How then?*

Renard strode ahead of her and opened the door leading into the second room on the left. It held a gorgeous piano against the far wall and elegant sofas to the right. Atalanta could see a fashionable crowd gathering here to hear an accomplished lady perform. But her grandfather had lived here alone. Had he invited friends over? Had he been close with certain families? Could she hope to meet people who would tell her things about him that helped her understand him better?

From one of the sofas a young lady rose to her feet. She had golden hair piled high onto her head and secured with a red feather fascinator. Her yellow dress had a red embroidered collar and cuffs. Her hands sparkled with rings and bracelets. She wasn't tall but she carried herself with an easy grace as she stepped up to Atalanta. '*Bonjour.* You are the successor mentioned to me?'

Before Atalanta could confirm, her client burst into panicked speech. 'You must help me remove this stain from my happiness. It can't be true. It can't be. But until I know for certain, I will not have a moment's peace.' She wrung her pale hands.

Atalanta spied her purse lying on the sofa with a pair of crinkled gloves. Apparently, Mademoiselle Frontenac had been extremely nervous waiting for someone to come to her, mangling her gloves to the point of tearing them. As she had been alone then, it suggested her distress was sincere. 'How may I help you?' she asked.

'I will bring some tea,' Renard intoned and retreated to the door.

'With chocolates, *s'il vous plaît.*' The young lady smiled at him. 'I need some sugar to restore me.'

She gestured for Atalanta to come to the sofas. 'Shall we sit here?'

Atalanta was slightly overtaken to be invited to sit down in her own home, but at the same time it was fascinating to see how quickly the mood of the client had changed from helpless to in charge. Of course, she was the youngest child, probably terribly spoiled and used to snapping her fingers and getting what she wanted. Atalanta had enough experience with such girls at school. It was best to indulge her client first and see how much information she could extract which might be useful in assessment of the case.

Case! She was about to take a case. Just two days ago she had been living her normal life and now she was in Paris following in the footsteps of her detective grandfather. *I won't fail him.*

Mademoiselle Frontenac said, 'You must know me and my situation.'

Atalanta silently thanked Renard for having informed her of everything she needed to know. It put her one step ahead. 'You are about to be married to the Comte de Surmonne.'

'Yes, and someone is trying to drive us apart.' The young woman threw up her hands in an exaggerated gesture of annoyance. 'I know people have been jealous of me ever since Gilbert proposed but that is only natural. He was considered a most eligible bachelor.' She smiled with satisfaction that she had secured him. 'He never had eyes for anyone after his first wife died.'

'Oh, he is a widower?' Atalanta asked.

'Yes, Mathilde died in an accident shortly after they were married. It happened at his estate. Very tragic. It took him some time to recover from the shock. He travelled and attended to business. He deals in art. He is like a treasure seeker, finding Renaissance paintings where no one expects them and bringing them to Parisian galleries. He is a genius when it comes to that.' She was silent a moment as if considering what more she could say about her fiancé.

Atalanta wanted to know if the marriage had been arranged, or if Mademoiselle Frontenac genuinely loved her fiancé, but knew it was a question that could never be spoken. She would have to find out some other way. 'How did you meet?'

'At a friend's birthday party in February. He fell head over heels for me.' Again, there was a little smile of satisfaction. 'We met in secret a few times and then my mother found out. She put him to a choice: break it off or marry me. He first thought it was too soon.'

She fell silent as if she remembered some other detail she was reluctant to share.

Atalanta wondered if the comte had ever conveyed to Mademoiselle Frontenac that perhaps their relationship hadn't been so serious to him that he considered marriage at all. What were a few secret meetings to a man who was in Mademoiselle Frontenac's own words 'a most eligible bachelor'?

Her potential client came to life again and continued. 'But after a few days away from the city he appeared out of nowhere and asked my father for my hand in marriage. He said we could start planning the wedding immediately and it would be perfect to do it in summer when the lavender fields are in full bloom. Maman had expected a long engagement so she could parade Gilbert at parties and get me the perfect dress, but of course she couldn't say *non* to a comte's wishes. Everyone was pleased.'

'Including you?' Atalanta queried. It was a direct question but one naturally stemming from the conversation. This way she need not inquire separately after Mademoiselle Frontenac's feelings. She hoped her grandfather would have approved.

Mademoiselle Frontenac seemed overtaken. 'Why would I not have been pleased? I am the first of three daughters to be asked. My sisters were so jealous. In fact, they still are.' She smiled again.

There was a polite knock at the door and as it swept open, Renard carried in a silver tea tray and placed it on a table nearby. 'Shall I pour?' he murmured, but Atalanta waved him off. 'I'll do it myself.' She didn't want the atmosphere to be broken by a strange presence.

As Atalanta poured the fragrant tea into delicate porcelain cups, Mademoiselle Frontenac asked again, 'Why would you think I wasn't pleased?' She sounded more vulnerable now, almost insecure.

Atalanta shrugged. 'You are so young. Do you really want to tie yourself to someone for life?' This woman was not much older than the oldest pupils at the boarding school, and some feelings of protectiveness swept over her.

Mademoiselle Frontenac shuddered a moment. 'When

41

you put it like that, it sounds like a sentence.' As she reached for the cup Atalanta offered her, her hand was shaking.

'I didn't mean to upset you,' Atalanta rushed to say. At the same time, the emotion spilling across her client's face was too interesting to simply let pass.

Her client waved off her apology, leaning closer to her as if to confess something. 'I do understand what you mean. My mother sheds tears that I'm leaving the house so soon, but I want to be free. Away from Paris and the constant gossip about what I can and cannot do.'

'And your husband will take you away? Does he not reside here for his business?'

'In winter he is often here. But in summer he stays at his estate amongst the lavender fields. I've never been there but Gilbert painted a wonderful picture of it. It's called Bellevue because of the gorgeous views across the surrounding land.'

'I see.' *And this is the same estate where his first wife Mathilde died?* she wanted to ask, but kept it to herself. Such an association was impertinent, suggestive, and potentially disastrous for her client's peace of mind. *Why, then, did I even think of it?*

'I wasn't unhappy with the match,' Mademoiselle Frontenac said. She sipped her tea and stared ahead of her.

Atalanta sensed an unspoken addition. 'Until?' she prompted.

'Until this letter arrived.' Mademoiselle Frontenac put her teacup down so wildly that brown liquid gushed over the rim. She grabbed her discarded purse and snapped it open, extracting something from within. It was a crinkled envelope. She smoothed it on her knee. 'This is so vile.' Her voice screeched on the latter word. 'So low and... I can't believe anyone could have the heart to send it.'

Atalanta looked at the plain envelope, which had a name written on it. *Mademoiselle E Frontenac.* No address.

Her client clenched her teeth. 'I still can't believe it. It must be some... trick to separate us. To destroy my chances for happiness.'

'What does the letter say?' Atalanta asked.

'See for yourself.' Mademoiselle Frontenac handed the crinkled envelope to her and stared as she opened it and extracted the contents.

Single sheet of paper, folded double. When opening it, Atalanta widened her eyes at the brightness of the ink used for the message. Bright red, like blood. 'His first wife didn't die in an accident. Be careful. Be afraid,' she read aloud.

She noted, almost absentmindedly, that the letters were formed carefully, avoiding any characteristic flourishes that could give away who had written this warning. The person had consciously been concealing their handwriting, something her pupils tried when composing notes that supposedly came from their parents explaining that Elisa could really eat no beans or Patricia should be allowed to play tennis every single day. Atalanta wondered if the twisted handwriting was simply a general precaution or whether it could indicate Mademoiselle Frontenac knew the person who had sent it and their handwriting. *Interesting.*

Here she was, extracting information from the smallest

details of this seemingly anonymous note as if she were a real detective. But her excitement died under the weight of the words entrusted to this letter.

The message itself was clear and left nothing to the imagination.

The man Eugénie Frontenac was about to marry was a murderer.

Stop, she admonished herself. *You don't know that. It only says that his first wife didn't die in an accident. If she was murdered, it could have been anyone.*

On the other hand, why warn the new bride unless the danger came from the man she was about to marry?

'Do you know how his first wife died?' she asked.

'Yes. Mathilde's horse threw her and she broke her neck. It was an accident for certain. No one could have prevented it.' Mademoiselle Frontenac looked Atalanta in the eye. 'This letter is a vile insinuation meant to make me break off my engagement, but I won't do that.'

'So your mind is made up?'

'Yes.'

'Then why are you here?'

'I want to know who sent this letter. I want to know who wants to harm my marriage. Or to paint my fiancé in a bad light. I want to know who wrote those accusing words and...' She almost choked and picked up her tea again to sip and swallow.

Atalanta said, 'Anonymous letters are notoriously hard to trace to a sender. This is plain paper without...' She held it up to the light to search for any identifying marks. *None*.

'Without further clues as to its origin. The handwriting isn't instructive either. The ink...' She studied it. 'I doubt we could trace it even if I tried. I see the envelope only has your name on it. How was it delivered to you?'

'That was the oddest bit of it. Our cook went out to buy fresh vegetables. She carried a large basket on her arm. When she came home and took the carrots and leeks from the basket, the letter was amongst it. She had the chambermaid bring it up to me. Of course, once I had read it, I went down to the kitchens myself to ask her how she had come by it, but other than that someone must have slipped it into the basket while she was at the market, I learned nothing from her.' It sounded deprecating.

Atalanta said, 'I see. And you can't attribute it to mere spite and leave it be? You wish inquiries to be made?'

On the one hand it was natural that a spoiled young woman like Mademoiselle Frontenac was outraged at this stain on her happiness, but to engage a private investigator to find out who had written it went beyond merely satisfying her hurt feelings. Her shaking hands earlier suggested she was genuinely afraid.

Mademoiselle Frontenac sat playing with the teaspoon. Her expression was pensive and almost sad.

Atalanta said softly, 'There is more, isn't there? You can tell me.'

Mademoiselle Frontenac sighed. 'This letter has poisoned my mind. I know it should not have, but it did. I started thinking... My fiancé's first wife came from a wealthy family. When she married him, she brought with her a substantial dowry. After her death, it was all his to spend on his business, his search for new paintings. My father loves me and he promised me that he won't let me go to my husband empty-handed.' She dropped into silence.

Atalanta nodded slowly. 'You're afraid you will also die, soon after the marriage, and the comte will have what you came with to himself.'

'It crossed my mind. I know it's wicked, but what else can I think? Why would anyone write such a letter?' Mademoiselle Frontenac exhaled in a hiss. 'I try not to think of it, but it haunts me at night when I'm in my bed. I see the horse throwing the woman off and I wonder if there was a thorn under the saddle. I lie on my back staring up at the ceiling, drifting into sleep, and then I feel like I'm suffocating because someone presses a wet pillow to my face. I can see a dark form standing over me and... I can only think that I too will die and all for money.' She gasped for air. 'You must not let that happen to me. You must find out for me, before I wed, whether this letter is just a mean trick to divide me and my fiancé or whether it is a genuine warning, else I will never have peace.'

Atalanta sat silently, considering the situation. She wasn't sure she would ever be able to determine who had written that letter. Or whether the death of the Comte de Surmonne's first wife had been an accident. How did one go about that?

Suddenly, everything she had done so far in life seemed child's play compared to the enormity of the task that lay before her. Her grandfather might have thought she could do something like that, but—

'Come with me.' Mademoiselle Frontenac gave her a pleading look. 'Come with me to Bellevue and meet the people involved in my wedding. See if there is someone amongst them who wishes me harm or wishes me well with this warning. Be with me if another letter arrives.'

'Why would you expect that?' Atalanta asked sharply. 'The sender has what he or she wanted.'

'They don't know that. They might think I threw it in the fire, not caring one bit for what it said.'

True, perhaps.

Most disturbingly, Mademoiselle Frontenac seemed to think that the person who wrote it would keep targeting her, even after she had left Paris to travel to her future husband's country estate.

Did she perhaps have an idea in mind who it might be? Did she truly want an investigator to put her mind at ease that it was *not* this person?

Mademoiselle Frontenac grabbed her arm. 'Please come with me.'

Atalanta considered that Bellevue was the very place where the first wife had met her untimely end. Perhaps there were still servants there, or neighbours, or friends, who knew what had happened. She could make discreet inquiries to find out if it had indeed been a tragic accident. If the testimonies lined up, the contents of the letter could be assumed to be a poisonous lie and the mind of this distraught young woman set at ease. That seemed doable.

The bride-to-be clasped her arm. 'Please. I need your help.'

The gilded pendulum clock on the mantelpiece chimed eleven. The notes reverberated in the chest of the gorgeous piano. This was all hers now; her grandfather had made it over to her provided she helped people in need. Such a person was sitting beside her right now. Begging her to at least come with her to the estate and see what she might do about the situation. Her grandfather had written that, as a woman, she might be able to achieve more, and that was already true for she doubted whether Mademoiselle Frontenac would ever have opened up to her grandfather in the way she had just now to Atalanta.

So his plan was actually working.

She smiled at Eugénie Frontenac. 'I'll come with you. When do we leave?'

Chapter Four

W hile Renard showed Mademoiselle Frontenac out, Atalanta's head was full of thoughts about things she'd have to prepare for her departure. They had decided she would travel to Bellevue in Mademoiselle Frontenac's company and pass herself off as a distant cousin. Mademoiselle Frontenac had assured her that her father's family was very extended and contained many cousins no one had ever actually seen.

Nevertheless, to get all the details right, Atalanta had asked her to supply her with as much information as possible about the branch of the family to which she allegedly belonged. After all, a wedding would be a family affair and she could expect close relatives of the bride to be present and interested in her.

Nothing worse than having to duck encounters all of the time and fear questions that could instantly expose me as a fraud.

Her heart beat fast at the idea she was actually going to

do this, and at the same time it gave her an energy she hadn't felt before.

Renard entered the room so softly she barely heard. He looked at her with a frown. 'Have you considered who to take along, mademoiselle?'

'Excuse me?'

'You must take along a maid or companion. Ladies of well-to-do families never travel without servants.'

'Perhaps in the last century, but this is the modern day,' Atalanta protested weakly. His reference to well-to-do families reminded her painfully that her father had fallen from his high position and she had never had the upbringing she might have had, had he been more prudent with his spending.

Renard continued, 'And you will need someone to assist you in the investigation. It can be very profitable to have eyes and ears amongst the staff.'

'No doubt, but I'm supposed to be but a distant cousin of the rich Frontenac family. Mademoiselle Frontenac asked me what my talents were, besides sleuthing...' Here Atalanta blushed slightly as she wasn't fully convinced yet she did indeed possess this talent. 'And I told her I teach French and music. She immediately brightened and said I could play the piano on the evening of the wedding feast as her fiancé has also engaged a well-known singer to attend the festivities. One Angélique Broneur.'

Renard afforded himself a discreet cough.

Atalanta was very familiar with that cough—whenever she and her father had arrived somewhere and people had drawn each other's attention to them, nodding and then whispering behind raised hands. 'Is there something you wish to tell me about Angélique Broneur?' she asked.

'I would not want to gossip, mademoiselle, or influence your judgment before you have even met her but...'

'Yes,' Atalanta encouraged him to continue.

'Angélique Broneur is considered one of the greatest musical talents of the past decade. Critics write that she has a voice sweeter than the nightingale. Rich ladies in Paris rather say that she is a siren.' He hesitated a moment. 'I assume that you are familiar with the myth?'

'About sirens? Naturally. Mythology is one of my favourite pastimes. I read anything remotely interesting, whether it's the well-known tales recorded in *The Iliad* and *Metamorphoses* or more obscure tales.' Atalanta stopped herself before she launched into a long list of everything she had recently discovered in a second-hand book she had bought in a small antiquarian bookshop in the village near the school. 'They call her a siren to denote that she lures men with her voice.'

'With other attributes as well,' Renard observed drily. 'But the fact that Angélique Broneur will sing at the wedding of Monsieur Le Comte is... remarkable, to say the least.'

'Has there been rumour he's... interested in her?' Atalanta phrased it delicately.

Renard held her gaze without flinching. '*Oui*, but that is not all. She also sang at his first wedding.'

Oh. Atalanta let this revelation sink in. 'She sang when

he married his first wife who died in an accident shortly after?'

'The accident happened while Mademoiselle Broneur was staying at the estate.'

'Really? Now that is interesting indeed.' Atalanta paced the room. A huge clue was offered to her and her mind rushed to make sense of it. 'So we might assume that the two of them had an affair before he married and that she then killed his wife... But why? It would have made sense if the affair had begun when he was already married and she would have murdered his wife to free him of the tie so he could then marry her. But if they were allied before he married and then she killed the wife, and he didn't marry her, but stayed on his own until he met and decided to marry Mademoiselle Frontenac... the murder would not have benefited her at all.'

'Perhaps at the time she believed that he married for money and that if the wife died and he had the money, he would marry her. Her belief would have motivated her, not the factual truth.'

'Hmmm.' Atalanta halted beside the piano and ran her fingers across the keys. 'That is of course true.' Especially when it came to feelings, it didn't matter what the truth was, only what someone perceived to be the truth. 'But if she did kill the wife and her hopes of becoming the new Comtesse de Surmonne didn't materialize, why would she still be in contact with him? Why would she sing at his wedding? She can't plan to kill the second bride as well. That would be so... obvious.'

Would anyone really have the nerve to try it? Atalanta had never thought deeply about the disposition of murderers before, but now she would have to.

After all, I might soon meet one at Bellevue!

Renard said, 'You call it obvious, but why would it be? The first murder, if indeed it was a murder, has never been investigated. Everyone saw the horse-riding accident as just that: an accident. Perhaps she believes she can contrive another accident for this new bride? Have you never heard of families pursued by tragedy?'

'But why? Merely to have the comte to herself? She knows he will not marry her—if he had wanted that, he would have done it by now.' Atalanta spread her hands in a questioning gesture. 'It makes no sense to me.'

If passion wasn't the motive, then what else might be? Her mind raced past the mystery stories she had read to find something plausible. 'Does she have money?'

Renard pursed his lips. 'Undoubtedly she has some savings as she has toured extensively and is well rewarded for her performances, but she also loves beautiful clothes and jewellery.'

'She spends most of what she earns?' Atalanta concluded.

'I would say yes. When she's in Paris, she stays in a house on the outskirts of the city. I could find out if she owns it or rents it from someone, but even if she owns such a house, she will never have what a daughter of Martin Frontenac has. By comparison, Mademoiselle Broneur can never win.'

'I see. That must be painful if she does love him.' Atalanta stared at the brightly coloured rug under her feet, deep in thought. 'Love is such a powerful motivation in life.'

'I would rather call it revenge,' Renard corrected. 'I do not believe for one moment that Angélique Broneur honestly loves the Comte de Surmonne. Or he her. They are both too self-centred to care deeply for another.'

'How can you tell? We only judge people from the outside. We don't know what is in their hearts.'

Renard seemed unconvinced but he said, 'You then will be the pianist for Mademoiselle Broneur's performance at the wedding feast. It does explain your presence in a satisfactory manner. And you can get to know Mademoiselle Broneur, which might prove useful in the investigation.'

'So you've pinned down the murderer without me even having set one foot on the estate?' Atalanta teased him.

Renard looked piqued. 'You needn't worry,' he said stiffly, 'that you will have a lack of suspects. I'm sure you'll soon discover there are many more viable candidates.'

'Was the comte's first bride so much disliked?' Atalanta asked with a frown. 'Why then was the accident never questioned? Were no suspicions raised that she had been killed?'

'I don't assume she had many enemies as she was, from what I heard of her, a very lively and engaging young lady. But people envy those who have good fortune. And the comte was very much in demand, even then.'

'More so now?' Atalanta pounced on the implied meaning of the latter two words.

'I would say so. He has gained an even better reputation as a Renaissance art expert and many rich men are willing to pay a fortune for a painting he can find them in Italy.'

'But if his services are so much in demand, certainly he won't need to murder his bride to have unbridled control of her dowry? Regardless of what happened in the past, he will now have no need to—'

She halted as Renard had put up his hand and said, 'We don't know if the motive for the first wife's murder—if there was indeed any murder—lay with his lack of money. There might have been other reasons for him to kill her. And in judging his financial position you must not look solely at his income but also at his spending.'

Atalanta nodded thoughtfully. 'You mean he might still have need of money as his expenses exceed what he earns.'

'I've been told—and the source is usually reliable—that he can lay down a thousand francs on a single poker game.'

Atalanta widened her eyes. 'That can become expensive unless he knows how to win.'

'Oh, he does, but some whisper that he is cheating. Many a father isn't pleased that the dear comte plucked their son.'

'So the comte has enemies.' Atalanta started pacing again. 'One of those might have written that blood-red warning to cause friction in the comte's personal relations. Perhaps even to prevent the marriage from taking place. To hurt his interests, his reputation. I assume if the engagement was broken off, people would whisper about it.'

'And Martin Frontenac would be furious. He isn't a man to be thwarted.'

'I see. All the more reason for enemies of the comte to try and hit him there where he is vulnerable.' Atalanta halted abruptly. 'Renard, you know so much. If anyone can help me, it's you. Why don't you come with me to Bellevue?' She surveyed him carefully to see if he displayed any subtle sign of satisfaction. Had he raised the topic of someone accompanying her solely to be invited?

Renard stood up straight. 'That will not do, mademoiselle. I'm your late grandfather's manservant. I can take care of his possessions for as long as you, his heir, let me, but I cannot travel with you to handle situations. People know me.'

Atalanta wanted to protest that people rarely paid attention to servants and that to her mind he looked like about any other butler or manservant did, but she didn't want to hurt his feelings. Besides, if there was even a small chance someone would recognize him and suspect something, her case would be ruined.

She could kick herself that she had even made the suggestion. She shouldn't make such silly mistakes as she was just setting out. But who would support her once she was there? Would she really have to do it alone?

'You're correct of course.' She met his eyes. 'I only wish I had such in-depth knowledge of the relations between the people I'm going to meet.'

This task is too big for me. How will I ever accomplish anything?

'It could also hamper you from forming an unbiased opinion. Your grandfather had a deep insight into human nature which helped him solve his cases. I think he believed you were cut from the same cloth, so to speak.' Renard suppressed a smile. 'I can tell that he was not wrong, because you are independent, like he was. It's a good thing when you're able to step into situations and adjust. Much can be learned by listening well.'

Renard frowned as he continued, 'As you explained to me that you are posing as a distant relation who earns her money as a music teacher, it is less likely you would have a maid traveling with you. Still, you do realize you will be alone there, amongst people you cannot trust? Each one of them could have an ulterior motive for being kind to you. You will constantly have to be on your guard.'

A cold shiver slipped down Atalanta's spine. In her excitement about Paris, about having her very own home where she could grow her mama's favourite orchids, about her first case and the prospect of seeing the lavender fields, she hadn't thought about it quite that way. Just how treacherous it might be. She was stepping out amongst people who might have secrets to hide. If one of them knew more about how the Comte de Surmonne's first wife died, they would of course be eager not to have anyone pry into the past.

As soon as she started asking questions, no matter how

57

innocently she tried to do it, someone might sit up and take notice.

Someone who knew very well that it was dangerous if that old matter was brought back to life.

Someone who might... decide she shouldn't look closer?

She wrapped her arms around her shoulders. Mademoiselle Frontenac feared she was in danger and had asked for her help. By accepting that task Atalanta might have put herself in the firing line. Unless she was extremely careful, her first case could... become her last.

Renard studied her. 'Are you aware of what you have taken upon yourself?' he asked gently. 'I don't want to see fear in your face, but understanding of your position. You must be very careful in everything you do. Lock your door at night. Make it a habit to look closely at your surroundings. See before others do. And never be too proud to ask for help. You can always write to me here. Or telephone me.' He held her gaze. 'And who knows, perhaps the first wife wasn't murdered at all and the letter merely written out of spite. There could be nothing in it.'

Renard walked to the door. 'If you have any special requirements for dinner, I can pass them to the cook.'

Atalanta blinked that he went back to their daily business like that, as if the whole topic of her first client was closed. As if he hadn't just instructed her to lock her door and look over her shoulder all the time.

But with his hand on the doorknob Renard said, 'Even if the letter was written out of spite, it denotes something is brewing. Someone doesn't wish the comte and the new bride well. That could be equally dangerous. You must be very careful. Your grandfather would not want you to get hurt.'

'My life hasn't always been easy but I have managed to get by.'

Renard stood with his head bowed. 'Forgive me,' he said softly, 'but fighting against difficult circumstances is not the same as facing malignant people. From all I've heard about you, you are a kind-hearted, loyal person. But don't believe others are like that as well. Don't trust anyone.' He opened the door and stepped into the corridor. 'Not even your client.'

'What did you say?' Atalanta called out, perplexed at his last words. But he had already closed the door.

She stood in the sunny room surrounded by her fashionable new possessions. But now it hit her fully that her vocation came with a whole set of challenges: to be wary of everyone she met and dealt with; not to take anything at face value.

Not even what her client had told her. She had seen Eugénie Frontenac as a slightly older version of one of her pupils: wilful, spoiled, brimming with emotions. But she had to give everything second thought. Look beyond her first impression and be aware of the other options. Eugénie Frontenac's tale was *her* version of events. She could have left out elements, by choice, or simply because she didn't think they were important. She could have embellished the truth or have told an outright lie to suit her purposes. Those need not be malignant even. Eugénie had perhaps felt embarrassed about something and decided that it was better not to mention it. But in making such a decision she could be depriving Atalanta of vital information.

Tapping her hand on the piano, Atalanta stood and thought for a few moments, then made up her mind. To ensure her information was factual and objective, she had to make her own inquiries. *Before I leave Paris for Bellevue, I have work to do.*

Chapter Five

An hour later, Atalanta stood in front of a beautiful house on one of the most prestigious streets in Paris. She was dressed demurely in dark blue and carried a basket on her arm full of flowers she had bought from a street vendor in Montmartre. Having looked at the façade for a few moments, she entered the alley beside the house, leading her to the servants' entrance in the back. She knocked and soon a boy in uniform came to open the door. He surveyed her with curiosity.

'I'm here to sell flowers for the dinner table,' Atalanta said. 'The cook knows about it.'

The boy looked doubtful but invited her in with a hand gesture. She followed him through a pantry where a maid was washing the dishes and into a large kitchen. A thickset woman was standing over a stove stirring furiously. The sweet scent suggested that it was some kind of custard dessert. The boy said, 'Madame Fournier, a flower girl saying she knows you.'

Madame Fournier looked over her shoulder. 'Do I know you, girl?' she asked, her sharp blue eyes taking in Atalanta's neat appearance and the basket on her arm. 'Those look like very nice flowers, but we don't need any.'

'Please, hear me out.' Atalanta placed her basket on the kitchen table. Ignoring the boy, who was gawking with his mouth half-open, she explained, 'I heard there is going to be a wedding soon. A large society wedding. I can do the flowers for you. I can do more than deliver them; I can also turn them into nice bouquets and table arrangements. I only want to make some money for my family. Please.'

The cook's expression softened. She stirred again, then put the lid on the pan and turned fully to Atalanta. 'You heard right about a wedding, girl, but it won't take place here in Paris.'

'It's at Bellevue, a country estate,' the boy declared.

'No one asked you anything,' the cook snapped at him. She said to Atalanta, 'Mademoiselle Frontenac is marrying a comte. He has a beautiful country house and they will wed there. I assume he has a large garden and can decorate the house with his own flowers.'

Atalanta lowered her head as if this was a blow to her.

The cook said, 'But those flowers look very nice. Jean...' She looked at the boy. 'Go and find Monsieur Vivard to ask him if he can use these flowers for the dinner table tonight. Go, go.'

Atalanta's heartrate sped up. Now that a senior servant

had been called, she had limited time to see to her purpose here.

'Merci,' she said to the cook with a grateful smile. 'You are very kind. I must admit I had an ulterior motive calling here. I'm not really a flower girl but a friend of Mademoiselle Frontenac.'

The cook looked confused. 'A friend?' She surveyed Atalanta's simple clothes.

Atalanta said, 'I'm very worried about Eugénie. She has not been her usual cheerful self lately. She confided in me that she had received a worrying letter. She told me you gave it to her.'

As expected, the woman immediately jumped to her own defence. 'I did not. The letter was in the basket when I returned from the market. It had been put in there, amongst the lettuces and leeks. I found it when I unpacked the basket. I had it sent up to her room. I had no idea it would upset her so that she came blazing in here to ask me where it had come from. I do not know.'

'She thinks you do know,' Atalanta said to exert pressure. She was sorry for the poor woman but she had to know more and quickly. Jean would return with Monsieur Vivard and the chance would be past.

The cook said, 'I don't know where the letter came from. The market is very busy and people push past me all the time. One of them could have slipped it in.'

'And when you arrived here at the house, did you come straight here and unpack the vegetables?'

'I came straight here and put the basket on the table.'

The cook pointed out where it had sat. 'The bell rang for the drawing room and there was no one here to go and answer it. I went into the corridor to see where the maids were. It was the afternoon off for our butler; I then keep an eye on the other staff.' She said it with some pride. 'I found the maids chatting in the library. I told them off and then I came back here.'

It was possible the letter was put in the basket while the cook was away from the kitchen, Atalanta acknowledged. *Someone in the household could have done it.* Eugénie had mentioned her sisters were jealous of her. Had one of them done it, to spoil her happiness for her?

'Did you know the handwriting on the letter?' she asked the cook, not expecting anything here.

The cook frowned hard. 'I don't think so. It was very neat and straight, not at all like how real people write. When Mademoiselle Louise writes a menu for a soirée, I can hardly make out what she wrote.'

Atalanta nodded. There were footsteps in the corridor and the door opened. A tall man with dark hair looked at her down his long nose. 'We don't buy flowers from peddlers,' he said in a grim tone. 'Please leave at once or I'll call the police.'

'I'm already leaving,' Atalanta assured him and picked up her flower basket. Her palms were clammy with sweat, but a smile bubbled inside her. *I actually managed to find information using a disguise.*

She was still in the alley when she heard a sound and swung round. The cook stood behind her. 'I know you told me the truth,' she said in a rush. 'Mademoiselle Eugénie told me not to tell a soul about that letter. As I said, the butler was out and the maids were working in the library. Jean took her the letter but then he left to run errands. No one was there when she came to me all upset to ask where I had found it.'

The cook swallowed and continued, 'She said no one should ever know about it. Especially not her father. He was so happy, she said. He should not worry. If she did tell you, confided in you, you must be a true friend of hers. And if you are and wish her well, you must tell her one thing.'

The woman's urgent tone drove goosebumps out on Atalanta's arms. What could she want to tell her? A big secret? Something that could assist her in finding the truth behind the warning in the letter?

She looked into the woman's apprehensive eyes. 'Yes, what is that?'

Taking a deep breath, the cook glanced over her shoulder as if to see that no one was near enough to overhear her and then she whispered, 'The ring is not real.'

'Excuse me?'

'The comte gave Mademoiselle Eugénie a ring for their engagement. It has a large stone in it. Not a diamond. Blue, it is. I don't know what that is called. But the butler has a nephew who works for a tailor. He came here to the house to fit a suit on Monsieur Frontenac for the wedding. While he was fitting the suit, making sure the sleeves were not too long, Mademoiselle Eugénie came in and spoke with her father. She put her hand on his arm and the nephew got a good chance to look at the ring and the stone. Now, he is a jeweller's son. He worked with stones since he was ten and helped his father. He was apprenticed in his shop but then he took up a fancy for tailoring, to his father's dismay. But he never forgot what he learned. He could see the stone well and he said later it wasn't a real stone, but a fake one. That the comte was deceiving Mademoiselle Eugénie.'

Interesting. So it could be true that he was low on money again and eager for a new bride to bring in funds he could then put into his business. Did that also explain his demand for a short engagement? To lay his hands on Eugénie's dowry as soon as he possibly could?

'Thank you for telling me.' She smiled at the cook to reassure her, although her own heart raced at the idea that the comte could be so cold and calculating. *An adversary to be reckoned with.*

The woman didn't seem relieved. She wrung her hands. 'Poor Mademoiselle Eugénie. It was bad enough that she wasn't allowed to marry the man she really loves. To fall into the hands of a dishonourable man, who gives her false stones...' She shook her head and walked off.

Atalanta stared at her disappearing figure. *The man she really loves...?*

Her client hadn't mentioned her affections for another. She had seemed delighted at the match with the Comte de Surmonne. Did Renard know more about this other man? Was that why he had told her that she shouldn't trust anyone, not even her client?

His warning had put a cold sensation in her stomach

and it increased now that she actually had proof of Eugénie withholding information. Her reasons for that could be simple. Perhaps her earlier infatuation had passed and she was embarrassed to be reminded of it.

But the situation could also be more complex than that. An ongoing attachment while she prepared to wed the man her parents approved of; the man who brought her a title and wealth.

Had this secret love interest written the letter to scare Eugénie away from her betrothed?

I have to ask Renard who it is or might be.

Chapter Six

'Oh look, look, that is it!' Eugénie Frontenac pressed her cheek against the windowpane of the Rolls Royce as they glided down a long, winding lane towards a white plastered house with turrets. On both sides of the road lilac waves of lavender moved under the breeze. Eugénie pointed at the house. 'Bellevue must be one of the most beautiful country estates I have ever seen. It's so white and pure, the turrets so sleek and elegant. Everything is sheer perfection, from the golden running-horse weather-cock on top to the fountain that is illuminated at night. It's a dream for our guests.'

Atalanta had to admit that the house and its surroundings painted a most appealing picture. Box hedges had been clipped into intricate cones and animal figures, yellow and orange roses grew against a bower, and a wrought-iron sign directed visitors to the shell grotto.

A grotto, here? What can that be?

The Rolls slowed and the driver steered it towards the bank on their right. On the left the road was obstructed by a simple wooden cart. Two men dressed in rumpled blue trousers and coarse linen shirts with rolled sleeves lifted something out of the ditch. Atalanta had the fleeting impression it was dark brown, muddied, and something hung limply, much like... *a human hand?*

Her breath caught and she turned her head to see better. But the men were already putting their load into the cart, obscuring it from her view.

'What is happening there?' Eugénie asked the chauffeur.

He shrugged. 'Probably a drunken tramp. They will take him to a farm nearby so he can sleep it off.'

Drunken, not dead. Atalanta suppressed a short laugh of relief. Her nerves were too highly strung for the arrival at the house where she was going to play an innocent guest while in truth hunting an alleged killer. She was already jumping to conclusions. Her grandfather would frown at her. *Ask questions first.*

But the questions that came to mind didn't exactly put her at ease. Why would people care to remove a drunken tramp from a ditch? It was none of their business whether he lay there or not. In the poorer parts of London it had been quite normal in summer for beggars or tramps to lie on the streets, in the blazing heat, getting close to sunstroke, and no one had lifted a hand to bring them into shelter.

But they were in the countryside here.

Perhaps people show more neighbourly concern to each other than they do in the city?

Eugénie had obviously taken the chauffeur's explanation at face value and her attention returned to the house up ahead as she said, 'At this time of day my fiancé is probably not here. Gilbert will be out riding, with friends, or visiting in the neighbourhood. He's very popular. I wonder'—she smiled indulgently—'whether that will grow less once he's married.'

Her expression changed a moment as if she considered something unpleasant and then dismissed it. She pointed again. 'Look, there's even a welcoming committee for me.'

The door of the house had opened and several people came out, lining up along the steps that led from the gravel up to the stone terrace surrounding the entire house.

The man in front—a butler probably—came to the Rolls as soon as it had halted and opened the door for the ladies. He lent a hand as Eugénie climbed out in her pink chiffon dress. 'Welcome to Bellevue, mademoiselle.'

'Thank you.' Eugénie stood and stretched slightly, turning her head to look around, 'What a lovely day.'

The butler assisted Atalanta and then gave instructions to the driver to take the car around the house and see to the luggage. 'Place it in the hall and I will take it up to the ladies' rooms.' He gestured for them to follow him past the waiting staff.

There were two footmen with tight expressions as if they were wax statues, a middle-aged housekeeper in a deep-purple dress and three maids in their twenties who curtseyed nervously. Then a girl of about sixteen in a loose-fitting turquoise garment came rushing through the open front door and joined the line. A small white dog followed her and circled her legs, wagging his tiny fluffy tail.

The butler cleared his throat. 'I do not think that is your place, Mademoiselle Yvette.'

'I dare say it is. I'm treated beastly here. I can't even come and go as I please. I can't ride the horse I want to. I'm not a baby anymore, you know.'

The daring tones were very familiar to Atalanta, who had often seen girls arrive at her school in this mood. *My parents sent me away to this prison; I can't do what I want here; I'm going to hate everything about it.* They were determined to be miserable and make everyone else miserable as well in the process.

'Yvette!' Eugénie exclaimed. 'How delightful you're here.' She leaned in and delivered two air kisses in the proximity of the girl's cheeks.

The little dog barked and snapped at her ankles. Eugénie stepped back and glared at the canine before pasting on another smile as she enthused to Yvette, 'I thought you were in Nice.'

'And how I wish I were,' Yvette sighed. Her gaze descended on Atalanta. 'Is she one of your sisters? Louise or... what was the other one's name?'

'Françoise, as you very well know.' Eugénie looked irritated a moment but forced a smile and said, 'This is a cousin of mine, Atalanta Frontenac. She's a pianist and will play at the wedding feast.'

They had decided to let Atalanta keep her own first name, as Eugénie had assured her that most Frontenacs had long names and no one knew exactly who was who, especially once they got into the shadier regions of the family tree. Atalanta was supposed to be the fourth daughter of a brother of Eugénie's father who had moved to Switzerland before the war. 'We barely hear from them ever,' Eugénie had said. 'And not even Grandmother knows exactly which daughter does what in life. It's safe enough.'

With a frown, Yvette studied Atalanta. 'I wager you can't play the piano as well as I can. Why can't Gilbert let me play at the feast?' She turned away and stormed into the house. The dog ran after her, his excited yaps suggesting he thought they were playing some game.

'You must forgive her manners,' Eugénie said to Atalanta. 'It's her age, I suppose. It's really kind of Gilbert to see to her education. He could have washed his hands of her.'

It sounded like Eugénie really meant to say: *should* have washed his hands of her.

Atalanta felt the staff standing so close, their expressions perhaps blank, but their ears striving to catch every syllable of something interesting to discuss later.

Let's not give them fodder for gossip.

She smiled at Eugénie and said, 'Shall we go inside and freshen up a bit? It was a long drive.'

The dutiful butler took them up to their rooms. Eugénie's was located in the east wing where elaborately decorated doors suggested that rich rooms lay behind them. Atalanta was transferred to the care of one of the maids who took her into the other wing. Here the tapestries on the wall were still colourful and the stained-glass windows overlooked the lush gardens outside, but the door into the room had a simple panel in the centre and a brass knob.

The room itself was furnished with a large bed, dressing table, and sofa near the window. All fabrics, from blankets to curtains, were kept in hues of lilac like the lavender that was so iconic of the region.

Can I see it from here? Atalanta rushed to the window to enjoy the lush land, but her room was facing the other way, giving a view of the forest behind the house. Large oak trees, birches, brush... and something scurrying away into the shadows—perhaps a deer?

The darkness of the dense forest contrasted sharply with the open, well-lit garden and Atalanta felt a thrill of excitement staring at its imposing shape. *Will that shell grotto be hidden somewhere in there?*

She turned to the maid, who asked her if all was to her liking. *'Oui, merci.'* The girl retreated and drew the door closed.

Atalanta breathed in and stretched her arms over her head. They had arrived. Her case was about to begin for real. For a moment the memory flashed through her mind of the limp hand she had viewed for but an instant before the men had taken the tramp away.

There's more than beauty and opulence to this place, she thought.

She wrapped her arms around her shoulders a moment and took a deep breath to dispel the unsettling feeling. Then she noticed that her room also had a balcony door and went to open it and step out onto the stone structure. The fresh air bathed her face, cooling her warm cheeks. It would be grand to bring out a chair and sit here for a while, in early morning or at night, watching the world wind down into hues of orange and red. Listening to the birds' evening concerto. *Perhaps there's an owl here like there was near the school?*

With a smile she placed her hands on the balcony's edge, leaned over, and followed the stretch of the forest all the way to the horizon. Would this all be the comte's property? He had to be a wealthy man indeed.

'Good afternoon,' a male voice called.

Atalanta jerked her head down to see who had addressed her from below.

A tall man with raven-black hair stood on the lawn under her balcony. He held a hand over his eyes to shade them against the sun. The light was bright indeed but Atalanta was quite sure the man's eyes would be deep brown, like those of the handsome stranger who had so often played a part in her travel fantasies.

That can't be. I made him up.

She tried to look calm and not flustered as she called down, 'Good afternoon. It's more than good actually. It's perfect.'

'High praise,' he retorted. 'But I must admit my

afternoon just got better.' A smile tilted the corners of his mouth upwards.

Did he mean because he had seen her on the balcony?

Of course not, she admonished herself. *Keep your mind on the case instead of getting distracted by a handsome stranger who might very well be teasing.*

Then another thought hit her like lightning. Eugénie had said her fiancé was out. What if this was the comte, returning to his house? She could certainly not appreciate the good looks of a man about to be married.

To her client, at that.

'Have you had a chance to look around?' he called. 'Have you seen the shell grotto? Come down at once and I'll show it to you.'

'But I...' Atalanta protested. The shell grotto was something she did want to see and while it was impossible to rush out and explore on her own, so soon after her arrival, this invitation made it perfectly proper.

'Hurry down then. I'll be waiting for you in front of the house.' Without awaiting her affirmation he strode away and vanished from sight.

Atalanta noticed she was gripping the balcony's edge and let go. Taking a deep breath, she tried to regain a cool attitude. It would be impolite to refuse an invitation of her host to show her around. And it offered her a chance to observe his behaviour right away, not in a crowd, but in a personal interaction. *What an excellent opportunity.*

She rushed inside and leaned down to the dressing-table mirror to check that her hair was impeccable and her little hat in place. She had bought some new clothes for this undertaking—nothing too expensive, but stylish enough not to embarrass Eugénie. She might be posing as a distant cousin, but she could still be one with breeding and taste.

She needn't pinch colour into her cheeks as those were bright red already. She forced herself to walk slowly down the corridor and then the stairs. In the hallway she spotted the man waiting for her. 'I came inside because you were taking so long,' he commented, offering her his arm. 'Why do women take forever to get ready for an outing? We're not even leaving the grounds.'

Atalanta ignored his arm as she didn't think Eugénie would appreciate her getting too close with the comte. Folding her hands together demurely, she smiled winningly to compensate. 'I'm so pleased to see Bellevue. What a beautiful house and such stunning surroundings.'

'Too bad one always smells like a perfume shop after a day or two here,' he commented. 'The lavender is everywhere.'

He leaned over to her. 'Did you know that the scent of lavender is considered to be sleep inducing? How odd that all of our visitors are not keeling over once they've been here for a few minutes.'

'It's not that overpowering, is it?' Atalanta asked. Had she missed it when getting out of the car? They stepped outside and she inhaled deeply. 'I barely get a whiff of it.'

'Good. I wouldn't want you to doze off. We have an exciting cave to explore.'

The words captured all of Atalanta's deepest dreams.

She was her own agent here, not a teacher under instructions from a school director or a member of the staff. No, she was a guest, distinguished and free.

She fell into step with him, craning her neck to look ahead. On both sides of the path were flowerbeds with lilies and dahlias. A gardener was cutting a bouquet, referring to a list he carried. *Perhaps the flowers for the dinner table?*

'The shell grotto is quite an old and authentic part of the estate. It was built in the seventeenth century and depicts Roman myths. Do you know any?'

'Oh, yes, I love myths,' Atalanta enthused. She almost blurted out that she had visited a Roman excavation site with her father once, but that would certainly call for questions. *Careful now, don't say something that gives you away.* 'I read a lot of books as I grew up.'

He seemed to suppress a smile. 'Another girl who loves to put her nose in the books.'

'Another?' Atalanta queried. 'Do you mean Eugénie?'

He waved it off. 'Down this path.'

It was narrower than the other one, made of trodden earth, and at one point she had to duck under the tendrils of a blossoming yellow bush hanging over the path. A painful twinge on her skull made her stop and reach up with her fingers to feel what had entangled itself in her hair.

'Let me do that.' He reached out and slowly untwined a lock of her hair from a twig. He stood so close she could smell his cologne. 'There you go. We can move on.'

Although he had not orchestrated her hair getting caught, he seemed at ease in such a situation, seeking more nearness than seemed appropriate for a man about to be married. Did that mean he didn't genuinely love Eugénie?

His dark-brown eyes didn't give anything away as he held her gaze a moment longer before turning away and leading her further down the path. 'Not far anymore.'

This was more exciting than anything else she had ever done before. But she shouldn't forget she was working. That she was on a case investigating whether this man walking ahead of her was a murderer.

A chilly feeling seeped through her, sharpening her senses. Renard's voice whispered in her ear, *See before others do.*

Ahead of them a rocklike structure sat, the entrance half obscured by a vine. Small grapes were already forming. 'How fitting,' her companion said. 'Wasn't there a myth about bunches of grapes dangling just out of reach?'

A moist scent rose into her nose as she entered the cave's mouth and she shivered involuntarily. But there was a hole made in the roof through which sunshine filtered, caressing the mosaic laid out in shells. Soft pink, beige, lilac, and brown, they formed a rich tableau of golden-haired youthful nymphs bathing, a hunter watching from the brush, a majestic antlered deer running frantically with dogs pursuing it.

'Actaeon,' she whispered. Desire being punished by death.

Birds were worked into trees and hares sat on the ground. A peacock spread its tail in the left-hand corner. The longer she looked, the more details she detected.

'Well, what do you think?' her companion asked.

'I think your forefathers had excellent taste.'

'My forefathers?' His voice sounded close beside her. He laughed softly. 'My dear lady, you didn't think I was the Comte de Surmonne in person, did you? I'm but a humble friend of his. Without a title or money.'

Really? How absolutely marvellous.

Atalanta suppressed any sign of delight and instead frowned on her new acquaintance. 'You could have introduced yourself when we met.'

'So could you.' He folded his hands behind his back. 'I mistook you for the bride. But I do assume you would know your own fiancé if you met him in broad daylight so I must have been mistaken as well.'

Atalanta's cheeks were on fire. This friend of the comte had believed her to be Eugénie and had graciously offered to show her around. Now she turned out to be a stranger and… he might feel his attempts at chivalry had been wasted on her.

'I must apologize for the misunderstanding,' he said in a formal tone, extending his hand. 'Raoul Lemont. I was asked to be a witness at the upcoming wedding.'

'Atalanta Frontenac. I'll play the piano at the feast.'

He smiled. 'So we both have our small part in it, this happy occasion.' He sounded slightly cynical.

Atalanta watched the emotion flicker across his features as they stood in the dim room. *What is he thinking?* 'Do you not believe it will be happy?' she asked.

Raoul seemed to shake himself from a distracting thought. 'What did you say?'

'Won't it be a happy occasion?'

He let out a sound caught between a laugh and a huff. 'I'm not particularly in favour of tying oneself up for life. But my friend seems set on doing it. Again.'

'Yes, I heard he had been married before and then tragically widowed soon after.' *There, now turn the conversation to the accident. But naturally.* 'Did you know his first wife?'

'Mathilde?' Raoul sounded surprised. 'As a matter of fact, I did, yes. But I had hardly expected someone called Frontenac to be eager to bring up her name.'

It sounded so accusing that Atalanta flinched. But she didn't look away. On the contrary, she tried to close in on the meaning behind his words. 'How do you mean? It's common knowledge the comte was married before.'

'Yes, of course, but very briefly. The marriage didn't last longer than a few weeks. Some people consider it barely worth mentioning. Especially as they think his choice of Mathilde was… a mistake.'

'I see.' *How fascinating in the light of a possible murder.* 'And why would they think that?'

He shrugged. 'Mathilde was young and wild, not really ready for marriage. Her choice to ride a stallion that even a man could hardly control was typical of her attitude to life. She always wanted more than she could master.' He frowned. 'Poor little thing. She paid for that mistake with her life.'

'So the horse was known to be hard to handle?' Atalanta asked, her heart beating fast. These were valuable facts to support the accident theory. 'It had thrown off riders before?'

'It certainly had. In fact, Gilbert was thinking about returning it to the man he had bought it from. He didn't consider the horse reliable enough to keep in his stables. But before he could put this plan into action, Mathilde took the horse for a ride—of course without Gilbert knowing a thing about it—and she was thrown off and broke her neck.' He threw his head back and stared at the hole through which the sunshine poured. 'She was reckless but she didn't deserve that.'

'Was she all alone when she died?' Atalanta asked. It might be an odd question so she rushed to explain. 'I mean, it's so sad to die like that, and even sadder if she was all alone, with no one to come to her aid.'

'No, she was with a friend.' Raoul looked grim as he said it.

Had it been a male friend? Why else would he take such a tone?

'But let's not dwell on the past,' Raoul said, lightly touching her arm. 'The dark clouds are blown away and the sun is shining again. Gilbert has brought another bride to the estate and we'll all dance at the wedding party. Come.' He turned and went back outside.

Too late to ask about the friend with Mathilde when she died. A sharp sense of failure stabbed her. Now she could hardly start the topic again. As a Frontenac here for the wedding, she might have some passing interest in the first bride, but showing too much curiosity, especially in respect to exactly how she had died, would look suspicious.

Raoul walked ahead of her as if he was suddenly in a hurry to get away. Just as they left the narrow trodden path, a man in riding costume came into view. He saw them and waved with his whip. He was in the company of a uniformed policeman who was gesturing with both hands as he explained something.

Police? Atalanta slowed her pace, her mind filling with questions of what this official did here. Estate business? Something innocent?

'That is the Comte de Surmonne,' Raoul said to Atalanta. 'In a foul mood, I presume, because I deserted him while he was riding.'

Atalanta looked at Raoul's neat, light suit. 'You're not dressed for riding.'

'How observant of you. I was acting as his fox. I was setting a trail he had to follow. But I grew bored with the game and abandoned him to go see what attractions were offered at the house.'

Attractions? Had Raoul wanted to know if Eugénie had already arrived? The cook had mentioned a man she had really loved. Renard hadn't known who it might be.

Could it be Raoul? Had he come here to flirt with the bride under the roof of the man she was about to marry? He wasn't afraid of risks then.

But no, how could he then have assumed she was

Eugénie? That mistake suggested they had never met before.

That didn't mean, of course, that he couldn't have wanted to meet her without his friend the comte present. To be honest, this handsome man with the raven hair, warm eyes, and engaging manners was probably used to ladies liking him at first sight and flirting with him.

Perhaps he had taken her interest in the shell grotto for a thinly veiled excuse to spend time with him?

But no matter how charming the grotto had been, this was all strictly in the interest of the case she conducted here.

The comte finished speaking with the policeman, who greeted him with a respectful bow of the head and took his leave. The comte continued his way to the house but he changed his mind and came over to them. He studied Atalanta head to toe. 'Mademoiselle Atalanta Frontenac, I believe? Eugénie wrote to me that she would bring you along. I must say I was a bit overtaken. In fact, I had already agreed that my niece, Yvette, would play the piano to accompany the singer we engaged for the feast.'

'Little Yvette to accompany the great Angélique Broneur?' Raoul laughed out loud, his head back. 'You know how Yvette feels about Angélique. Last time they met, she put a wet broom in her bed.'

'Yvette was younger then.' The comte said it confidently, but still his neck reddened. 'She will behave this time.'

'Still, I think it's an excellent idea to keep her away from Mademoiselle Broneur,' Raoul insisted. 'If Mademoiselle Frontenac here can play the piano well and your dear bride asked her for the occasion, you must oblige.'

He leaned over and tapped the comte on his arm. 'Men must listen to their wives. It prevents so much misery.'

The comte withdrew his arm as if stung. Anger flickered in his eyes and for a moment Atalanta was certain he would raise his whip and strike at Raoul. But then the fury had already passed like a flash of lightning in broad daylight when you are barely certain whether you actually saw it or it was a trick of the eyes.

Of course he won't lash out at a friend.

Not over something so innocent as that remark made in jest.

Still, it was remarkable how all these people shared a past connected with the dead Mathilde and seemed so touchy whenever the subject of wives and marriage was raised.

'Did I see a policeman with you just now?' she asked. 'I hope nothing has happened? A burglary perhaps? Thieves seem to become more audacious by the day, even coming to grand houses in broad daylight. And as an art collector you must have so many valuable objects at hand.'

'No, he merely informed me about a poacher who died on my land.' The comte made a dismissive gesture. 'It was an old man and he drank too much. He was bound to end up in a ditch someday.'

In a ditch? Her breath caught as she realized the implication. The man they had seen being removed when they were on their way to the house had not been drunk, but dead?

I knew it. That awfully limp hand...

Death amongst the lavender. And Eugénie had called everything about this place sheer perfection. Atalanta wouldn't say anything was perfect when death was a part of it. Another death, after Mathilde's.

But Mathilde had died in a horse-riding accident and this old man had drunk himself to death. It had just so happened to have occurred on the comte's land. A coincidence.

Still, coincidences like that made her uncomfortable. A good investigator would take nothing for granted. *See before others do*, Renard had told her.

How could she learn to do that?

Chapter Seven

They sat at the dinner table. After an excellent soup—or perhaps it could better be called a bouillon, for it had been light and aromatic, perfect as an appetizer—they were now on the main course: venison with duchess potatoes and ratatouille. Wine sparkled in the crystal glasses and the dahlias Atalanta had seen the gardener cut earlier that afternoon were arranged skilfully into a stunning centrepiece.

Upon entering the dining room and spotting Yvette's dog, Eugénie had complained that it should be removed, but Yvette had protested that Pom-pom was never far away from her and after a few pleading glances at Gilbert, the comte had yielded and allowed her to keep him by her side.

Yvette now kept sneaking the dog bites of food under the table, and seeking Eugénie's eye as she did it, to rub in her win. Eugénie would do better, in Atalanta's opinion, to pretend she didn't notice, or care, but it didn't seem in

87

Eugénie's nature to ignore slights. She picked at her food without any appetite and kept glaring at Yvette whenever her hand disappeared under the damask tablecloth.

The comte made a few attempts to start a conversation about the delights of summer in the country but when he noticed the absolute lack of enthusiasm this was met with by his bride, he concentrated on his venison and sampling the rich red wine served with it.

Raoul cast Atalanta an amused look.

Is he contemplating how right he is to shy away from marriage and everything related to it?

Suddenly a vivacious honking outside the windows broke the silence and the comte looked up with a jerk. 'Who can that be?'

Yvette jumped to her feet and went to the window, lifting the lace curtain. Pom-pom ran after her and stood on his hindlegs against the wall underneath the window as he tried to reach the windowsill and look out.

'It's a gorgeous sports car,' Yvette exclaimed and left the room at a trot, the dog hard on her heels.

'Now I'm also curious,' Raoul said and took the place at the window Yvette had vacated. He tutted. 'A gorgeous sports car, she calls that. I call it rather a tame thing.'

Her curiosity piqued, Atalanta was tempted to go and see for herself, but she remained seated out of respect for her host, who was frowning at the disturbance of his evening meal.

From the hallway laughter resounded and then a tall man with blond curls stepped in, a pair of goggles in his hand. A woman dressed in turquoise draped herself against him and waved an elegant hand to the people in the room. 'Hello, there. I dare say we're late for dinner.' She pulled herself away from the man and rounded the table to the head, leaned down to the comte, and kissed him on the cheek. 'Gilbert, how delightful to meet you again.' Then she turned to Eugénie. 'Sister, dear...' Eugénie had turned a fiery red. 'What are you doing here?' she croaked.

This had to be one of her sisters. Louise, or whatever the other was called, as Yvette had put it. This led Atalanta to assume that the third sister was somehow rather forgettable. This new arrival certainly wasn't. Her blonde hair caught the light of the chandelier above and her eyes sparkled with a daring expression as she let her gaze run past the guests.

The man at the door smiled at Eugénie. 'Surprise! We thought we'd come over early and spend a few days extra breathing healthy country air.'

'It won't be very healthy if you spoil it with the exhaust fumes of your new toy.' Gilbert sounded spiteful. Nevertheless, he snapped his fingers to the butler. 'Bring extra plates for these guests.'

'We had dinner on the way,' the woman assured him. 'It was too delightful. A little inn, a narrow table, candlelight.' She had returned to the man and ran her hand across his arm in a loving gesture. 'We had better go upstairs and freshen up for the dancing later. We will have some dancing?'

'Grand!' Yvette exclaimed. She cast the man admiring looks.

The two new guests retreated from the room and voices resounded in the hall as they spoke with the butler.

Gilbert looked at Eugénie. 'Did you know Louise was coming?'

Louise, yes, it was as she'd thought. Atalanta nodded to herself as she picked up her wine glass and sipped, studying the interaction. Each correct deduction gave her a thrill of pleasure, like when she had played chess with her father and made her moves step by step, lulling him into a false sense of security while she prepared her checkmate.

Eugénie leaned back against her chair. 'Why would I ask her what she was doing here if I had expected her to come?'

'I thought you might have suggested it to her.'

'Nothing of the kind.' Eugénie cut her venison with a vicious gesture. 'And I certainly didn't ask *him* to come along.' She managed to put a world of loathing into the word.

The comte seemed to relax a little. 'I see. Well, we'll just have to make the best of it. I can hardly turn them away.'

'I wouldn't mind if you did.' Eugénie threw down her cutlery. 'You must excuse me; I feel a terrible headache coming up.' She cast Atalanta a pleading look. 'Would you mind accompanying me on an evening stroll? Some fresh air will revive me.'

'I don't mind at all.' Atalanta rose. She caught a hint of laughter in the features of Raoul Lemont, as if he thought she was jumping to do the beck and call of her relative.

The idea that he took her for a less well-to-do relation, someone not quite in their league, was painful. For the first time in her life she had met a truly intriguing man and how different it would have been if they had been introduced at a party in Paris, where she would have entered among envious gazes as the new heiress in town. The granddaughter of the respected Clarence Ashford. But here she was playing the part of someone who didn't have the status of the others she associated with and while it was a role she was very familiar with, it now grated.

It is just as well, she soothed herself with reasonable arguments as she had often done. *Remember the lawyer's warning that you should not share news of your wealth or people will take advantage of you. Imagine Raoul flirting with you, merely because he knew you have money. That would be far worse than him snubbing you now.*

Still, where such rational thoughts usually helped, they now failed to convince her, and something of the longing lingered to fit in with these people and for once feel like she belonged instead of being on the outside, looking in.

Soon the two women were outside walking away from the house. 'I can't believe the nerve Louise has in coming here like that. With him!' Eugénie pulled a delicate lace handkerchief from her sleeve and dabbed at her eyes. 'I feel totally humiliated.'

'I don't see why you should feel uncomfortable about your sister coming over a few days early. I'm sure the comte is the perfect host.'

'Louise is only doing it to make me feel bad.' Eugénie

gasped for air. 'First she pushed me towards an inappropriate alliance so Father would disown me...' She shivered. 'Louise is evil. She has a pretty face and nice manners when she wants to, but her heart is pure night.'

Would she have written the letter to scare her sister? Atalanta walked slowly, trying to work out what she could ask without being rude. On the other hand, Eugénie had engaged her to look into the anonymous letter and possible threat from her husband-to-be, so it was natural she would have questions.

'You aren't good friends with Louise?' She opened the interrogation with an obvious question.

'We used to be quite close. Louise is just one year older than I am. We often played together, had the same nannies and teachers. Some people even thought we were twins.' Eugénie's expression softened. 'We shared all of our secrets. I never thought she would ever betray me.'

She stopped to pick some lavender and sniffed it. 'I wish we could go back to what it was like back then, when I believed I could rely on her. But I guess it all changes when you grow up. You have different interests and...'

She stared into the distance. 'Louise always wanted to marry young. But although she is charming and accomplished, men take no lasting interest in her. I've often told her she makes it too easy for them. She shows that she wants them to like her and they don't find that appealing. They like to have to take trouble to make a woman care.' She glanced at Atalanta. 'So Louise took it upon herself to play matchmaker for people in our acquaintance. She even takes credit for having introduced Gilbert to his first wife.'

'To Mathilde?' Atalanta asked. 'Was Mathilde a friend of Louise's then?'

'Yes. They went to boarding school together.'

Atalanta recalled that Raoul had told her Mathilde had, on the fatal ride that had led to her death, been accompanied by a friend. *Louise?*

Eugénie said, 'At the time I had no interest whatsoever in being matched so I was just happy for Mathilde and Gilbert. I still think they made a very good pair.' Her expression became pensive, almost sad.

'A better pair than you and him?' Atalanta asked softly.

Eugénie jerked upright. 'I would not want to say that, but... Mathilde was something different. She was kind-hearted, soft-spoken, and infinitely elegant. There was no evil bone in her body. She would never gossip or laugh at someone less fortunate. I think... I think Gilbert adored her, put her on a pedestal, took her for a saint. It was quite unhealthy, if you ask me. We're all just human.'

'I guess so,' Atalanta confirmed, to keep her talking. The picture Raoul had painted of Mathilde had been very different. Wild, doing whatever she wanted, even if her husband had forbidden it.

Or had that been part of her attraction? 'And still, after Gilbert lost this very special woman, Louise thought she could make him fall in love again?'

'Yes. With her.' Eugénie cast Atalanta a blazing look. 'It was a source of gossip in our circle for some time that

Louise was at Gilbert's side comforting him immediately after his wife died. It was… unseemly. But when we tried to tell her, she got angry and said we were just misinterpreting her meaning.'

Still, was it possible that after Louise had matched her perfect friend Mathilde with the attractive Comte de Surmonne, she had realized her mistake as she herself began to feel affection for him? Had she contrived an accident in which Mathilde died so she could comfort the bereft widower and become the new comtesse?

If she wanted that, she had failed.

But how? Had she tried to show Gilbert her feelings and had he rejected her? Was that the reason why he had traveled for months, allegedly busy with his art acquisitions, but in reality to avoid Louise?

That would have been very painful, almost unbearable. Was Louise Frontenac a bitter woman driven by a need for revenge?

Eugénie said, 'While Louise was making a fool of herself pining for Gilbert, who was not in the least interested in her that way, she was also trying to find someone for me. I believed she meant well and I went out on a few occasions with a man she had found for me. She told me he was an heir to a large factory in Germany but later on it turned out none of this was true and she had even damaged my reputation. I think she did it on purpose. My parents weren't happy with her for her infatuation with a widower and she wanted to divert their attention. But I found out in time who and what he was.' She clenched her hands into fists crushing the lavender. 'And now he is here.'

'The man with your sister is this alleged heir to the German factory?'

'Yes. But he is no heir. He's just an opportunist who wanted a slice of our family fortune—via me or via Louise, that is all the same to him. I can't believe she brought him here and is behaving like...'

'They are involved.' Atalanta nodded slowly. The reference to a candlelit dinner certainly implied as much. 'Perhaps they are. She might have accepted that the comte will never return her affections and has made another choice.'

'Choice?' Eugénie fumed. 'What choice is there in falling into the arms of a man who only wants to get into our father's chequebook? I despise her for it.'

'And him?' Atalanta asked softly. Eugénie considered a moment. 'I suppose Victor can't help the way he is.'

Such a kind assessment after she judged her sister so harshly. Did Eugénie still retain some soft feeling towards the man she had been matched with on her sister's authority?

What a tangled affair this is. 'And you did not invite her here?'

'I did invite her to the wedding of course, how could I not? Maman would never forgive me if I passed over Louise. But I assumed she'd be coming over with the others on the day before the wedding. Not ahead of time and in this... ostentatious manner.' Eugénie opened her hands and looked at the crinkled lavender stems. 'They do smell delicious now.' She inhaled the scent. 'I must put these flowerheads into a small linen sachet and keep it under my pillow. They say the scent of lavender helps one to sleep. I will need it. The wedding is causing me so much anxiety.' She cast Atalanta a look. 'Have you any idea yet who wrote the letter to me?'

'I'm sorry, no.' Atalanta shook her head. 'How could I establish anything so quickly?'

'I wish I felt like there is enough time, but I don't. There is... a sense of foreboding in the air.'

Atalanta swallowed, thinking of the dead poacher. The comte hadn't mentioned it over dinner; a logical choice, perhaps, as it was an unpleasant situation he would rather conceal from his guests.

Or is there another reason for his reticence?

Eugénie said, 'It's a feeling I can't quite explain. A weight pressing on my chest and preventing me from breathing freely. No matter how clean the air is out here.' She wrapped her arms around her shoulders.

'Are you not well, Eugénie?' a male voice inquired.

Both women spun round.

The man with the blond curls, Victor, stood smiling at them. He had a cigarette in his left hand, but it didn't seem to be lit. Had he used his intention to smoke as an excuse to go outside and follow Eugénie?

Victor stepped up and reached out a hand, touching Eugénie's left hand. 'You're cold. You mustn't walk about in the evening air.'

'It is high summer,' Atalanta observed. 'It must still be well above twenty degrees.'

He turned his twinkling blue eyes on her. 'And you are her chaperone?'

'Does she need one?' Atalanta countered.

There was a sudden silence after this rather forward question. Eugénie might get angry at her for acting in this fashion, but if Victor had lied about being an heir to a German business empire, he deserved to be kept in check.

'You can go back to the house now, Atalanta,' Eugénie said softly. 'I'll be perfectly fine.'

Would she? Her client had told her, minutes ago, that she sensed something sinister here. 'I thought you had such a bad headache,' she said. 'Are you certain it's not too much of an exertion?'

'You just said the evening air is warm,' Victor observed with a challenging smile. 'And with me by her side, Eugénie is in no danger of being attacked by a wild animal or a tramp.'

That was not to say that in his presence Eugénie was in no danger, Atalanta thought, but she couldn't convey her worries to Eugénie with him standing beside them. She smiled. 'I rely on you, monsieur, to be chivalrous.'

The double meaning of the words didn't seem to escape him. He gave her a searching look as if he wondered how much she knew about his forbidden liaison with Eugénie.

Atalanta tried to maintain a blank expression. Victor seemed to understand he would get no further with her and said to Eugénie, 'You must forgive me for barging in, but Louise can be very persistent. She wanted to surprise you.'

'You could have hurried so you'd be in time for dinner.'

And avoided the tête-à-tête Louise had alluded to? Atalanta wondered as she walked away. When she was close to the house, she glanced back and saw Victor standing with his hands on Eugénie's shoulders speaking to her urgently, it seemed. She wished she could hear what it was about.

'Dismissed?' a cynical voice asked, and Raoul stood before her. He looked past her to the pair in the distance. 'Three's a crowd?'

'I was just asked to return to the house ahead of them. I'm sure they will follow shortly.' She added, 'Whatever they have to discuss is none of my business. Or yours.'

Raoul's eyes narrowed as he kept looking. 'I wouldn't be too certain of that.'

Atalanta studied him. 'You must be a close friend of the family that you care so much for what is happening here.'

Raoul seemed to shake himself and faced her. 'I have eyes in my head.'

'So?'

'I have them and I use them.' He turned away from her and strode to the house.

Atalanta had to run a few paces to catch up. *What does he plan to do?* 'Are you going to tell the comte that they are together?'

'Why on earth would you think that?'

'Perhaps you want the engagement to be broken?'

98

He halted as if stung. His eyes flashed as he studied her. 'Why would you think that?'

'I don't know.' Her heart hammered in her chest. Had Raoul written the letter?

He shook his head. 'No evasive answers now, Mademoiselle Atalanta. You know exactly why you said such a thing. You are the quiet type who never speaks much but who is constantly watching and listening and... waiting for a chance to use something to her advantage? Do you think I will give you money to buy your silence?'

The suggestion struck her dumb. *Me, a blackmailer?*

Disbelieving laughter welled up inside her, but his expression made it die in her throat.

He means it. He thinks I'm here to play people against each other to my own advantage.

Just because he knows I have no money? A cold feeling seeped into the very core of her. Would it be the same always? The prejudices and the lies? She didn't want to flaunt her newfound wealth but it was so tempting whenever people assumed the worst merely because they thought she had no money.

'That is some insult,' she said. She stood up straight and eyed him. 'You have barely met me. You know absolutely nothing about me, aside from my situation in life. Just because I am but a piano teacher—' Anger shook her voice.

'If you think you can manipulate me,' he cut across her with a growl, 'I would think again. I'm not a man to be toyed with.' He swung round and strode off.

Atalanta watched him go. Indignation made her legs

tremble that he had actually had the nerve to accuse her of something so despicable. *To my face, no less.*

She held her palms against her cheeks and took a couple of steadying breaths. He thought he was in command here, but he had also betrayed himself. Why assume she wanted to take advantage of the situation? Nothing untoward had happened.

Unless Raoul knew much more than he had admitted to. *I'm onto something here.*

But was it helpful for the case she was engaged in? She now knew that Louise had set up the comte and his first wife Mathilde, that Louise was still playing a part in what happened here, that Eugénie might have loved another before she had agreed to marry the comte... but how did Raoul fit in? Why had he become so angry at the idea she was watching him?

She rubbed her temple. She had to make some notes of everything she learned and try to establish order in this chaos.

Chapter Eight

A talanta sat at her dressing table making short notes in the code she had always used at the boarding school. She had kept track of her pupils' progress, little quirks, traits that might be beneficial or harmful, and in the beginning she had simply written everything down in a notebook. But after a clever pupil had taken the notebook and used it to manipulate others, Atalanta had developed a code to ensure that neither curious colleagues, like Miss Collins, nor eager pupils could ever get into her thoughts again and use her ponderings to their own advantage.

First of all, she used the Cyrillic alphabet, as in her experience not many people in her circles knew it, and as an extra precaution she used a simple transposition cipher to ensure that even if someone could recognize the letters he could still not make out the words. It was a little thing she had always enjoyed as it made her job more exciting, and right now as she scribbled her notes in the familiar spidery lettering, she felt the thrill of it rush through her veins. This information was more important than any earlier observation had ever been.

Perhaps she should be ashamed of herself that it was thrilling, as a woman had died here. Death was tragic and had an impact on all involved, even when it was accidental. If, however, it had been murder, it was even worse. It should repel her and in part it did, when she considered how a young life had been brutally taken. But that exact fact drove her to look closer and want to know more. What had happened? If it wasn't an accident, whose hand had been behind it? Why?

It was like standing in the shell grotto looking at the mosaics and wondering how the maker had been able to create them when the wall had still been blank. How had he known where to put each little part in order to create such a magnificent whole?

The murder case was like a mosaic in which shells had been glued in the wrong places. Superfluous information or conscious lies had changed the picture. But if she understood what to remove and what to leave in place, she would be able to discern the pattern. And find her way, inevitably, to the truth.

A knock on her door made her stiffen. She slipped the coded notes into a drawer and called, '*Entrez!*'

It was Louise Frontenac, dressed in an exquisite white evening gown with pearls around her neck. She stepped into the room and closed the door softly. 'I want a word with you.'

Atalanta rose to her feet at once. Standing up made her feel stronger and better able to face whatever this woman with the handsome, cold face wanted.

'I don't know how you managed to get in contact with Eugénie,' Louise said, 'but I'm well aware that your branch of the family has never been able to support itself. You've always had to depend on others who were more fortunate, or should I say more able and hard-working?'

Atalanta flinched. If anyone in this house shouldn't be accused of being lazy, it was her. *First Raoul and now Louise...*

But springing to her own defence too readily could defeat her purpose of wanting to know what others thought and felt. She had to act like she cared but little, provoking the other woman to continue.

She tilted up her chin slightly.

Louise seemed to take the challenge. She narrowed her eyes and said, 'You may think that Eugénie is an easy target, but I can tell you she has family and friends who will protect her. You'll not be getting anything from her.'

'I assure you, you're mistaken.' Atalanta forced a casual, almost smug tone to her voice. 'Eugénie only engaged me to play the piano at the wedding feast.'

'Then why are you here ahead of time?'

'We met in Paris and she invited me to join her for the journey. It's quite boring to travel alone.'

Louise seemed to want to laugh disparagingly. 'You may have told her that, and she believed you, but I do not. I won't hesitate to warn her against you.'

'Then why are you not with her, warning her against me?'

Louise's face turned even colder, her cheeks paling with rage. 'How dare you speak to me like that?'

'I'm not a servant who has to do your bidding. I'm my own woman. I came here at Eugénie's request.' *And you have no idea what potentially explosive consequences that request may have, if I find out you are involved in Mathilde's death.*

She added, 'Perhaps you should accept that she is her own woman too, and forging her own path in life, without needing her older sister to tell her what to do.'

'So that's it. You're poisoning her mind against me, suggesting I'm overbearing and trying to steer her in a direction she doesn't wish to take.' Louise looked Atalanta over as if she had turned into a viper rising from the grass. 'You've destroyed what we had to come between us and take my place in Eugénie's confidence. For your own gain. But rest assured'—she took one step closer and hissed —'you'll regret it. Soon.'

She then spun away and left the room, slamming the door shut.

Atalanta drew breath. *That is the second enemy you've made, and all that since dinner,* she told herself. But the glint of humour was doused quickly, and she sank onto the tabouret in front of her dressing table with a sigh.

That Louise didn't like her was of no great concern to her, as Eugénie obviously didn't trust her sister and wouldn't listen to her tales even if she went to her to malign Atalanta.

In fact, it could be quite fruitful if Louise felt threatened and obliged to act to secure her position.

But Raoul Lemont was a different matter. She had genuinely liked him and now he had turned against her for no apparent reason. Did his anger hide hurt? Had he been betrayed by someone before?

She wished she could redo that conversation and somehow change it so the outcome would be different. But that wasn't possible, of course. And Raoul might even laugh at her if he knew how she worried about it, while he had long put it behind him and was preparing for the dance feast. *I should also get ready.*

She picked up her pen and finished her notes with a short addition about Louise. Then she went to her half-unpacked suitcase to find a suitable gown to wear. Amongst the few garments she found a plain white envelope addressed to her in a strong hand. She had no idea how it had come to be there.

From Renard?

She slid it open and read.

My dearest granddaughter…

Her heart skipped a beat. It came from her late grandfather again. And it wasn't *dear* he had chosen in order to express their connection, but *dearest.*

When you read this, you will be handling your first situation. I will ask Renard to send this letter with you so you will find it as soon as you arrive at your destination. I have no idea where that may be, in France or abroad. The situations I've handled have taken me across the border many times, into Switzerland, Italy, Austria, and even Poland, and I'm sure that with your youth and talents you can even go further, perhaps across the ocean to America.

New York! Atalanta felt a shiver of excitement at the idea.

I don't know what situation you are working on at this moment so I cannot tell you what to do. That is a good thing as there is nothing more bothersome than an old hound that keeps barking when the hunting signal sounds even though he has been long retired as he can no longer keep up with the horses, let alone run ahead of them.

You were not that old, Grandfather, Atalanta muttered to herself, *and I believe your mind was sharp till the end.*

I can instead give you some general council. Always go back to the beginning. Think of motive as the engine that sets everything in motion. Danger is like a magnet to some people and the idea of risk—even of death—only pushes them to be more audacious. Desperate people stop at nothing. Don't trust anything you hear, but examine the truth behind it. Find support for information you receive, the more factual the better.

I did that, she told him quietly. *I went to the Frontenac home to speak with the cook. You would have approved of that.*

Opinions have value, but never forget whose interest they serve.
I could go on as so many experiences come back to me while I
write this, but I must allow you to embark on your own journey
and set your own course.

I have faith in you.

Yours faithfully...

And then there was a signature consisting mainly of a strong C and A. Clarence Ashford. The man she had never talked to but to whom she nevertheless felt so connected. She would always cherish this letter.

And hide it, as it revealed too much of her purpose and her identity.

She used the small knife from her sewing kit to open the lining of her suitcase and slipped the paper inside. The first letter he had sent her, via the lawyer, was also in there. She sewed the lining shut neatly and then did what she had meant to: she dressed in a red evening gown. Her grandfather's advice was imprinted on her brain. But first and foremost she felt excited that he had spoken of her own journey. One that would take her places she would never have otherwise gone.Descending the stairs, she admired the grand flower arrangement placed in the bend where the stairs separated: a marble vase filled with tall pink roses and sweet peas piled around their stems like a garland. Would there be a conservatory here somewhere, full of orchids? She longed to see them and make plans for the ones she'd buy herself. *If only you knew, Mama, what I'm doing now...*

A burst of awkward music swept over the house like a tidal wave. She turned around in a jerk, listening, although she really didn't want to hear this. False notes crashed over one another, piercing her eardrums. *Who is abusing the piano in such a fashion?*

Resisting the urge to cover her ears with her hands, she rushed to follow the nerve-racking sounds to a room where several people were gathered. Yvette was banging the instrument with both hands, luring a storm of discordant notes from it, while Eugénie shrieked at her to stop it.

Pom-pom had hidden behind a sofa, his ears flat against his head. Still, he had not quit the room, clearly wanting to keep an eye on his mistress.

Gilbert stood at the window lighting a cigarette. As the flame of his lighter flickered across his features, Atalanta thought she saw concern there and sadness. She walked over and said, 'It can't be easy to take care of a girl at that age.'

He looked at her, raising an eyebrow. 'What do you know about that?'

'I teach music. Pupils often confide in me about their frustrations in life—parents who don't understand them; friendships that break apart.' *Falling in love for the first time, with someone unattainable.* 'And besides, although it might seem difficult for you to imagine, I was once sixteen myself.'

Now he had to laugh. 'My dear mademoiselle, I would never dare insult you by suggesting this was a long time ago.'

Atalanta answered his smile. 'You're most gracious. But when I see her throwing a tantrum like that, I feel as if it were a lifetime ago. Once one is grown up and responsible for so many things, it becomes impossible to let go.'

The comte sighed. 'That is too true.' He gestured with his cigarette at the girl at the piano who was almost tearing off the keys in her wild play. Eugénie had stopped shrieking and now stamped her foot, gesturing along with her hands as if she were trying to tone down the sound.

The comte said, 'I wish Eugénie had a way with her, you know. That she could provide that soft feminine touch I lack. Mathilde...' He fell silent.

Was that why he had looked so sad before? 'Your first wife,' she supplied, 'she had this touch with Yvette?'

'Oh yes, they were the best of friends. Mathilde indulged her fancies, but Yvette did listen when she asked her to be serious about her studies or...' He pointed at the sofa where Pom-pom was peeking out, uncertain whether he wanted to appear or hide even further away. 'That little dog was Mathilde's idea. She believed that Yvette would calm down if she had something to care for. But I'm afraid that no matter how much she loves the dog, it's not helping her. She's only getting worse.'

'I'm sure that your wife's death was a shock to her and she is still coming to terms with it. Grief doesn't pass as quickly as some people seem to think.' There were still moments when she became suddenly, achingly aware that her father was never going to walk into the room again shouting that he had at last found the way to end their streak of bad luck and make them happy; that he would never again put his arms around her and lift her off the ground to whirl her through the room, swearing it would all be different this time.

Even after she had stopped believing him, his laughter had still been infectious and she had got caught up in the way he had always seen new chances on the horizon. Whatever could be said about her father, he hadn't been a quitter.

The comte lowered his cigarette and looked around him for an ashtray. Atalanta fetched a silver one from the mantelpiece and placed it on the windowsill beside them.

'*Merci.*' He tipped off the ash. 'I quit smoking for Mathilde. She disliked the smell of it and the way it ruined the curtains.' He gestured across the white lace which had indeed attained a vague yellowish glow. 'I agreed only to smoke in my study. She never set foot there anyway so it wouldn't bother her if I restricted the smoking to my own territory. She was a very good influence on me.'

'And Eugénie?' Atalanta asked. 'Does she not object to cigarette smoke staining the curtains?'

'I don't know if she cares for any of this.' He swept his hand in a circle to encompass the room with the oil paintings on the walls, statues on pedestals and the world beyond the windows, bathing in gorgeous evening light. 'Any of Bellevue's attractions.'

'But she does. She enthused about them when we drove over here. She was ecstatic when the house came into view.

Even in Paris, she told me about it in a way that had me longing to see it.'

'She's often like that. Exuberant with strangers and...' He fell silent and smoked.

Atalanta felt sorry for him. He probably understood as little of Eugénie as he did of Yvette, and must feel he had failed as a fiancé as much as he did as guardian of his unhappy niece.

She wanted to say something uplifting but a sound distracted her. A thud and wail. Eugénie stood half bent over Yvette, who had fallen off the piano stool.

Or had Eugénie dragged her off it?

'I won't forget this,' Yvette shrieked. 'You ugly hag. You should die. Die!' She scrambled to her feet and ran from the room. Pom-pom followed her, his sharp barks echoing in the hallway.

Now that the music had stopped it was so very silent in the room. As if all life had been sucked out of it and only a vacuum had been left. Eugénie looked at the empty door frame with contorted features. Then she turned to her fiancé. 'Did you hear that? She called me a hag! I'm not even twenty-three. And she wants me to die.'

'Just an outburst of emotion.' Gilbert's voice was remarkably level. 'Why didn't you let her play?'

'Play? You call that raging madness play? She should be locked up in her room until she comes to her senses. Yes. Can't you lock her in?' Eugénie's eyes sparkled with glee as she stepped up to the comte. 'Order a servant to do it. You needn't do it yourself.' The latter sounded a bit like she was taunting him, suggesting he wasn't up to it.

The comte's neck reddened. 'I will do no such thing. She's not an animal to be locked in a cage.'

'Then she should stop behaving like one.' Eugénie straightened her evening dress. 'My headache has returned full force because of her... eccentric behaviour. How can I dance this way?'

'Then don't dance.' The comte's eyes flashed. 'No one is forcing you.'

Eugénie audibly gasped for air. Her expression changed from triumphant to defeated. Then she hissed, 'Of course. You wish to dance with others rather than me.'

He raised a hand to stop her, but she continued, 'Very well. If I am too much, I will not stay.' And she turned around and walked off with her head held high.

The comte raised both hands. 'Women! You can never please them.'

Atalanta suppressed a smile. 'Perhaps I can persuade her to return?'

'Actually no, don't bother.' His expression was cold again. 'If she wants to behave just as childishly as Yvette, she must do it. I don't want to see her sulking face all evening.' He turned to the window and stared into the garden where the evening sunshine kissed the roses.

Atalanta said softly, 'She is your bride. You will be wed in just a few days' time. You must try to make up and—'

'Face judgment.' He sighed. 'It's all my fault for wanting to marry again. I should have known no good would come of it.' He stubbed out the cigarette in the ashtray and muttered, 'Excuse me...'

As he left the room, Atalanta found herself all alone in the silence that pressed upon her like a dead weight. All the people here were so unhappy despite having all the conditions to be perfectly at peace with life. They had this beautiful house to live in, each other's company... but they let themselves be guided by raw emotions that turned them against each other and broke everything that was precious.

But perhaps I'm just deluded by an idyllic notion of what family can be because I never had much of it.

She wanted to quit the room, uncomfortable with lingering alone, when her eye fell on a photograph on a small table in the corner. It was sepia but still she could make out some familiar faces. The comte, Raoul Lemont, and some other people. They looked younger, more carefree, and were raising glasses. They were mostly men but there was one woman amongst them, smiling serenely, with a sort of quiet beauty you would remember later on. *Was that Mathilde?*

Atalanta took a good look at the faces and then turned away.

Chapter Nine

As their plans for the previous evening had been so rudely disturbed by the argument between Eugénie and Yvette, and their host's subsequent decision not to have any dancing after all, Atalanta expected a rather dull mood at breakfast the next morning.

But to her surprise everyone was perfectly cheerful and pleasant to each other. Eugénie praised the workings of the lavender she had put in the sachet under her pillow, declaring she had never slept so well, undisturbed by any bothersome dreams. Yvette said that she wanted to take out her painting things and spend the morning in the forest, while the comte declared that unfortunately he had to leave on some business but would return later and take all of them on a picnic at the nearby lake.

Plans having been made, they parted and Eugénie told Atalanta she wanted to write letters and didn't need her.

Excellent. That gives me time to read the newspapers and see if the dead poacher is mentioned anywhere.

With the local newspaper that had just arrived folded in her hand, Atalanta walked into the garden and sat on a bench beside the bower with the climbing yellow and orange roses. Some were still half-closed, others fully open, showing their many silky petals.

The front page of the newspaper was devoted to a village festival taking place soon and on page two there was mention of the distinguished guests arriving ahead of the wedding of the beloved Comte de Surmonne. Unfortunately, there were no interesting details provided about Raoul Lemont.

There were announcements of births and marriages, calls for lost objects, including a wedding ring of solid gold, and salesmen offering services. An agony aunt answered the questions of married ladies about problems with domestic staff and of young girls seeking to attract the attention of a man that had caught their eye.

Only on the last page was there a short mention of Marcel DuPont dying, having been recently released from prison where he completed a twelve-month sentence for poaching.

Poor man, free at last and then dead so soon.

During his confinement he had naturally not been able to drink alcohol so perhaps upon his release he had indulged in so much it had killed him?

It all seemed logical enough and Atalanta was about to dismiss the whole thing when her eyes fell to the last line of the article.

A medical examination has revealed that M. DuPont was stabbed and the police request anyone who has information about an argument he might have had before he died which can lead to the apprehension of the murderer to come forward.

Death amongst the lavender?

Murder amongst the lavender.

Stabbed, it said. No accident, no case of too much alcohol in combination with the hot weather, a weak heart perhaps, or an unfortunate stumble into a muddy ditch. No, this was cold-blooded murder.

The cold-blooded murder of a poacher who had been in prison. A man who might have made enemies who had been waiting for his release. It seemed unlikely that his death was somehow related to that of Mathilde, Comtesse de Surmonne. They had moved in completely different circles.

Still, I have to follow the news about this murder as it becomes available. I must find out whether the police receive any tips as to who might have administered the fatal stab.

Atalanta put the newspaper aside and took in her surroundings to steady her racing heartbeat. The morning glow lit up the petals on the roses and a butterfly sat on the stones of the path, spreading its wings to soak up the warmth of the sun. A woodpecker hammered deeper in the forest.

It seemed unthinkable that the previous evening such tension had reigned amongst the people staying here. Or that Eugénie had claimed to sense something sinister around. How could any danger come from this lush garden, the shaded forest, the gorgeous shell grotto with its intricate mythological figures she had explored with Raoul the previous day?

Raoul... Where had he gone?

Over breakfast he hadn't expressed any plans but had cut up his toast with a preoccupied expression. *Perhaps I should have stayed at the house to spy on him?*

But after his accusation that she wanted him to pay for her silence, it felt wrong to shadow him. Should he even be on her suspect list? After all, he seemed to be no part of the triangle Eugénie was caught up in with the comte and Louise.

Or the one consisting of Eugénie, Louise, and Victor.

Ah, the inscrutable Victor. He was still an enigma to her. Where others had carelessly shown their hand, seeking confrontation with her, he had stayed carefully away and refrained from even speaking to her. At breakfast he had shown no interest in either Eugénie or Louise, but had piled his plate full of scrambled eggs, ham, and apricot compote as if he never ate a decent meal. Did that make him all the more suspicious? Quiet, in the background, but still watching and waiting? He had arrived on the same day the poacher had died.

But so had Louise.

And Raoul had already been here, but separated from the comte in the forest when he had put out the trail for him. The comte, for his part, had also been away from Raoul.

And both of them had been in the photograph with the beautiful woman who was possibly Mathilde.

Such a tangle!

If only Renard was with me to tell me more about all the people present. He had recounted all facts about the Frontenac family with such ease; he would undoubtedly know something useful about Raoul.

Or Yvette. Why was the comte her guardian? Were her parents no longer alive?

A piercing scream rang out and echoed in the still air.

Atalanta jumped to her feet. The screaming seemed to come from the forest.

Yvette! A girl of sixteen alone with her painting things.

Victor had mentioned a tramp last night. Had he meant in general, or was there one around? A tramp who might come over to a girl alone and ask her for money? Become aggressive when she said no?

The same killer who had stabbed Marcel DuPont? Why had the comte, who knew of the death, not forbidden Yvette to go into the forest alone?

There it was again, a frantic, petrified scream. Atalanta broke into a run in the direction of the sound, her heart pounding in her ears. She was used to walking in the mountains and had good stamina, so the dash didn't immediately wind her. She clenched her hands into fists to keep going, faster even.

Under the first trees she saw a figure coming for her. It wasn't the slender Yvette, fleeing danger, nor was it a man searching for his quarry. But still it looked like a tramp with ugly brownish dirt covering him top to bottom, as if mud had poured from the sky engulfing the poor creature. The figure kept wailing as it ran for Atalanta. Startled, she halted. Only when she was within two feet of it did she realize who it was. Eugénie, covered in mud. Much like the lazy daughter from the tale of Frau Holle, a Brothers Grimm fairy-tale in which two girls fall down a well and one proves herself dutiful and is rewarded by a shower of gold, while the lazy and disrespectful one is covered in tar. Eugénie stopped in front of her. 'Someone tried to kill me,' she wailed.

'I thought you were indoors writing letters,' Atalanta said. What was her client doing here?

'I needed a breath of fresh air. I only wanted to see the shell grotto.' Eugénie swallowed hard. 'It collapsed on top of me. I'm certain someone tried to kill me.'

The shell grotto? Atalanta's mind whirled. When she had been in the grotto with Raoul it had seemed very stable and reliable. Not a contraption which could suddenly collapse on top of someone.

Besides, while Eugénie was dripping with smelly, dirty liquid, she didn't seem to be injured like you'd expect if rocky debris had landed on top of her.

'Did you get hit by stones?' Atalanta asked.

'No. Yes. I don't know.' Eugénie raised her hands. 'Look at me. I could have been killed.' She stretched the latter word into a long yowl.

Atalanta shrank back from the high-pitched intensity of it. 'Let me go and see what happened at the grotto.'

'Someone is after me and I want to know who it is,' Eugénie lamented. 'Can it have been Gilbert? He said he had to leave on business but...'

'Mademoiselle Frontenac, you told me that you fear he is after your dowry. How can he attain that by killing you *before* you are even wed?'

In her state of mind Eugénie didn't seem to be open to this logic. 'I want to leave this place,' she sobbed. 'It's a nightmare.'

Atalanta should probably have put an arm around her and guided her to the house, but curiosity drove her to go and see the grotto before any traces of what had transpired there might have been cleaned away. Certainly, that was the best decision to gather evidence for the case. She said, 'I'll join you later,' and turned to head towards the grotto. Eugénie cried out in dismay and then walked on to the house.

Atalanta found the grotto easily and stood a moment studying its layout. Nothing seemed to have changed. The roof didn't appear collapsed or in any way damaged.

She walked up to the entrance and looked in. A foul stench rose in her nose. The same swampy scent that had risen from Eugénie's sodden clothes. *What happened?*

She took a deep breath and walked in. Making sure her back was protected by the wall, she stood looking up at the opening through which sunlight came in. There was brownish liquid there, dripping down.

The cave hadn't collapsed. Someone had poured mud through the hole, on top of Eugénie.

But why was Eugénie here in the first place?

Frowning hard, Atalanta went outside again and looked up at the cave's rock face. It was probably manmade, constructed especially to hold the shell mosaic and impress visitors to the estate. Did she dare clamber onto it to see if there were traces of the culprit?

If the construction was unstable, it would be very unwise. She could break a leg, or worse.

And what if whoever had attacked Eugénie was still around?

Go carefully then. You've done this often enough at the burg ruins near the school.

She clambered onto the rock. Once safely on top, she inched over to the opening. Someone had been here before her. The moss that covered the rock was scraped off in places. And it seemed something had rested on the edge of the opening. *A bucket filled with mud?*

'Hello there! Are you mad?' The voice was half-wondering, half-accusing.

Atalanta pushed herself up and spied Raoul standing on the forest floor looking up at her. He squinted against the bright sunlight.

Of course, it has to be him catching me in this compromising position. What to say?

'I'm coming back down.'

As she was at the point where she could lower herself conveniently, he appeared and before she knew it, she felt strong hands around her waist helping her down. He lifted her off the rock face and put her on the ground. He held her a moment longer, eyeing her probingly. 'You are more agile than a mountain goat.'

'My family lives in Switzerland.' Atalanta followed the story she and Eugénie had devised together. *But better not expound lest I slip up.* 'I'm investigating what happened to Eugénie.'

'Investigating?' Raoul echoed with a flash of curiosity in his brown eyes.

Wrong word choice. 'I mean,' Atalanta rushed to say, 'Eugénie shrieked in panic that the shell grotto collapsed and that seemed so strange to me that I wanted to see for myself what happened. The structure didn't give way; someone poured mud through the opening on top of her.'

Raoul raised an eyebrow. 'I can imagine some dirt falling through but... someone did this on purpose? Who? Why?'

'That I can't tell.' *Unfortunately.* 'I can see that someone was on top of the rock and used a utensil to pour something down the opening. It must have taken strength to haul a bucket full of mud up to that height. I saw Eugénie up close and what hit her was not a little bit of dirt that fell through because of a breeze in the forest.'

'Birds make nests in trees. Sometimes they come loose and fall down.'

'It was too liquid to be a nest. Didn't you see her appearance?'

'I saw a dishevelled figure running inside, babbling about the cave. I came here to see what had happened.'

Had Raoul perhaps done it himself? To humiliate Eugénie or to scare her?

'While you came out here, did you see anyone?' she asked, studying his response.

'No. You?' Raoul surveyed her in return. 'Did you expect to see someone? The culprit? He or she would have rushed off as Eugénie started to scream.'

'How do you know she screamed? Were you outside when it happened?'

'I can't imagine her not screaming. She shrieks when a butterfly brushes her arm.' Raoul shrugged. 'But where were you, dear Mademoiselle Frontenac? Are you not supposed to be her dutiful shadow?'

'I'm not her maid.' Atalanta heard how defensive it sounded and added more gently, 'She claimed to be writing letters and said she didn't want my company.'

'She claimed? You don't believe her?'

'She told me she wanted fresh air and stepped out later. But perhaps it was her plan all along.'

'Why?'

'I don't know.' Atalanta turned down her eyes. She had her suspicions that Eugénie had wanted to meet Victor, away from the house, but as she hadn't actually seen the blond man, it was mere speculation she didn't intend to share.

Raoul stepped closer to her. 'Are you really here to play the piano at the wedding feast?'

'Yes, you know that.' Atalanta felt a treacherous blush creep up. He was getting nearer to her, and to the truth, than she could allow. She turned away from him. 'I had better go and see how Eugénie is doing.'

124

'And what will you tell her? That someone lurked on top of the grotto to pour a bucketful of mud over her on purpose? It will only further shatter her nerves.'

'*Further*?' Atalanta queried. She wanted to escape his probing looks but this word choice was too interesting to let pass. 'You already found her... anxious before?'

'I don't know the Frontenac sisters well, but Eugénie struck me as rather highly strung with her headache yesterday, and her lavender sachet she thinks she needs to sleep well. Such girls start imagining things at the slightest encouragement.'

'But you can't deny she was covered in mud. She can hardly have poured it over herself.'

'There you have something.' Raoul walked beside her. 'Then what is your theory?'

Atalanta hesitated a moment. The temptation was real to discuss the matter with Raoul, if only to see how he responded to it. She need not share too much. Just a hypothesis. 'Someone is playing a game with her. It could have been Yvette. She vowed to get even with her last night.' She briefly sketched the events of the piano incident.

Raoul laughed. 'Such a small contretemps? It hardly warrants action, let alone something so dramatic as this.'

Atalanta tilted her head. His light-hearted response set her mind at ease a little, but wasn't he underestimating the girl? 'Yvette has a temper. And as she is mostly alone here, and doesn't have girls her own age to talk to, she might think up extraordinary ideas.'

Raoul caught her arm. 'You're not going to suggest she is

mentally unstable.'

'Did I mention such words?' Her pupils had sometimes acted in inexplicable ways when they felt slighted, but before she could explain her meaning, he was already squeezing her arm and saying, 'I won't have it. Stop persecuting her.'

Persecuting her? She blinked. Why would he one moment dismiss Yvette's behaviour as harmless and the next believe someone could actually argue she was mentally unstable? 'I don't understand what you are warning me against. I'm only noting that she has a temper and that, when left to her own devices, she might think up a silly plan of revenge like pouring mud over Eugénie.'

Raoul let go of her arm. 'Yes,' he said, suddenly calm again. 'I can see what you are thinking. Just a prank like schoolgirls play. Something innocent.' It sounded as if he was trying to convince himself of it.

Without much success.

She would bring it up again another time and try to lure him into saying more about what he thought of Yvette and why it mattered to him, but not right now. Her arm hurt where he had seized it. Again, he had believed the worst of her. First accusing her of blackmail, now of persecuting Yvette.

Why focus on me? I'm a perfect stranger here.

They came in view of the house. Louise and Victor were sitting on the terrace, drinking coffee. A statue of a Greek god towered over them. Atalanta deduced from the items he carried—bow and arrow, sword and shield—that it was probably Ares, god of war. *How oddly appropriate.* There was nothing but tension at this house, war between people, as if something in the air affected their brain and made them jump at each other's throats.

Glancing at Raoul beside her, disappointment pricked Atalanta. She had certainly not expected this antagonism when she had first seen him from her balcony.

Louise waved at them from afar. 'Come and join us. It's perfect here in the shade. And the cook made fresh macarons.' She pointed at a porcelain plate filled with the delicacies in pink, yellow, and green.

Victor said, 'Pistachio isn't too sweet.'

'I want to see how Eugénie is,' Atalanta said. She added, keeping an eye on both of their responses, 'Were you not here when she came back, all panicked?'

'Panicked?' Victor echoed. He dropped the macaron he had just selected beside his cup. 'Why, did something happen?'

Louise stared into her coffee and said nothing.

'She had a little accident in the forest,' Atalanta said.

'Accident?' Victor scooted to the edge of his seat. 'You mean she is injured?' He looked genuinely shaken.

'I'm sure it's all exaggerated,' Louise said in a sharp tone. 'Eugénie likes the attention.'

'I'll go and see how she is,' Atalanta repeated and Raoul joined the others, asking Victor to ring the bell for coffee for him too.

Inside the house, a benign silence reigned. A maid was quietly dusting the stairs, putting an extra shine on the polished oak and Atalanta smiled at her as she passed to go up. 'What room is Mademoiselle Eugénie in?'

'I'll take you there.' The maid tucked the dusting cloth into her apron's pocket and led the way. She knocked on the door and at the reply, announced around it, 'Mademoiselle Atalanta Frontenac to see you.' She stepped aside to let Atalanta pass.

The room was bigger than the one allotted to Atalanta, with a four-poster bed draped with heavy velvet curtains held up by elaborate gold embroidered sashes. A wooden contraption was attached to the top of the bed, which could be put into motion by pulling an embroidered rope. Atalanta had only read about this until now; it was meant to work like a fan and provide cool air during hot summer nights.

Eugénie had changed into her nightgown and sat in the windowsill, sobbing in her hands. The scent in the room was pleasant, not at all like the swamp stench of the grotto. Had she cleaned herself in the bathroom?

Atalanta came to stand near her. 'Are you well now?'

'How can I be well when someone wishes me harm? The whole grotto collapsed on top of me. I saw a sort of shadow fall over me and then it began to fall in and I ran.' Eugénie shuddered. 'I should never have come here. I'll leave again, this very day. I'll tell Papa I cannot marry this horrid man. This… murderer!'

'You think your fiancé had a hand in the grotto incident?' Atalanta asked.

'It must be. Who else would do something like that?

Gilbert must hate me or something. You said it can't be for the dowry. But you don't know how he is. Last night, when Yvette attacked me, he didn't even come to my defence.'

Atalanta opened her mouth to point out that Eugénie had rather attacked Yvette by dragging her off the piano stool, but in her present state of mind Eugénie would not be open to reason. She said softly, 'He obviously cares a lot about Yvette. And she is very young and impressionable. She still has to get used to the changes... you coming to live here.'

'But I don't want to live here and I'm leaving. Pack my suitcases.' Eugénie gestured wildly at the closet and the bed.

'I'm not a servant. And I don't think it is wise to leave. The grotto didn't collapse. You were in no real danger.'

'No real danger? How dare you say that! I had such a fright I almost died. There. Now you need not care. Why would you? A stranger.'

'Not so loud,' Atalanta admonished her. 'You'll give away everything.' She glanced at the door. It was firmly closed.

'Do you think someone is listening at the door?' Eugénie asked with a panicky expression.

'I don't know, but we can't be too careful.' Eugénie sniffed but did tone down her voice as she continued. 'You don't care at all for how I feel. No one does.'

Perhaps, to be taken seriously, you should stop acting so dramatic all the time. Atalanta bit back this observation, which would only serve to throw her client into new hysterics. She had to soothe her and convince her that it wasn't the time for drastic action. Not without her having discussed the matter with the comte first.

'I'm certain your fiancé will be upset when he hears what happened,' she said in an encouraging tone. 'And I went to the grotto to investigate, quite closely, in how much danger you have been. The grotto did *not* collapse.' Eugénie seemed to listen now and Atalanta emphasized, 'I looked at it from all angles. I've been inside of it and on top of it.'

'On top of it?' Eugénie gave her a curious look. 'You actually scaled it?'

'Yes, I take my duties towards you very seriously. I could see traces of someone having been there before to pour mud inside and scare you. But it was never meant to kill you; it couldn't have.'

'Still, I could have had a heart attack...' Eugénie spluttered. But she seemed to think it through more dispassionately now. Her hands crinkled a wet handkerchief. 'So you think it wasn't meant to kill me? Just give me a fright?'

'It feels more like a prank,' Atalanta said.

At the word *prank* Eugénie seemed to want to splutter again, but Atalanta raised a hand to cut her off. 'A mean prank, I admit. I don't condone it or say you have no right to be angry about it, and whoever did it should be ashamed of themselves, but it wasn't an attempt on your life. You believed so because the warning letter upset you. You must not, however, connect things that might be totally unrelated.'

'Even so…' Eugénie drew breath slowly. 'I don't feel at ease here. Especially now that Louise and Victor have come.'

'But you're engaged to be married. This is going to be your home. You are the hostess.' Atalanta leaned over to her and said with insistence, 'Take your rightful place. Engage your fiancé, be at his side. Show you care about what he thinks of you.' Eugénie wanted to protest but Atalanta pressed on. 'You are so caught up in a struggle with Yvette and your sister that you forget what really matters: your marriage to a man you can hopefully respect and care for.'

Eugénie was now silent, sitting there like a girl with her bare feet.

'Of course you can leave if you want to,' Atalanta said. 'I can't stop you. But I do feel that your fiancé deserves an honest chance.' The comte had seemed genuinely distraught the other night when he had shared his concern over Yvette with her. 'You don't know for certain that he was involved in any way in the accident that killed his first wife. If that letter contained a lie to harm you both, you're playing into the sender's hands by behaving as you do now.'

Eugénie sat up. Her expression changed to one of determination. 'You're correct. I won't give them that satisfaction.'

'That's better. Now tell me one thing. Did you really step outside for a breath of fresh air, on impulse?'

The sudden question was meant to throw her client, and it worked. Eugénie flushed. 'No. I received a note. It was

131

pushed under my door. It said to come to the grotto at eleven.' She lowered her head. 'I thought it was from Victor... I thought he wanted to see me.'

'And you wanted to meet up with him like that, away from the house?' Atalanta tilted her head. Here she was, persuading Eugénie to make amends with Gilbert while she was sneaking away from the house to meet a former love interest.

Renard had been so right. She couldn't trust her client. 'If your fiancé had found out...'

'But he was away on business. And I never got a chance to explain to Victor... I only wanted to tie up loose ends. End our contact decently.'

The way Eugénie wrung her handkerchief and refused to meet Atalanta's eyes as she spoke strongly opposed her claim. Was there still something simmering between Victor and Eugénie? Or was it merely her need for attention, her sense of feeling flattered by his continuing advances even though she was engaged to be married to someone else?

Had it been motivated by the idea that she could hurt her sister's feelings if she could prove that Victor was still under her power and had not succumbed to Louise's charms?

How to make sense of all these emotions...

'I'll dress for the picnic,' Eugénie said, sounding strong and in command. 'I'll show everyone I'm not letting myself be driven away from here. Bellevue is my new home, the place where I belong.'

Atalanta nodded. 'That's the spirit. I think I hear a car. It must be your fiancé coming back.' She left the room. It was good Eugénie had calmed down but something about her responses had been off. One moment she was desperate to leave, then she wanted to stay again. Was it all an act? *Meant to deceive me?*

But first she had to check on the comte's alibi.

She went downstairs to find the comte stepping into the hallway, humming a tune. She passed him with a greeting and went out where the chauffeur was just about to drive off. She halted him and asked, 'Where did you take monsieur? I mean, I need not know exactly where, but… has he been away from the estate since you left here?'

The chauffeur looked confused. 'But of course. I drove him into Saint Michel where he met with an acquaintance.'

Suspicion flashed in his eyes and Atalanta added hurriedly, 'Mademoiselle Frontenac, his fiancée, is preparing a surprise and was worried he might have returned earlier than expected and seen something to spoil it all. Please put her mind at ease.'

'I can do that at once.' The chauffeur gestured. 'While they discussed business at Café Sur Mer, I waited in the town square reading a newspaper. After he came out, I brought him back here. He was there all the time.'

No chance for him to have poured the mud over Eugénie at the grotto, Atalanta thought with a hint of relief. Her advice to Eugénie not to depart seemed sound enough. 'That's very helpful, thank you.'

He stared after her with a bit of befuddlement as if he wasn't quite sure what to make of the whims of women. But

Atalanta had her information. She hadn't harmed her client by saying she should try and stay for the time being. The incident at the grotto had not been the work of a murderous fiancé.

Whose work it had been she still had to decide. Yvette came to mind.

And that's exactly why Eugénie's response was so odd. Atalanta stood frozen as the realization sank in. Why had Eugénie not jumped at this chance to accuse the girl she couldn't stand? Yvette had insulted her the night before and even said she wanted Eugénie to die. Wouldn't it have been logical to think it had been her at the grotto?

But Eugénie hadn't even mentioned her as an option. She had jumped to the conclusion that it had been Gilbert. Not even Atalanta's reference to a prank had brought Yvette to Eugénie's attention as the likely culprit.

That seemed almost impossible. Why would she not try to blacken the girl she disliked so much?

Merely because of the letter? The accusation of earlier foul play readymade for her to build upon?

But if she were still attached to Victor somehow, she might not be totally innocent herself. Might even have reasons to want to cast her fiancé in a bad light?

Atalanta's grandfather had advised her not to trust anything she heard, but to examine the truth behind it.

She had to bear that in mind. Also his next words: *Find support for information you receive, the more factual the better.*

Perhaps events during the picnic would enlighten her?

Chapter Ten

The small lake was clear blue under the summer sky and on its grassy bank the comte had spread blankets. Eugénie distributed the food and drinks from the baskets like a perfect hostess, while Pom-pom explored the nearby brush and came running back with a yap as a bird suddenly flew away.

'That animal is afraid of his own shadow,' Raoul teased Yvette.

'Not true. He's very courageous for someone his size. Imagine being so little.' She draped herself across the blanket. Her skirt rode up exposing her knees over her stockings and Louise cast her a warning glance, which Yvette ignored.

Atalanta surveyed the young lady's knees, searching for bruises or scraped-off skin that might indicate she had scampered up a rock this morning. Admittedly the knees didn't look pristine but those injuries weren't fresh.

Raoul pulled out a packet of cards and engaged Yvette in a game of *chemin de fer*. Whether he let her win, or she was good at it, Atalanta could not determine, but with every triumphant outcry as she bested him, the girl's smile became broader and the general mood of the company improved.

Louise told a lively tale about a visit to Rome the previous year, while Victor had put a sketchbook on his knees and was absorbed in the drawing he was doing with a bit of charcoal.

As new refreshments were passed around, Atalanta got up to have a look at his creation and held her breath as she saw a rather good likeness of their party. Victor had exaggerated all of their features just a touch: there was the sharp liveliness of Yvette's hungry face, the elegance of Louise's head posture, Eugénie's dreamy look.

Her fiancé was portrayed as looking away from the company, as if he was expecting something or someone just outside the circle the drawing captured. In that direction was a shadow. Someone stood there, invisible, but still casting the shade of its presence into the lively scene.

Victor looked up at her. 'How do you like it?' he asked.

'You're very talented. I can draw a little but I could never sketch such a stunning likeness in so short a time.'

He waved off the compliment. 'When I was a student in Paris, I earned a little money doing drawings of the tourists.'

'You mean you lived like one of those artist tramps on

Montmartre,' Gilbert said sharply. 'Your father can't have approved.'

'My father never cared what I thought of him and so I decided to care as little as possible what he thought of me. It was a decent enough arrangement while it lasted.'

'It seems he did care what you did or he would not have disinherited you.'

'Gilbert!' Eugénie looked half-shocked, half-amused. 'Victor is always the first to admire frankness of speech but we need not discuss such intimate family matters, especially not on a joyous occasion like this.'

Yvette sat up, throwing her cards down. 'It's so hot! I could do with a swim.' She held her gaze on Eugénie to see how she took this suggestion.

'Neither of us brought bathing suits,' Louise said, but Yvette cut her off with a an abrupt 'I don't need one.' She stood up and walked to the edge of the lake, kicked off her shoes and leaned down to pull her stockings off her feet.

'Don't make a fool out of yourself,' Eugénie warned, her cheeks turning red. She cast a look at her fiancé as if to demand of him to do something.

But the comte sat staring into the distance, not responding at all to his protégée's antics.

Yvette had removed her stockings and stepped into the lake. The water was shallow and played around her bare ankles. 'It's so nice and cool,' she called. 'Will no one join me?'

'Best to ignore her,' Louise said with a high colour suggesting she was mortified.

'Show us your sketchbook, Victor,' Eugénie said, and soon the three of them were huddled close together, the women exclaiming in admiration as Victor flicked past his drawings.

Raoul leaned back on the blanket, folded his hands behind his head and closed his eyes.

Yvette walked further and further into the lake, her arms spread as if to balance herself. Suddenly, with a shriek, she tilted forwards and splashed into the water. Her entire body disappeared from view. The surface rippled and became still.

That's not good. Why is Yvette not thrashing about?

Raoul was up on his feet already and rushed into the lake fully clad. He used his arms to feel in the water for the vanished girl.

Where is she? Atalanta's heart pounded painfully, and her hands were clenched into fists by her side.

The comte stood up straight, his hand up to his face, while Louise and Eugénie looked disapproving, as if the rescue was as inappropriate as the bathing had been to begin with.

Atalanta took a step forward, then stopped herself. Should she try to lend a hand or let Raoul take care of it? He was a strong and sporty man who obviously knew what he was doing.

His agile arms fished something from the water and he slung the dripping girl over his shoulder, carrying her back to them.

'You are a true hero,' Louise said, batting her lashes at

Mystery in Provence

him, while Victor rolled his eyes and Eugénie suppressed laughter.

No one rushed up to check whether Yvette was well. Her legs dangled limply as if she were...

The memory of Marcel DuPont's hand flashed through Atalanta's head and her stomach contracted. She tried to tell herself that healthy young girls didn't just die like that, but cold anger gripped her that no one had bothered to pay real attention to the unhappy girl and had allowed this accident to happen.

Accident?

The comte stood waiting as Raoul stopped and panted while lowering his wet charge to the ground. He was very pale and his voice shook as he spoke Yvette's name, while leaning down over her.

With a burst of laughter the girl sat up and shook herself. 'Got you all, didn't I?'

The comte stepped back a pace, his eyes widening. His mouth pinched into a tight line. 'How can you be so silly?' he burst out. 'You could have hurt yourself.' He seemed to want to say more and then turned and abruptly walked away.

'Gilbert!' Eugénie got up and followed him, grabbing his arm and speaking to him, but he shook her off and left her standing alone.

Visibly chastised, she came back to the group. Her eyes sought Yvette with a venomous look that shocked Atalanta. She had only read in novels about looks that could kill but here she caught one fierce enough to scorch the girl off the earth.

Yvette sat in the grass, raking back her wet hair and laughing. 'I wasn't drowning. I didn't even misstep. It was just so boring. All I wanted to do was shake things up. Have a little fun.'

'You call it fun to give other people a heart attack?' Louise said. She looked at Victor. 'I think Gilbert should find a boarding school for her with the strictest rules to bend her into shape.'

Yvette looked up with a jerk. Her eyes seemed hollow for a moment in her pale features. 'He would never send me away.'

'Why not?' Louise challenged. 'He certainly won't keep you here forever. He will be married soon.'

'If there even will be a wedding...' Yvette jumped to her feet and shook herself like a wet poodle. Then she ran off on her bare feet.

Raoul called after her, 'Don't make it worse, girl. Come back.' He let out a sigh of frustration. Water dripped from his hair and out of his expensive suit.

Atalanta's knees still felt rubbery from the shock of thinking Yvette was dying before her very eyes. And it had merely been a joke? A provocation of the women she didn't like?

This young lady needs some straightening out.

She said, 'Let me try and talk to her.'

Throwing all her pent-up energy into action, she ran after the girl, who was making her way down a country road past high sunflowers. 'Yvette! There's no point in running off. You must come back with us to Bellevue.'

'Why should I if nobody wants me there?' It sounded angry, but most of all forlorn.

Atalanta bit her lip. The anger clashed with a wave of compassion for this lonely girl who didn't know how to communicate without turning everyone against her.

Moments before, she herself had wanted to give her a shaking for being so stupid; now she could hardly resist the urge to put her arm around the girl's narrow shoulders. But that wasn't a good idea. Despite her obvious pain, Yvette desperately wanted to be grown-up, to be taken seriously. Treating her like a child would only alienate her further. Atalanta had to reason with her on an adult level. 'The comte does want you there. Your fall into the lake gave him a real scare. I saw his expression. He feared for your life.'

Yvette's angry expression softened a bit, but she huffed, 'It's not that he doesn't care, I know. But all these silly women... He cares more for their opinion than he does for me. They try to make me sit up like a little dog.'

'Is it really that bad?' Atalanta leaned over. 'You could try and be pleasant. Just when they are around.'

'You have to be pleasant to people because you have no position. You are just some piano teacher who must smile at others to get money.'

The words stung, even if the girl was just lashing out at the first victim at hand. For a moment Atalanta was tempted to reveal she had plenty of money of her own. That she could buy anything she wanted and travel far beyond where Yvette had ever been.

But the satisfaction of retaliation would be brief and the damage lasting. As so often in her life, she had to be sensible, take the insults flung at her, and not reveal how she felt about them.

Yvette barked at her, 'I have money. I should have had a title too. I'm the eldest. Stupid rule that says boys are more important even if they are born later.'

'So you have a brother.' *Why have I never heard of him before? Where is he?*

Yvette nodded. 'I haven't seen him in years. Not that I care.'

Atalanta waited a few moments. She had to tread carefully here. 'I can understand how you had to fend for yourself. I had to, myself.' Perhaps the poor lifestyle Yvette envisaged for her could help to draw them closer? Create the sympathy she needed to get through to the girl?

But Yvette grimaced as if struck. 'Don't act like you understand because you don't. They all tried that with me. Eugénie, Louise. "Oh, tell me your secrets, girl, I want to be your best friend." But I don't believe them. They laugh at me behind my back. They think I'm silly and I don't know my mind. But I do know. They'll see. Soon enough.'

Yvette stopped and looked at Atalanta. The obstinacy died in her eyes. 'I will come back with you, of course,' she said. 'I have no other place to go.' She made a sharp turn and began to walk back.

Atalanta blinked. The change in her was so sudden.

From full-blown anger to acceptance. As if a switch was flicked and her whole being changed in a heartbeat.

As if another person had taken over.

She shivered a moment, rubbing her bare arms. Raoul's words echoed in her mind. Mentally unstable. He had been worried she would say that. Did she now have reason to do so?

Or was it all just an act? The cry for sympathy, the mood swings...

Yvette had just admitted she hadn't been drowning either. She was a very smart girl who loved to play people against each other. One moment their group had been content, looking like a unit, and the next they had been divided, attacking each other and placing blame. Yvette seemed to enjoy that.

Raoul met them a little away from the others. He had rubbed dry his face, and his hair, though moist, wasn't leaking anymore. 'How are we?' he asked Yvette with a probing look in his dark eyes.

'Not that I needed you,' she said with a tilt of her chin. 'And you only wanted to play hero for Eugénie. I know how you pine after her while you can't have her. But if you want to get into her good graces, you should have let me drown. That is what she wants. To see me dead.'

With this parting shot she crossed the last few steps to the picnic blanket and threw herself onto it. Pom-pom ran up to her and began to lick the hand she had pushed against the fabric. A hand formed into a fist.

'Drama, drama.' Raoul rolled his eyes but didn't meet

Atalanta's gaze. She wondered if Yvette was right that he was a bit enamoured with Eugénie. Her client could be very charming when she wanted to. Atalanta hoped a level-headed man like Raoul would see through that, but how well did she know him? What could she gather about his life, his choices, the women he fancied?

She didn't understand any of his behaviour. For all of her working adult life she had been surrounded by women, and men were like creatures from the moon to her. What did they want? How did they reason? Would they stoop to writing a letter like Eugénie had received?

Atalanta sighed. One moment the atmosphere at Bellevue was pleasant and peaceful and she was certain nothing dark and sinister lurked here; the next she was witness to the charged altercations between the inhabitants and guests and there was such a strong undertow of tension she could feel how it waited to sweep them away.

And she herself wasn't impartial either. She wanted to be; she demanded it of herself. But she couldn't help but feel sorry for the motherless Yvette and her uncle Gilbert who struggled to raise her. It didn't seem like Eugénie was the right person to stand by his side in that endeavour. *Regardless of any truth in that letter, should those two get married?*

But that wasn't what she was here for. She had to keep an objective view of the personal affairs at hand to be able to uncover the truth about Mathilde's death, and that of Marcel DuPont the poacher. Her opinion about the comte, Yvette, or her client didn't matter.

But she felt like she was wading around in quicksand, getting nowhere and slowly but surely being sucked under. Perhaps her grandfather had been too optimistic in his assessment of women's instincts? Second to none, he had called them. But she had always relied on her common sense sooner than something vague like instinct. Something unreliable like... feelings.

Atalanta bit her lip. Understanding people's emotions without attaching her own seemed nigh on impossible.

And uncovering their secrets could prove to be a dangerous thing to do.

Chapter Eleven

They arrived at the house in a sombre mood. An unfamiliar car was parked in front and when they ascended the steps to the house, the door opened and the butler appeared with a flustered look. 'It is Madame Lanier,' he said. 'She says she will stay for the wedding.'

Gilbert turned pale. 'For the wedding?' he repeated as if the words were in a foreign tongue.

'Did you invite her?' Eugénie asked in a shrill tone. 'How... odd.'

'I didn't invite her.' Gilbert shot her a murderous look. 'Not that it is any of your affair if I had.' He turned to the butler. 'Where is she now?'

'In the salon.'

'I'll go and see her. Persuade her...' He entered.

'To leave?' Raoul whispered to Atalanta.

She asked him softly, 'Who is Madame Lanier?'

'Mathilde's mother.'

Atalanta widened her eyes. 'Her daughter died and now she wants to attend her former son-in-law's wedding to another woman who is taking her daughter's place?'

Raoul shrugged. 'If you phrase it that way, it does seem unusual. But you must understand the circumstances. Madame Lanier always loved Gilbert. They were as thick as thieves. After the accident she stayed here for a few weeks. I don't think she ever...' He sought for words.

'Blamed him?' Atalanta supplied, curious how he would take this word choice.

But Raoul didn't even blink. He nodded with relief. 'Exactly. She might have as the horse was his and it was quite a wild beast. But she knew how Mathilde always got what she wanted. That she didn't take no for an answer.'

Atalanta was only half listening. She had been dejected on the way home, a feeling of failure taking control of her mind to the point where she couldn't think at all. But now light shone in that darkness. The arrival of Mathilde's mother could be a real break in the case. She dearly wanted to speak to that woman and learn more about the deceased and the way in which she had died.

Could Madame Lanier dispel the notion that Gilbert had anything to do with his first wife's death? If so, nothing stood in the way of a marriage between Gilbert and Eugénie. Whether it would be a happy one remained to be seen, as they seemed to be very different and there was Yvette to come between them. But that lay outside the scope of her investigations.

And what about Marcel DuPont, the dead poacher? a small

voice inside whispered. *Another death at Bellevue, and certainly not an accident.*

First things first, she retorted. *Madame Lanier is my object.*

They all entered the house and dispersed. Atalanta walked upstairs with the others, pretending to be headed for her bedroom, but after they had all gone to their respective rooms, she slipped back down again and approached the door leading to the salon. Her heart beat fast in anticipation of her doing something as despicable as listening in on a conversation but this chance was too good to let it pass.

The door, however, was firmly closed and she could hear absolutely nothing.

She stood for a moment, half-annoyed, half-relieved that she didn't have to stoop so low. But private investigators had to be resourceful. Perhaps there was another way?

She left the house and quickly walked to the salon's French doors. As she had hoped, with the hot summer weather, they were open and voices drifted out from inside.

Gilbert said, 'You are of course welcome to stay here and attend the proceedings. My house will always be your house as well. To honour Mathilde's memory. But I... I don't want you to hurt yourself. I can marry again, but you will never have your daughter back.'

'I know,' a woman's voice said, strangled as with tears. 'Still, I must show my face here. I cannot let people whisper that I don't wish you well. That I somehow blame you for what happened. I know it is silly, for no one could have contained that horse and she wasn't supposed to ride it, but you know what people are like. They assume the worst. All to feed their gossip and have something to prattle about.'

Gilbert seemed to pace the room as Atalanta clearly heard footfalls. 'You are too kind thinking of my reputation. But I can't demand of you to live through a wedding so reminiscent of that happy day when I took Mathilde's hand in mine and...' He fell silent as if he was unable to go on.

A rustle of fabric. 'My dear boy...'

Atalanta dared peek into the room and saw a petite woman dressed in black with her arms wrapped around the sturdy figure of the Comte de Surmonne. He rested his head on her shoulder and made a sound suspiciously like subdued sobbing.

Atalanta retreated hurriedly. Her cheeks burned. It was low to listen in on people and this intimate conversation had certainly not been meant for a stranger's ears.

Still, it strengthened her feeling that Gilbert was innocent of Mathilde's death.

That, however, didn't exclude the possibility that another had contrived to kill her. Eugénie still might not be safe. Who had thrown mud over her at the shell grotto and why?

Atalanta went to her room and made coded notes again. She had to investigate a few specific matters to try and clear up the identity of the mud thrower, and the letter writer. It would also be most useful to learn if the police had already made progress with the case of the stabbed poacher. If they had established that he was killed by a rival poacher, for instance, she could cut the potential tie between the two deaths.

Suddenly, a sharp scream rent the silence. *What's that?* Dropping her pen, Atalanta jumped to her feet and ran from her room. In the corridor she tried to determine where the sound had come from. The other wing, it seemed.

She rushed over. Louise appeared ahead of her, in a silk dressing gown that trailed her in flutters of pale yellow, and knocked on the door to Eugénie's room. 'Eugénie? What's happening? Why are you screaming?'

As no answer came, Louise opened the door and went in. Atalanta followed her. She braced herself for some horrible scene.

Eugénie sat on the edge of her bed. She held a linen sachet in her hand and on the blue bed cover was something dark brown that was spreading a pungent odour.

'What on earth is that?' Louise exclaimed. Her nose wrinkled as she backed away. Eugénie sobbed. 'It's dung. Someone exchanged the sweet lavender in my sachet for dung. It's horrible. I wanted to take a few relaxing sniffs and then... I smelled it wasn't lavender. Not the blooms I plucked myself. Who did this and why?'

She jumped to her feet backing away from the horrid substance. 'It must have been Yvette. That little witch is trying to destroy everything, but I'll get her.' She pushed past Louise and Atalanta into the corridor and stormed to Yvette's room. She threw the door open and marched in.

The other two women followed hurriedly, Louise calling

to her sister not to be silly now.

Yvette sat in the windowsill, with an album clasped to her chest. Eugénie ran to her and tore it from her hands. Yvette shouted, 'No, don't do that!'

Pom-pom yapped anxiously but ran out of Eugénie's path as she dashed from the room and into the nearby bathroom. She opened the tap and moved to hold the album under the stream of water.

Yvette had come after her and shrieked as she fought to retrieve the album before it got wet. She slapped at Eugénie who let go of the album, but fetched a nearby jar and filled it with water, then splashed it over Yvette who was clutching her album.

Yvette cried out and grabbed a wooden bath brush, slamming it down on Eugénie's head. As Eugénie pulled back instinctively, the brush grazed her temple, and the force of the strike drew blood. Eugénie whipped up her hand and felt her cheek. Her palm came away tainted with red liquid. She turned pale and gasped. 'She tried to kill me.' She staggered backwards, her bloodied hand feeling for a hold.

Louise caught her before she sagged to the tiled floor. 'Help me,' she said to Atalanta, 'to take her to her room.'

Blood trickled down Eugénie's jaw. Atalanta grabbed a clean washcloth and pressed it to the wound. She helped Louise support her sister. Eugénie didn't respond to their questions of how she was feeling. *Is she unconscious?*

It took them quite an effort to move her into her room and place her on her bed. When Atalanta lifted the cloth, the graze on Eugénie's temple was still bleeding and Louise urged, 'Bring me a fresh cloth and water to clean this wound.'

'At once.' Atalanta hurried back to the bathroom, hoping she could tell Yvette to wait for her there so they could speak about what had happened. Dealing someone a blow was a serious matter, but Atalanta couldn't deny Yvette had been provoked. She had fought like a wildcat for that album. *What can be in it?*

But the bathroom was empty; the girl had gone already. Where to? In an angry mood, Yvette was capable of anything.

And that with Madame Lanier in the house. Atalanta shook her head to herself as she filled a bowl with water and took it with a washcloth back to the sisters. Eugénie was moaning that the little monster had to be locked up and she had told Gilbert before to have a psychiatrist look at her. 'She's mad, stark raving mad,' she declared.

Having handed the bowl to Louise, Atalanta excused herself and left the room, rushing to Yvette's room to find her. She shouldn't be allowed to do something dangerous again.

If she's not careful, she really will be declared mentally unstable.

Raoul would be appalled. Atalanta didn't want to analyse why this mattered to her. She merely wanted to act and douse the fire for the moment.

Yvette wasn't there.

Neither was Pom-pom.

Atalanta looked around the room to ascertain there were no hiding places there, checked the balcony, which was also empty, and rushed down to see if she had gone to the piano again to maltreat it in her anger.

No one in the music room. She strained her ears to catch the sound of sobbing, angry reproaches, or the yapping of the little dog, but it was so silent. Almost threateningly quiet, as if everything held its breath waiting for the big outburst.

The lethal one?

In the hallway Atalanta almost bumped into a maid and asked her if she had seen Mademoiselle Yvette but she hadn't. 'Perhaps she went outside?'

Atalanta rushed out of the front door and spotted a gardener at work trimming the box hedges. When asked if he had seen the girl, he nodded and gestured with his shears. Atalanta thanked him and followed the path, listening for anything that might give away where Yvette had gone to.

The gardens were large and offered several secluded corners with seating arrangements. Perfect hiding places for an upset girl.

Finally she heard sobbing and found Yvette huddled at the foot of a stone statue of the goddess Minerva, clutching the album she had tried to save against her chest. Pom-pom stood at her feet, leaning his head on her ankle.

Compassion tightened Atalanta's throat as she knelt beside the girl and placed a hand on her arm. To feel so all alone in the world...

'Go away,' Yvette said.

'I won't go away.' Atalanta's head was full of things she wanted to say to this sad young woman but Yvette wouldn't be open to it. How to handle this?

Wait. At school she had learned that the easiest way to earn her pupils' trust was by asking them for their side of the story instead of assuming, naturally, that a teacher or parent was right. What if she took that same approach here? 'Did you put the dung in the lavender bag?'

'What if I did? She was going on and on about it. How well it made her sleep.' Yvette pulled a face. 'I just wanted to play a trick on her. The idea she'd push the bag to her nose... inhaling hard to calm herself, and she'd be sniffing horse poo! It was just too brilliant.'

Atalanta fought a laugh. She had to admit there was a sort of irony in it that could be quite amusing, but she tried to look stern. 'You are a guest here at the comte's estate. You can't misbehave and harass other guests.'

'She doesn't think she's a guest here. She thinks it's all hers already. I can see it in her face as she walks around. She will change everything about it. Sell furniture and buy new things. Change rooms. She demanded that one room upstairs be painted red. They are doing it now. Red, I ask you. It's horrid. But he is like wax in her hands.'

'The comte?'

Yvette sniffed. She relaxed a bit and leaned the album on her knees. Atalanta looked at it. 'Is it a photo album? Of your family?'

Yvette nodded. 'Eugénie can't stand that my mother was beautiful. She wants to destroy all I have of her.'

'It seemed more like her grab for the album was a response to your sachet filled with dung,' Atalanta pointed out gently. 'And you could have really hurt her at the grotto.'

'What grotto?' Yvette asked. 'The shell grotto?' Her eyes were wide and questioning. 'I haven't been there in days.'

'Someone attacked her at the grotto.'

'It wasn't me.' Yvette looked at the album and caressed the embellished front with a finger. She looked younger now and lost in her thoughts. Happy memories of when her mother was still alive?

Or just pain that those days were over for good?

How bittersweet it could be to dwell on the past.

Grief changed people. For a while or forever. Had grief and anger eaten their way so deep into Yvette's heart that she had become a danger? To herself and others? Atalanta asked urgently, 'Can you promise me, honestly, it wasn't you who threw mud over Eugénie at the shell grotto?'

Yvette looked her in the eye. 'Why does it matter?'

Atalanta sighed. If she told Yvette people were whispering about her mental condition, she would only frighten her. She had to protect this young woman against the consequences of her own reckless behaviour. 'Eugénie blames you for everything that happens but I think she's overreacting. Her nerves are suffering from the tension here.'

Yvette shrugged. 'Why should I care?' She scratched

Pom-pom behind the ears. The little dog closed his eyes in contentment.

'If things go on like this, there might be no wedding,' Atalanta said and then, slowly, as if she was just picking up this idea, 'Or is that what you want? Are you doing all of this to drive her away?'

'It's not about her.' Yvette huddled again, turning her back on Atalanta.

'What is it about then? The comte's affection? A competition to see who can win him?'

'I'm family.' Yvette sounded indignant. 'She's a stranger.' She turned to Atalanta again and said with wide eyes, 'Why do there have to be strangers coming along and ruining everything? It was perfect after Mathilde died.'

'Because you had the comte all to yourself?'

'He taught me how to play chess and took me to a nearby chateau. Finally, he had time for me.' Yvette pursed her lips. 'But I should have known it wouldn't last. Good things never do.'

Atalanta studied her. 'That Eugénie came into his life doesn't mean he can't play chess with you or take you places.'

'Of course it does mean that. She will be there all the time. She is the kind of woman who throws herself at him constantly. If we played chess, she'd be in the room prowling like a tiger, distracting him, yawning, saying it was so boring, until he quit to go with her and then she'd look at me to show me she had won.'

'It's not a competition. People love many other people in

157

VIVIAN CONROY

different ways. The comte can love both Eugénie and you.'

Yvette sank into stubborn silence. Atalanta said, 'Mathilde's mother has arrived. Do you like her?'

Yvette didn't respond. Her eyes followed a butterfly dancing from flower to flower in a nearby bed. Then suddenly she said, 'She tried to be nice to me. I don't know why. I never know why people are nice to me.'

How difficult it had to be to feel so suspicious of everyone's good intentions. To be constantly on guard and defending herself. 'Perhaps she is genuinely interested in you,' Atalanta suggested gently.

'Why would she be? I'm just a child nobody wants. After my mother died, I was passed around like a parcel.'

'That's not completely true. The comte has asked you to live here. You already lived here when Mathilde came.'

'That's just a year ago. I mean before that.' Yvette scrambled to her feet. 'But you wouldn't know that or understand. And I don't even want you to understand. I don't need you or anyone else.'

'Did you or did you not attack Eugénie at the grotto?' Atalanta asked.

Yvette tilted her chin up. 'If I say I did, what would you do? Call the police to tell them I'm trying to kill her? They won't come. They're far too busy with the dead poacher.' There was a triumphant gleam in her eye.

'How do you know about that?' Atalanta asked. 'Did you see something?'

'The police were here to report about it. They stand in awe of Gilbert because he is the comte. They will never

158

touch his family.' Yvette smiled contentedly. 'Goodbye.' And with that she scooped up her dog and walked off.

Atalanta stood and let her gaze wander over the smooth marble features of Minerva. Such features gave nothing away. But although Yvette's face was made of flesh and blood, and easily betrayed anger and pain, it was as hard to determine what she was really thinking, and why she acted the way she did.

Yvette had admitted to having placed the dung in the linen sachet right away but she had denied having attacked Eugénie at the grotto. Why lie? She took obvious pride in her treatment of her uncle's bride.

So if she accepted that Yvette had no part in the grotto incident, who could have done that? And why? Pouring mud over someone wasn't a genuine attempt on their life, she supposed. More of a humiliation.

Had it been a joke?

Louise?

Victor, whom Eugénie had scorned? There had been a note luring Eugénie to the grotto. That aspect was relevant, she felt. Whoever had invited Eugénie to come out had known she would come if she believed Victor waited for her.

Was it a test?

A sound close by made her jerk round. Raoul stood with his feet planted apart, his hands in his pockets, watching her with an unreadable expression. The sun reflected off the gold watch around his wrist. 'You won't get into Yvette's confidence just like that, Mademoiselle Atalanta.'

Unease rippled through her. How much had he overheard? What had he wanted to learn?

'And why would you even want that?' He tilted his head. 'Are you blessed with that typical teacher's gift of a real interest in your pupils' affairs?'

He sounded so cynical she blushed. 'Yvette is not my pupil.'

'No. In fact, she is nothing to you. You're a guest here, invited to play the piano at a wedding feast. Why are you so interested in what is happening here?'

'Why are you interested in the reason I'm interested?' Atalanta countered. He kept approaching her, wanting to be with her, to talk to her. Was he suspicious of her? Or did he want to spend time with her?

Her heart skipped a beat as soon as he was near. Under different circumstances she might have…

But the circumstances weren't different. She was here for work. She shouldn't like him, couldn't trust him.

Then why do I want to be with him anyway?

She walked past him back to the house.

Raoul followed her. 'I wonder what's in it for you.'

'In it for me?'

'Yes. You're a relation of the Frontenacs. Not as wealthy as they are nor as privileged. Do you hope to endear yourself to Eugénie by standing up for her?'

'Why would you think I'm standing up for Eugénie?' That was just it. She should be supporting her client, but the more time she spent here, the more she started to doubt whether the wedding she was supposed to save should take place at all.

Raoul stopped so abruptly she also halted. 'Am I supposed to believe,' he asked with exaggerated confusion, 'that you want to stand up for Yvette? That would be very unwise in your position. Eugénie hates Yvette. By choosing the girl's side you'd be alienating her.'

It was even worse. By feeling such sympathy for Yvette she was potentially hurting her client's interest. It was unprofessional and still she couldn't help herself. Yvette was an orphan like she was, aching to feel at home at Bellevue and constantly facing the threat of being sent away. There was nothing worse than having to pack up your things again and leave for another unknown destination. And the damage done to the album with her mother's photographs... If anyone dared touch Atalanta's only picture of her mother, she'd also be beside herself.

'Alienating,' Raoul repeated, 'the very person you need in order to get ahead in the world.'

Of course he would see it in that light. Financial gain is all he can think of.

'You have concluded that I need her in order to get ahead in the world?' Atalanta said with dignity. 'I am my own person and I can choose whoever's side I want to.' She added quickly, 'Not that I've chosen sides already. I'm still making up my mind.'

Raoul stared at her and then burst out laughing. 'My dear Atalanta, you are so precious in your indignation. Your genuine conviction you're somehow... rational about all of this. That there can be something like objectivity. Is it not so that people make up their minds instantly? You see someone, you find them attractive...' He held her gaze a moment, letting the words linger.

Atalanta swallowed. Her throat was very dry.

Raoul continued, 'You hear an opinion and you agree with it or you don't. It's not like a court case where you hear all parties and come to a hopefully impartial judgment.'

'I like to think I'm impartial as much as I can be.' *I have to be, to succeed as a detective.*

'Impartial and without emotions?' Raoul asked. He stepped closer to her, his dark-brown eyes holding her captive with the glow deep inside them. 'You can just stand and watch and listen and judge without taking part in any of it? Without feeling and being hurt?'

Atalanta couldn't look away, or reply with some witty retort. Her mind was empty and her knees wobbly.

'There are no bystanders in life,' Raoul said in a low voice. 'We are all part of the game. We make choices, good ones or bad ones, but choices nevertheless. We're involved, we take responsibility. Or blame.'

'Or guilt, even?' Atalanta whispered. She wanted to see some sort of response in his eyes, but no matter how she looked, she wasn't certain it was there. They stood in silent battle, neither of them willing to look away first.

Then a voice called out for Atalanta and they broke apart, Raoul walking away deeper into the garden as if he had forgotten he had wanted to return to Bellevue.

Atalanta hurried to meet the servant who came for her.

Her breathing was shallow as if someone was chasing her. His question echoed in her mind. She was far from being without emotions in this case. She blamed herself for it and still, she couldn't stop feeling all of these things. Feeling quite powerless, most of all, to change anything for the better.

The servant said, 'Your dresser has arrived.'

'My dresser?'

'Yes, with your gown for the wedding. It needs a few last-minute adjustments, she said. She is waiting for you in your room. I took the liberty of showing her up.'

I have no idea who this is. I certainly didn't order her.

Trying to look calm, Atalanta followed the maid inside and up the stairs. In her room, a slender blonde girl in a fashionable crepe day dress was waiting for her. She had opened a large bag she carried and had extracted a garment she put on the bed.

Atalanta stared in awe at the finely tailored silhouette in lilac with elegant loose sleeves. 'Is that my dress?' she breathed. The maid had already left. The new arrival checked that the door was closed and said softly, 'Monsieur Renard sent me. He wanted you to have this dress for the wedding, and the information he has collected for you.'

'Information?' Atalanta queried. A breath of hope filled her heart that he had discovered something useful and could put her on the right track again.

'Please put on the dress so I can see how it fits and make some adjustments. We must play the part.' The girl winked at her.

Atalanta asked, 'Did you know my grandfather? Have you worked for him before?'

'Via Monsieur Renard, *oui*.'

Atalanta took the dress and disappeared behind the screen to change. She asked, 'Did you come all the way from Paris?'

'Monsieur Renard arranged for a car and chauffeur.'

'He is very thoughtful.' *And apparently thinks I need a hand. I can't deny that I do as this is all very confusing. Fortunately, he doesn't know how poorly I'm handling all of this.*

She slipped into the garment and enjoyed the smooth sensation of the fabric on her skin. The length was perfect but the waist a little too wide. She appeared and the girl cast a quick look across her. 'I'll see to it.'

She circled around her, rearranging, putting in pins and muttering to herself.

Atalanta felt quite special, almost like the bride-to-be. What would it be like to fall in love so irrevocably that she'd want to commit herself to another person for the rest of her life?

But I mustn't forget about the case. 'What did Renard tell you to tell me?'

'He gave me a letter to pass on to you. He told me that you must keep it safe so no one can find it and read it. Or destroy it after you read it.' She grimaced. 'He can be very cloak-and-dagger sometimes.'

Atalanta smiled. 'I'm sure it is a wise precaution. There are eyes and ears everywhere here.'

The girl asked her to take off the dress again and made

the adjustments while Atalanta, with a dressing gown slung around her, sat in the windowsill reading Renard's letter.

I do hope you will not think it forward of me to seek contact with you in such a manner. But I believe it cannot hurt to remind them you have friends away from that place and that you are not alone.

She smiled. He had no idea how welcome these words were to her.

I have made inquiries, via servants at both houses and clubs, what the opinion was about the late Comtesse de Surmonne's horse-riding accident and it seems no one ever thought anything of it. Ever since she was a child, Mathilde Lanier was most wild and she had several accidents growing up, falling out of trees and off her pony. She had to spend six weeks in bed with a concussion after she hit her head exploring a cave in the Ardennes with friends. People shake their heads about her and think all of it rather sad but not suspicious in any way. I have also had the good fortune of being able to ascertain that there was an agreement made when they were married that the dowry Mathilde brought with her upon her marriage would go straight to her children and, if she died childless, would revert to her family. This means that the Comte de Surmonne didn't gain financially by her death.

Atalanta muttered to herself, 'So it seems the accident truly was an accident and he had no motive for murdering her. At least not a financial motive. He didn't gain money or assets by it.'

The letter closed with:

I trust you are well and will be careful. If you need information,
send your request back to Paris with Mademoiselle Griselle.

Atalanta looked at the girl. 'Are you still busy? Can I write a return letter for you to take?'

'Yes, naturally. Monsieur Renard told me to make certain I gave you time to write an answer if you wished. I can even undo this hem and stitch it anew…'

'No, no, please don't change a thing about that beautiful gown. I'll write quickly.' Atalanta sat down at her dressing table and wrote in a strong hand.

Dear Renard,

Thank you for your information. Very useful indeed. I would like to know more about Yvette, a girl of about sixteen staying with the comte. She is family, I understand, a niece, but the exact relationship is not clear to me. She also seems to have a brother who is younger than she. Do find out all you can about her—especially if she has a history of illness or other things of special interest.

She hesitated, her mind cast back to the strange confrontation in the garden which still made her head spin. Then she wrote determinedly,

I would also like to know all you can find about Raoul Lemont.
He's a friend of the family and I saw him in a picture with the
comte and others taken a while ago, I would guess. How long I
do not know. I trust you will handle all of this with the greatest
discretion.

Yours faithfully, AA

She put the letter in an envelope and shut it.

Griselle had finished work on the dress and put it on the bed again. 'See how it is now, mademoiselle.' She accepted the letter and put it in her bag. 'I'm traveling back to Paris tonight. Renard said it was all very urgent.'

Having put the dress on again, Atalanta looked at herself in the mirror. The garment's cut emphasized her narrow waist and made her look even taller. Its lavender colour was both fetching and appropriate. If she showed herself around Paris like this, people would wonder who this dashing new heiress was.

But Paris was far away, and she couldn't go to parties and enjoy a carefree existence. Even wearing this apparel she would be playing a part: a role she had assumed in order to do her work as a private investigator. The dress brought her glamour and at the same time it was like a working uniform. *The two sides to my inheritance rolled into one.*

Caressing the fabric, she said, 'You must thank Renard for this great gift.'

'It's not a gift,' Griselle corrected with a smile. 'It was no doubt paid for by your grandfather's money, which is now

167

all yours.' She studied her with a frank interest. 'You look a bit like him. He was also tall and carried himself as if the world belonged to him.'

Atalanta didn't know whether to feel flattered or put in her place for acting too self-assured. Was that what irritated Raoul?

'Was my grandfather a happy man?' she asked Griselle.

The seamstress gave her a puzzled look. 'I think so. He had money, he travelled, and he helped people. That meant so much to him. Before he investigated cases, he was often alone at his estate, but the cases took him out and gave him puzzles to exercise his mind.'

His mind, yes, but not his emotions. She wagered he had been very cool about everything, keeping a proper distance from the people involved.

But I can't.

For a moment she wanted to tell Griselle she was going back to Paris with her, because she really couldn't do the work that was expected of her. She simply wanted to enjoy her new house, eat macarons at fashionable teahouses and buy hats from the best couturiers, instead of having to wade through all the tension here and feel the responsibility weighing upon her.

I've already had too much of that in my life. It's time for something completely different. It's time to... think about myself for a change.

Griselle tidied away her things and said, 'I wish you good luck, mademoiselle. It must be exciting to stay here and watch everything unfold.'

'Exciting?' Atalanta echoed. 'It doesn't feel like that most of the time. It feels like there is a constant expectation in the air, of something about to happen. It could be good, or bad.'

'But you can influence the outcome. You can make it better for everyone involved. Renard told me once that that was the greatest satisfaction his master took from his cases. To be able to change people's lives for the better.'

Yvette... could her life be changed for the better? Having sensed how unhappy the girl was, Atalanta certainly wished to see her smile again, to create an environment for her where she would feel safe and appreciated. But would a marriage between the comte and Eugénie ever create that kind of home?

Why was she even thinking of Yvette foremost, while Eugénie was her client? Her loyalty should lie with her. Shouldn't it?

What had her grandfather written in his letters to her? She would have to take them out again tonight and reread them to make sense of what he had tried to tell her.

Hurriedly, she put on her day clothes and accompanied Griselle down the stairs to see her off. As the car disappeared down the lane, regret washed through her that she wasn't on board. But there were too many questions left on her mind. Not about the case, but about herself. What she really wanted of life, now that her father was no longer there to look after and no more of his affairs were left to be settled. The void caused her to ache.

Louise came from the salon and asked, 'Oh, you had a visitor?'

'Just some preparations for the wedding.'

Louise pushed her heels hard against the carpet. 'Do you think there will be a wedding?' The challenge in her eyes couldn't be missed.

'I don't see why not.'

'My sister has a bruise and a cut on her face. I doubt she will want to marry looking like that.'

'The wound is on her temple. We can do her hair in a way that covers it. She will also be wearing a veil, I assume.'

'She got this injury because some dramatic girl smashed her head with a solid wooden bath brush.' Louise looked appalled. 'I do wonder whether it's safe for her here as long as Yvette is around. Gilbert should know better and send her away.'

'To a boarding school?' Atalanta asked. Louise had suggested this before and might even have made inquiries in that direction.

Louise made a soft sound as if she swallowed ridiculing laughter. 'I doubt any will have her. She was at three different ones before Gilbert took her in, and got expelled each time. She's not... like other girls.'

'I suppose her mother's death hit her hard,' Atalanta said, hoping Louise would reveal something about this. But Louise looked bored and said, 'I've heard that excuse so often I can't stand it anymore. Gilbert lets her get away with anything because he feels sorry for her. But he should know better really. Mathilde might have indulged her, but Eugénie won't. If he keeps the both of them here, there will be war.'

There already is. But she didn't say so. 'Mathilde managed to become close to Yvette?' she asked.

Louise shrugged. 'Mathilde was a bit like Yvette, I suppose. Wild and unpredictable. The two of them got along because they didn't abide by any rules. Mathilde used to say they were treasure hunting together. I think they made that up to be interesting.'

Atalanta perked up. 'Treasure hunting? What on earth could they have referred to?'

'I really wouldn't know. I never asked. I don't care for people who spend their days fantasizing about what can never be.'

'It seems rather incredible you were friends with Mathilde,' Atalanta ventured. 'After all, you sound totally different.'

Louise blushed painfully. 'We weren't close friends, but we did get along tolerably. Not that I need explain myself to you. I'm sure that when Maman arrives she will have a question or two for you.' She leaned over and hissed, 'To determine exactly which Frontenac you are.'

Cold trickled across Atalanta's spine at the idea of being questioned by the matriarch and failing that test. Perhaps she should have taken the opportunity to leave.

But the car back to Paris was miles from Bellevue already and she was still here, determined to find out where she stood, who she was, and whether her grandfather's faith in her had been justified or misplaced.

She kept smiling. 'I look forward to meeting your mother.'

Chapter Twelve

Coming down for dinner, Atalanta found Madame Lanier in the dining room alone. She stood staring up at a large painting of a sea view on the wall and turned in the last instant. 'Oh, you startled me.' Her clear blue eyes surveyed Atalanta. 'I don't think we've met before.'

'Atalanta Frontenac. Allow me to express how sorry I am about your daughter's accident. It was a year ago, I understand, but I only learned of it recently and... it seems almost unbelievable that such a beautiful place as this can have been the scene where someone died.'

Madame Lanier sighed. 'When the news reached me, I couldn't believe it. I was certain some mistake had been made. My lively girl couldn't be dead. Not at the time in her life when she was so happy, when she had finally arrived and found peace.'

'Peace? Here at Bellevue?'

'Yes. She adored this house and the gardens, the forest

with the shell grotto. She could wander for hours. She felt like it offered the tranquillity she had always been looking for. A world of her own she could hide in. She wrote to me how happy she was when she was at the forest stream watching the water rush by.' Madame Lanier shook her head. 'It amazed me she was actually happy. I had my doubts when she accepted the proposal to marry Gilbert. I knew he wasn't a society man. He is content at his estate and on his travels to Italy to find the paintings he sells. He wouldn't go to balls with her or to the opera. And Mathilde loved those things. She was an avid dancer and loved music. She played the piano so well. And the flute. I couldn't imagine her here at a remote country house with no parties to attend. I expected her to have dived into it with enthusiasm only to tire of it soon.'

Had she tired of it? Had she asked Gilbert to return to Paris? Had they quarrelled about it? It did seem unbelievable they had never quarrelled. That they had always agreed about everything. *The perfect marriage. Does such a thing even exist?*

Madame Lanier said, 'I was anxious whether it would work. But it did. Her letters were cheerful. She made many plans. To change the gardens and even have a concerto in the shell grotto.' Her eyes filled with tears. 'She was so alive and then... one fall off a horse... My only comfort is that she died quickly. That she probably didn't suffer.'

'I'm so sorry for you.' Atalanta put a hand on the older woman's arm. 'You must feel quite undone coming back here and seeing the rooms she lived in.'

'But it isn't a bad feeling. She was happy here. Walking through the corridors I can hear her voice and it is almost as if she could still walk in again and start speaking to us.' Madame Lanier blinked away the tears. 'I won't deny her. I won't pretend she never lived or died. It's sad, but we must acknowledge her.' She wrung her hands together, repeating with urgent emphasis, 'We *must* acknowledge her.'

Did Madame Lanier fear her daughter's memory was being forgotten? Now with the new bride about to take her place...

The others walked into the room, greetings were exchanged, and places taken. Gilbert said, 'I must excuse my fiancée, Eugénie. She has a headache and can't attend.'

'You needn't lie for my sake,' Yvette said. She sat up straight, her eyes flashing furiously. 'I caused Eugénie's headache. I beat her with a bath brush.'

Madame Lanier's eyes widened. 'What for?'

'She wanted to destroy the photographs of Mathilde.'

A deep silence descended. Atalanta sat motionless. She had assumed the album Yvette guarded contained only photographs of her own family. Her deceased mother. But of Mathilde as well?

This had to be a blow to the bereft mother.

Madame Lanier looked at Gilbert. Her voice was shrill as she asked, 'Did you agree to that? Did you give your fiancée permission to do such a thing?'

'Of course not. I can't see why Eugénie would even want to do something like that. She never felt like—' He fell silent.

Madame Lanier rose from the table. 'Excuse me but I'm not feeling well. I'll lie down.' She stumbled her way to the door.

Gilbert shot to his feet. 'May I assist you?'

'No. Don't bother.' Her tone was curt, cold. The door slammed shut.

Gilbert turned to Yvette, eyes blazing. 'Why did you say that?'

'It's true. Eugénie tried to destroy the photographs I have of Mathilde and me. She's jealous. She's an ugly, jealous monster.'

There was a quick flash of triumph in Louise's eyes. Victor looked uncomfortable and Raoul was engrossed in smoothing the napkin across his knee.

Atalanta cleared her throat. 'Actually, it wasn't quite like that. Eugénie was angry because someone had exchanged the lavender in her linen sachet for horse dung.'

Victor made a smothered sound as if he was stifling laughter.

Atalanta continued. 'Eugénie believed it was Yvette and went to her room to ask her about it. Entering, she found her with an album. On impulse, she snatched it and threatened to hold it under water to damage it. I think it was just an act of anger. She was not intending to... I doubt she even knew it held photographs of Mathilde.'

'She did know.' Yvette sat up straight. 'I showed them to her earlier. She came to my room on purpose to destroy them. She even said there is not one trace of Mathilde allowed to remain around here.'

'I didn't hear her say that,' Atalanta protested. *What is Yvette doing?*

Her heart beat faster. *Is she lying to gain sympathy and avoid being punished for what she did? Or is it deliberate? Manipulative. Even... devious?*

She glanced at Raoul. He kept his eyes on his plate, not betraying any particular interest in the subject.

Louise came to Atalanta's aid. 'I didn't hear her say that either.' She cast Yvette a cold look. 'You're making it up to be interesting. You're a pathetic little liar.'

Yvette grabbed her glass and splashed wine into Louise's face. It stained the damask tablecloth like blood spreading. Louise yelped.

'Yvette!' Gilbert was ashen. 'Apologize at once.'

'I won't. She's a monster just like her sister. You can't see who they really are.' Yvette stood up. 'I won't eat dinner with them.'

'Then you won't have dinner at all. I'll instruct the servants not to give you anything. You hear?' These last words the comte had to call after her as she was already running out the door.

Louise dabbed her face and spluttered, 'Such a scene. She can't control her impulses. You have to get a psychiatrist in to see her, Gilbert. This isn't normal.'

'I agree,' Victor said. 'If she really hurt Eugénie with that bath brush, she's dangerous. You can no longer protect her.'

Gilbert gestured at the footman who had stood with a blank expression at the door during the entire scene. 'Please serve the soup.' He cast a quick look at Louise.

'That album means the world to Yvette. It's all she has of her mother.'

Atalanta again saw the grabby hands of the debtors snatching her mother's jewellery from the box beside her bed and her heart broke all over again. She had often dreamed she fought them, lashing out at them with anything at hand, to stop them.

'Eugénie should not have touched that album,' the comte said.

Louise looked as though she wanted to protest but Gilbert continued. 'You're all behaving like toddlers. Show some dignity.'

As he said it, the doorbell rang. He dropped his spoon, which clattered in his plate.

Louise gasped and pressed a hand to her throat. 'The tension here is destroying my nerves.'

The door opened, and the butler announced, 'Monsieur Joubert to see you.'

A uniformed policeman pushed past him and said stiffly, 'I apologize for disturbing you at dinner but I must have your immediate permission to search your grounds and the shell grotto. I have brought a few villagers to assist me. We believe that the poacher DuPont died there.'

Atalanta sat frozen. *I knew it.* There's a connection between DuPont's death and Bellevue.

Gilbert rose to his feet. 'On my land?' he thundered as if it were a crime in itself.

'Yes. There was a shell in his pocket. We believe it came from the grotto. He must have gone there to meet someone.

Even while he was in prison, he was threatened by your gamekeeper, Guillaume Sargant.'

The comte relaxed a little. 'Oh yes,' he said. 'The ongoing feud between DuPont and Sargant. You believe they finally settled it?'

'It wouldn't surprise me if they had,' the officer said, jumping on the comte's more accommodating tone. 'If we can find some trace of Sargant's presence on the scene, we can arrest and charge him.'

'It would have been natural for him to go there as he walks my grounds freely. But you must do whatever needs to be done. Don't bother us with it. I'm getting married the day after tomorrow.'

'I know, my comte.' The officer bowed his head. 'We will be very discreet.' He left the room in a rush.

'Discreet,' the comte rumbled. 'He doesn't know the meaning of the word. But it is best to get it over with. Sargant and DuPont have been at each other's throats for years. Sargant takes his duties as my gamekeeper very seriously and won't tolerate even one hare or pheasant on my grounds being poached. But DuPont often managed to outwit him and laugh about it with villagers. Sargant was livid and threatened to avenge himself. One of them had to kill the other sooner or later.' He shook his head. 'Inevitable.'

'Wasn't DuPont arrested for poaching on your grounds on the very day that Mathilde died?' Raoul said.

What? Atalanta stared at Raoul in shock. He had known this and never mentioned it before? Hadn't he read the newspaper and wondered why a poacher would be stabbed?

'Yes,' the comte affirmed. 'He would never have been caught if it hadn't been for her accident and people being in the woods to find the runaway horse.' He picked up his spoon. 'Bad luck for him.'

He added, after a few moments, 'The horse ran all the way to nearby Saint Ponière. Poor beast must really have been spooked by something.'

Atalanta ate her soup, her thoughts whirling, trying to reconstruct the scene as vividly as possible. Because of Mathilde's accident the woods had been swarming with people looking for her runaway horse and the poacher had been caught in the middle. Normally DuPont was clever enough to evade capture, but finally the situation had overtaken him. That made sense.

But no one seemed to realize a very important thing. If the old man had been traipsing about when Mathilde's accident had happened, he might have seen something. He might have been an actual witness.

And now he was dead. Stabbed by this old enemy, gamekeeper Guillaume Sargant?

Or...

Was it possible he had been killed to ensure he never talked about what he had seen that day? Until his release he had been in prison, safely locked away, no danger to anyone. But once released, he might have...

She barely tasted what she ate, working on her theory and a way to verify it. As soon as she could reasonably leave the table, she went into the kitchens and asked where the butler was. He came from the pantry, carrying more wine. 'Mademoiselle?'

'Could I speak with you for a moment, in private?'

'Naturally.' He put the wine on the table and followed her, his expression not betraying what he thought of her unusual request.

'The day Mademoiselle Eugénie and I arrived here at Bellevue, had there been a visitor calling on the comte? An old man, a bit shabby.'

The butler raised his eyebrow ever so slightly. 'The comte is not in the habit of seeing shabby old men.'

'It's very important. Do you recall? Did the man ring at the door? Or come round to the servants' entrance? Was he seen lurking in the gardens?'

'I really couldn't say, mademoiselle.'

'Could you ask the rest of the staff and let me know?'

'I could, possibly, but...'

'I assure you I have the comte's best interests at heart. You see...' She hesitated a moment. 'There's a police investigation into the death of a poacher. It seems he came here before he died. I only want to make sure he didn't call at the house so the comte won't be involved and the wedding can take place without a shadow hanging over it. I do wish the comte and Mademoiselle Eugénie the greatest happiness.'

'I assure you that if the police ask us anything, we will tell what we know.' His tone suggested the police would most likely not ask anything, and that she would do wisely to follow that example.

Atalanta nodded, realizing she wasn't achieving any more with this man. She should have brought someone who could get friendly with the servants as Renard had suggested. *My mistake.*

I seem to be making more of them than I can afford.

Her hands were cold and clammy. How could she encourage Eugénie to continue with the wedding when so much was unclear?

She went back into the hallway and up the stairs to see how Eugénie was doing. The bath brush had grazed her temple more than it had actually struck her, but still, blows to the head could be treacherous. Perhaps she was now convinced she wanted to leave Bellevue?

As she approached her client's door, she heard raised voices from within. The door stood ajar and, stepping closer, Atalanta caught Eugénie saying, 'I assure you, that little liar twisted the entire story. I never meant to damage any photographs of your daughter. I only wanted to show her she can't hurt me and get away with it.'

'I'm sorry to see,' the moderate voice of Madame Lanier spoke, 'that my daughter's place will be filled by someone so unlike her. Mathilde was kind and compassionate. She loved that young girl like a sister. You, however, belittle her and try to turn Gilbert against her. That is an evil act towards a helpless child.'

'Helpless child?' Eugénie fumed. 'I'll have you know that Yvette is far from helpless or a child. She's throwing herself at Raoul Lemont. I will advise Gilbert to send her away from here before we get embroiled in a scandal we can't control.'

'*We?*' Madame Lanier said. 'I'm certain Gilbert will never agree to part with Yvette. And if he should entertain any thoughts in that direction, I'll convince him to dispose of them right away.'

'He doesn't have to listen to you. You are nothing to him. You got your money back. What do you even want here?'

There was a deep silence. 'How do you mean I got back my money?' Madame Lanier asked with a treacherous calm.

'The marriage arrangement determined that Mathilde's dowry would go to her children, or, if she died without offspring, back to her family. Gilbert didn't get a franc from her. He doesn't owe you anything.'

Madame Lanier breathed in sharply, as if struck.

Atalanta flinched. This was no way to speak to the mother of a woman who had tragically died here and who obviously still felt attached to the house and her former son-in-law.

And if Eugénie had known about Mathilde's dowry arrangements, then why had she told Atalanta when she had come to her to ask for help that she feared Gilbert had killed Mathilde for money?

Madame Lanier said, 'He owes me respect and he shows it to me whenever we meet. I can't say as much about you.'

The finality in her voice seemed to signal the end of the conversation. Atalanta stepped back hurriedly as the maltreated lady would likely leave now and would see her for sure. She looked about her for a hiding place but didn't find one.

The door opened and Madame Lanier stepped out. When she spotted Atalanta, she stopped and looked at her questioningly. Atalanta forced a smile. 'I came to see how Eugénie is doing. Is her head wound any better?'

'I'm not sure. Judging by her behaviour, she might be delirious.' Madame Lanier sailed away with her head held high.

Atalanta knocked.

'No, I don't want to hear anymore!' Eugénie cried furiously.

Atalanta entered and closed the door. 'It's only me. I wanted to see how you were. Is your temple very painful?' It was difficult to hide her indignation but sympathy would get her more answers than reproaches.

The anger in Eugénie's expression died instantly and she raised a limp hand to touch to her temple, wincing and retracting it at once. 'It stings so badly. I wish I had tossed her album in the fire. But there is no fire in the hearth in high summer and...' Eugénie turned her face away and made a sort of sobbing sound.

Atalanta took a deep breath and said, 'I can't believe how Yvette twisted the whole thing around in her favour.' It was treacherous to present things this way but she had to gain Eugénie's confidence to learn more. 'Do you know what she said over dinner? The nerve she had to—'

'Unfortunately, I'm already acquainted with her evil lies.

Madame Lanier was here to tell me that I'm unworthy of taking her daughter's place. Apparently, Mathilde was a saint.' Eugénie huffed.

Is that it? The constant need to fight a shadow? Even Victor had captured an undefinable presence at the edge of their group at the picnic.

Atalanta sat down on the edge of her bed. 'You can't blame her for missing her daughter. People often idolize those who are no longer with us.'Eugénie turned her face to her. 'I do understand. I'm not a complete fool. And I would never have been so unfeeling towards a grieving mother if it weren't for Yvette. She is making my blood boil. She just can never let us be in peace. I think she wants to ruin the wedding.'

Atalanta couldn't deny that the result of Yvette's behaviour was that everyone jumped at each other's throats. Eugénie might be manipulative, but so was Yvette. Her lie that Eugénie had claimed to want to erase all traces of Mathilde had played into Madame Lanier's worst fears. In that respect Eugénie and Yvette were each other's equals. 'You can apologize to Madame Lanier,' she suggested softly. 'If you explain to her that...'

'No, I will *not*.' Eugénie's eyes sparked with defiance. 'Yvette should apologize. She should explain she lied about the album. I didn't want to destroy photographs of Mathilde. Why would I even try? Gilbert adores her. I do know he loves her and always will. But he has to marry and...'

Atalanta said, 'If you are now convinced he still loves

her, you must have abandoned your belief he did anything to harm her.' She wanted to mention the dowry, but how to explain that she knew about it without betraying that she had listened at the door?

'I have.' Eugénie nodded firmly. 'The letter was meant to warn me that Mathilde was murdered, but not by Gilbert. I think it was Yvette.'

'What?' Atalanta stared at Eugénie. 'Yvette killed Mathilde? But I heard they were the best of friends.'

'Madame Lanier says so because she can't accept that Mathilde was anything but perfect. I, however, think Yvette didn't want to share Gilbert with Mathilde any more than she wants to share him with me.'

Atalanta's throat went tight. Hadn't Yvette herself said something to that point? That it had been better after Mathilde had died because then her uncle had had time for her? Eugénie said, 'Yvette might not have done it on purpose. It could have been one of her ill-timed pranks. Popping up from behind a bush and scaring the horse. She doesn't think about the consequences of her actions at all.' Eugénie touched her sore temple again and winced. 'But Mathilde died because of her. She knows it and feels guilty about it and that is why she is so unbalanced.'

It wasn't as farfetched as Atalanta would have liked. There was a real possibility that something Yvette had done had spooked the horse. And couldn't guilt eat away at people, leaving but a shell of what they had once been?

'Raoul mentioned to me that there was a friend with

Mathilde the day she died. On that horse riding trip. Do you know who?'

'Raoul? When did you speak about Mathilde?'

Atalanta waved it off. 'That doesn't matter. Do you know?'

'Yes, it was Angélique Broneur. But she wasn't with her when the accident happened. They had parted ways because Angélique thought the path was too rough and it was too risky. Mathilde pushed on ahead by herself. Angélique was already back at the house when word of the accident reached her.'

'I see. Who discovered that an accident had happened?' Atalanta asked.

'I think it was a farmer or salesman seeing the horse run without its rider. He reported it. Then people went into the woods to look for her. They found her later that day.'

'I see. And that was also when the poacher was arrested?'

'What poacher?' Eugénie frowned and flinched as her temple hurt.

'The police are on the estate looking for traces of a struggle between two people which led to the death of a poacher. You do remember that the Rolls had to avoid a cart when we arrived here? They had picked up a man from a ditch? He wasn't drunk. He was dead.'

'Oh, how terrible.' Eugénie sat up and stared at her. 'And the police are now looking for the murderer on the estate?'

'They believe that he might have been killed on the

estate because he had been embroiled in a feud with the comte's gamekeeper. Seems the two of them couldn't stand each other and the gamekeeper even threatened him while he was in prison.'

'I see. It sounds like something peasants do.' Eugénie shuddered. 'Nothing we should worry about.'

Atalanta studied her nails. Should she explain how DuPont had been around on the day Mathilde died? Or wait a few hours longer? The police were conducting their investigation at the grotto right now and might soon have proof of Sargant's guilt. Via the murder weapon perhaps? It seemed logical that a gamekeeper would carry a knife.

She said briskly, 'I think we'd best focus on the wedding. The date is so near already. Do you wish to go through with it?' Part of her ached for Eugénie to deny this. If she decided to leave Bellevue, Atalanta's task would have ended.

'If you don't want to do it,' she said, 'you must tell the comte as soon as you can. You cannot decide on the wedding day itself.'

'I do know that.' Eugénie looked piqued. 'I had decided I would go through with it until Yvette hit me with that brush. I don't want to share this house with a violent maniac.'

There was a knock at the door. Louise put her head in. 'Maman is here.' Eugénie's expression changed. 'Maman? Show her in at once.'

Atalanta wanted to take her leave quickly before the mother arrived, but apparently she had been hard on the heels of her other daughter for Louise had barely pulled back her head before the door opened wide and a lady in red sailed in. She threw her arms wide and cried, '*Ma fille!* How are you? What happened?'

She closed in, leaned over, and studied the bruise. '*Ma pauvre fille!* You must rest. Take it easy. Oh, my darling.' She clucked and rounded the bed. 'You must look your prettiest on your wedding day. I've looked forward to it for so long.'

Atalanta withdrew to the door. 'I'll bring up some tea.' She stepped into the corridor and shut the door behind her.

Louise stood waiting for her. 'You seem very close with Eugénie,' she said with a cold look. 'And I had never heard of you before.'

'There was little contact after my father left for Switzerland.' Atalanta forced a smile. 'I promised to fetch tea.'

She went to the kitchens in person to make sure that the very best was prepared for the new arrival. Tea, cakes, fondants, macarons. While she was pointing out what bonbons she wanted added to the tray, a maid touched her arm. 'Excuse me, mademoiselle, can I speak with you? One moment.' She glanced around her and drew Atalanta aside. 'You asked about Marcel?'

'Marcel?' It took Atalanta a moment to recall who she meant. 'Oh, you mean DuPont, the poacher.'

'Yes. You asked if he came to the house before he died. I don't know if he did. But I do know something else.'

'Yes?' Atalanta encouraged her. Perhaps she could learn

something worthwhile from the servants even without her having a contact amongst them.

'When he was caught the day the mistress died, he made a fuss. He said he wanted to speak with the comte. They thought he wanted to claim he had permission to catch hares on his land. But old Marcel said he wanted to see the comte because he knew something very important.' Her blue eyes went wide. 'I've always wondered what that might have been.'

I do too. 'Did the comte go to see him?'

'Oh no. He had his mind on other things. Preparing for the mistress's funeral. He was so sad we all feared he would die of a broken heart. That he would join her in the grave soon after. He didn't go out for weeks on end and then he left for Italy again. I don't think he ever talked to Marcel. Marcel was convicted and locked away... until he was released this week.'

'I see.' And right away Marcel had returned to Bellevue. With his news for the comte.

He had already served his sentence so it seemed unlikely he wanted to claim he had been in the right poaching on the land. What then could he have known?

And had it led to his death?

'After his release did you see him near the house? If not, have you heard of anyone who saw him?'

'The gardener says he might have seen him. At least, he saw some figure skulking about. But the gardener is given to telling tales; as soon as there is something up, he always says he knew all about it.' The maid made a gesture, palms up. 'I can't tell you anymore. I do hope it won't spoil the wedding. We've all been looking forward to it. The house was so desolate all those months when the comte traveled to Italy and then spent time in Paris in spring. We feared that the comtesse's death here had turned him against the house forever and he wouldn't want to live here anymore. But now he's back, to stay. The chapel is all done up with flowers and the house full of guests. Life will come back to Bellevue at last.'

Yes, life would come back to it. But death had also come back to it.

And Atalanta wondered with a cold feeling inside if the hand that had driven the knife into Marcel DuPont's body belonged to anyone she knew.

Chapter Thirteen

When Atalanta entered the bedroom followed by a maid with the refreshments, laughter rang out. Eugénie was sitting up, colour in her cheeks, holding up a necklace with shimmering stones. The maid gawked in awe as she carried in the tray and Atalanta took over before the girl could trip and drop the whole thing. '*Merci*,' she dismissed her. The girl cast one last longing look at the glittering necklace and vanished.

'Shall I pour?' Atalanta suggested.

Madame Frontenac shook her head. 'Come to the window, child,' she commanded.

When Atalanta hesitated, she gestured with a beringed hand. 'Come, let me look at you.'

Atalanta joined her reluctantly. *What does she expect to see?*

Madame Frontenac seized her shoulders and turned her this way and that, studying her profile. She frowned hard.

Atalanta's heart raced. If Madame Frontenac was searching for a family resemblance, she'd look in vain. There wasn't a drop of Frontenac blood in her veins.

What if she was exposed?

Could Eugénie persuade her mother to keep the truth under wraps in the interest of the investigation? Her new knowledge about DuPont confirmed he had known something vital. That he had died because he wanted to reveal this to Gilbert.

'Yes,' Madame Frontenac spoke at last, 'you do have something of the Frontenac features. The nose, the earlobes.'

Relief washed over Atalanta, but she tried to hide it behind a polite smile.

Madame Frontenac added with a scowl, 'Though you are really just a distant relation. I had never heard of you—and I know everyone.'

There you have it. Now she will question me and I won't be able to answer to her satisfaction. Her mind raced to keep hold of the information Eugénie had provided her with. *My father's first name is Guillaume. My mother… I can't remember.*

And how many brothers do I have? Three or four?

This is a disaster!

Madame Frontenac let go and returned to the bed. 'Pour the tea, will you? And what are those? Little delights.'

A narrow escape. 'Yes, I assumed you would want refreshments after your long journey. I trust it was pleasant?' Atalanta rushed to offer her tea and cakes and Eugénie showed off her new necklace once more. 'Real diamonds. Papa sends it with all of his love,' she explained.

'He can't be there for the wedding. Prior engagements and all that.'

But at the Frontenac home in Paris the cook told me a tailor had come to fit a suit for Monsieur Frontenac for the wedding. So, originally, he had intended to come.

'He's so busy with his affairs.' Eugénie pouted but her eyes betrayed that the necklace made up for a lot. 'He will be here later to see me, I'm sure.' She held the necklace against her chest and pressed her chin down to see how it looked. 'How do you like it, Maman? Is it not too ostentatious?'

'It must be ostentatious,' her mother declared with pomp. 'The comte has a title *bien sûr* but we have more money than he will ever have, and I intend to let him know. These comtes are all so full of themselves and their family history. But I tell you, you can be related to all the aristocrats you want but when you have no money to buy bread…' She clicked her tongue.

'I dare say the Comte de Surmonne can buy bread,' Atalanta said, gesturing across the sweet delights she was offering to her guest.

Madame Frontenac cackled. 'Of course he can. I wouldn't dream of marrying my daughter to a man in debts. But I mean to say that while he has something to offer here, we are not nobodies depending on his grace. We can afford luxury and we will show it. Tomorrow you must try on the dress, my dear, and you will look like a dream, a mirage.' She kissed her fingertips. 'You will look more beautiful than anything they have ever seen around these parts.'

Atalanta withdrew to the door. 'I'll leave you to catch up. I'm pleased to see you so much better, Eugénie.'

Her client barely seemed to hear her. She caressed the precious stones and let her mother put a cognac bonbon into her mouth.

Atalanta stepped into the corridor and sighed. While it was good to have some tension defused by this visit, it didn't lessen the burden weighing on her to discover what had happened on the day Mathilde had died. And on the day Marcel DuPont had been released from prison only to be dragged from a ditch, dead, hours later. If he had witnessed the 'accident'...*Could I speak to a police officer discreetly, to discover what they are expecting to find here?*

Not likely. He will certainly believe it's none of my business, especially as I'm a woman.

She sighed in frustration. *I wager if my grandfather had been here and went out to stroll around the garden and start a conversation, he would have got something.*

Still, DuPont was very important and she had to take action to learn more. Time was running out.

She went to her room, collected her binoculars from her luggage, and stood on her balcony to look at the forest with the shell grotto. Could she discern any police activity? Could she make out by their actions what they were looking for?

And if she saw them leaving, could she determine whether they had been successful or not?

She stood there for a long time, leaning against the

balcony's stone edge, letting her gaze wander the entire stretch of forest. But she saw nothing but a few birds flying and a deer looking for food. At last, the light became so weak it was pointless to continue and she turned to go inside.

Failed again.

Her legs were stiff, her knees locked, and she massaged them before attempting to hobble to the doors back into her room. She had shut them to prevent flies from getting in, but now as she turned the handle, they wouldn't open.

What is this? She pushed down the handle repeatedly, and put her weight against the doors, but nothing happened. Someone had locked them from the inside, shutting her out.

Darkness now closed around her and the eerie cry of an owl resounded in the distance. Gooseflesh formed on her arms. Who had done this and why? Was someone aware of her interest in the case?

Raoul Lemont had confronted her several times. But surely if he suspected her of anything, he wouldn't have let on that he did?

Anyway, she rallied herself, *I'm not going to cry for help and look like an idiot. I can no doubt find some way out of this predicament.*

To the left of the balcony there was just thin air, but to the right was another balcony attached to the room beside her. She wasn't certain who was staying there, but light was seeping through the half-closed curtains so she could at least try to clamber from her own balcony onto the next one and knock on that door to be let inside.

Long walks in the Swiss Alps had taught her to navigate narrow ledges and not fear heights; even Raoul had called her a mountain goat.

Grimacing, she put her hands on the stone balustrade and pushed herself up. *Don't look down. Focus on the destination.*

Holding her breath, she stepped across the narrow open space between the balconies to reach the next one. Her balance wavered and she gasped, but her reflexes restored her weight to her right foot and she found a hold with her hand. *Careful now.*

She lowered herself onto the solid stone floor and exhaled in relief. She took a moment to smooth down her dress and catch her breath, else she'd sound hopelessly squeaky when she spoke.

Then she peered into the room. Raoul was standing at the door leading into it. She could only just see his face as a woman stood in front of him, inside the room, obscuring her view. She was dressed in an elegant white gown and had just removed a little hat from her dark hair. Suddenly she flung the hat on the bed and reached out to hug Raoul.

Atalanta held her breath, wondering how he would respond to it. He ducked her arms and stepped back, saying something with a shake of his head. Then he shut the door.

The woman stood motionless, her one arm still up. She formed her hand into a fist and bashed it against the door. The sound was even audible on the balcony. With her fist up, she whirled around, her beautiful face a mask of frustrated anger. Her gaze searched the room as if looking for something to pick up and throw.

Atalanta was too late to step away. The woman caught sight of her.

Atalanta cringed, expecting a piercing scream that would have people running to see who was being attacked now. Her little action to avoid detection of her painful situation had gone massively awry.

But the woman didn't scream at all. She came to the doors, opened them, and asked, 'What on earth are you doing on my balcony, peeking in? Are you poor Raoul's fiancée? I can't imagine why else he wouldn't have wanted to kiss me.'

She added in a lower tone, 'He used to enjoy that so very much.'

Atalanta flushed at this frank admission. She had been fairly certain Raoul could attract women as much as he liked, but being face to face with one who had been close to him was something different. A new and rather painful experience.

The woman laughed. 'Do step in. With the sun having gone down, it's getting chilly.' She underlined her invitation with a wide arm gesture. The room smelled of her rose perfume.

Atalanta spotted elegant suitcases with inlaid ivory handles standing near the door.

'Angélique Broneur,' the woman introduced herself,

retrieving the hat from the bed and placing it on her dressing table.

The friend who was with Mathilde before she died. Exactly the person I need. 'Atalanta Frontenac. I'm your pianist.'

'Really? Is that why you knock on my window at night? To rehearse?' Angélique laughed, a soft sound deep in her throat. 'I have no piano here. And my voice is loud enough to shatter windows if I so choose. I would wake all the other guests.'

'I was locked out of my room,' Atalanta confessed. She could not help but like the woman's boldness. A little confidentiality could help to create the atmosphere in which she could ask questions. 'While I was on the balcony, enjoying the summer evening, someone locked my doors.'

'I can guess who.' Angélique rolled her eyes. 'You must not let Yvette get under your skin, Mademoiselle Frontenac. She only comes after you as long as you respond. If you ignore her and pretend you haven't even noticed the wet broom in your bed, she leaves you in peace.'

She frowned a moment. 'I had hoped, though, that with age she'd mellow. Or should I say, get other interests?' She winked. 'Unfortunately, she may be a little late with that. Not too odd considering she is stuck here. There's not a decent distraction for miles around.' Angélique sat down and crossed her legs. 'Do you wish to see if you can enter your room through the door? Or shall we chat some more? I can even mix you a cocktail.' She gestured at the suitcases. 'I always bring my own bar.'

'I would love a cocktail.' Atalanta was determined to

take advantage of the odd situation by finding out as much about this woman as she possibly could. Renard had seemed to think her highly suspicious when he had first told Atalanta everything about Angélique's close relationship with the comte.

I need to spend time with her, purely in the interest of the case, of course, and not at all because she tried to kiss Raoul.

That he had ducked her attentions gave Atalanta a secret satisfaction she would rather not explore. It was really none of her business what he did or did not do.

'Here we are.' Angélique clicked open a small case, extracted liquor bottles and a shaker and set to work. 'I call this my very own cocktail of seduction.' She grinned at Atalanta. 'If you dare try.'

'You came at exactly the right moment,' Atalanta said in a confidential tone. 'I was rather tired of the whole charade.'

'What charade?' Angélique asked.

'Oh, everyone behaving as if they had been allotted a part in a play. The widower who is remarrying, the obstinate girl who tries to make life hard on the new bride, the bride herself who is constantly in tears because she is so happy...'

'Is Eugénie actually happy?' Angélique raised a perfectly sculpted eyebrow. 'I thought she was merely greedy.' She handed Atalanta a glass with bright-orange contents. 'Cheers.'

Atalanta sipped. *Fruity with a good amount of alcohol. I'd better be careful or it might go to my head.* 'Delicious. How do you mean greedy? Her mother assured me that the

Frontenacs have more money than the comte will ever have. They don't gain by this alliance.'

'Of course they gain.' Angélique waged a finger at her as if she was correcting a slow pupil. 'They may have money but they don't have access to the highest circles. By giving Eugénie's hand in marriage to the comte, they step up to his level. I can imagine Madame Frontenac already sees herself taking tea at all the estates. She is a very vain woman, but also educated and able to blend in. I think she will do very well.'

'And what about Eugénie? Will she do well?'

'I doubt she'll enjoy life in the country. Not like Mathilde.' Angélique sat down with her own cocktail and stared into the green liquid. 'She threw herself into anything with zeal. She had planned to change the gardens, wanted to breed horses. She wasn't pining for Paris. I think Eugénie will last here for about... oh, three months. Then she will want to go back or she'll grow absolutely mad.'

'Does the comte know?' Atalanta clenched her glass. Why was everyone intent on letting a marriage take place that seemed destined to make both partners utterly miserable?

'I doubt he cares. He travels a lot and I assume she can visit her friends in the capital whenever he is away. In winter, there really isn't a lot to do here.' She gestured at the curtained window. 'It looks so perfect now with the lavender fields in full bloom, the sunflowers and the peasants carrying their baskets of earthenware to market. Just like those paintings in the art galleries everyone wants to have in the drawing room these days. The idyllic countryside. They have no idea of winter in this place. How it is all grey and dull and the rain beats against the windows.' She shivered. 'I wouldn't like to be in Eugénie's shoes.'

So much for the theory that Angélique Broneur expected the comte to be interested in marrying her.

Unless she is lying, of course.

But why would she? She doesn't know who I am.

Angélique added with a wink, 'Not that I ever ran the risk of being in that position. Gilbert knows me too well to ever want to marry me.'

Atalanta looked her over and exclaimed, 'It is you in the photograph! The comte, Raoul Lemont and you, with other young men. Taken a while ago, I wager.' It was not Mathilde, but Angélique, on display in full view...

'Does he have that photograph standing around? We were much younger then. It was during an art course in Italy. Florence.' Angélique's expression became dreamy. 'We had a wonderful time. We were all so full of dreams. Gilbert discovered his love of the Renaissance painters and... Raoul and I just discovered love.'

'That sounds wonderful.' Atalanta ignored the little stab inside her and sipped her cocktail.

Angélique said, 'Of course there was no way he was going to marry me. We are both too independent for that. If I were married, people would frown upon me traveling to sing. They do frown upon it now, but at least I am my own woman. And he... I can't say I'd enjoy watching him gamble with his life in his Maserati.'

'He owns one?' Atalanta exclaimed.

'He drives one for sport. In races. You must really not have talked to him much to have missed his greatest passion.'

Atalanta blinked. She knew of the growing interest in races where men got into fast cars and risked their lives to cross the finish line first. It was called a sport of the future. If the drivers stayed alive long enough.

Angélique said, 'You look quite overtaken. I assume you are used to a quiet little existence as a music teacher or something. Or do you perform? You must excuse me, I've never heard you play so I cannot determine how good you really are. But I'm sure we will make it a performance to remember. For the happy couple.'

With difficulty Atalanta put the image of Raoul risking his life in sports car races out of her mind and tried to lead the conversation back to where she wanted it to go. *Mathilde's death.* 'So after this time in Italy for the art course, you stayed in touch with the comte?'

'Oh, yes. I was a guest at his wedding. I was staying here with Mathilde when—' Angélique emptied her glass and got up to mix herself another cocktail. 'I should have prevented her from getting onto that wretched horse. Cyrano was his name, I think. It was a black beast with the temper of a tiger released. It didn't obey any orders. But Mathilde never listened to good advice. I even laughed about it. Told her Gilbert would strangle her for having disobeyed him.' She shook her head. 'He never got the chance. She broke her neck.'

She drank from the new cocktail, a pink one this time, and continued. 'I wasn't with her either. I had turned back. The path was rough after rain and there were even dead trees in the way. She told me carelessly we could jump those, but I'm not half the rider she was. I refused. I left her alone.'

The four words were laden with regret. Reproach even? Atalanta wondered.

'I'm sure you made a wise decision. It was indeed dangerous.'

'Yes, but then I had to face Gilbert's questions of why did I leave her? Where was I?' Angélique put down her glass in a thud. 'He wasn't there either, but... he put the blame on me.'

'I'm sure he doesn't blame you. Why else would he have asked you to come and sing at his wedding? It is natural people are upset and say things after such a shocking event. He didn't mean it.' Angélique seemed to steady herself. 'Yes, of course. I do know that. I'm just... tired from my journey over here.'

'Then I'll no longer keep you. I had better go to my room.' Angélique accompanied her out of the door and watched as she tried hers. 'Open,' she whispered. Angélique nodded and mouthed, 'Good night.'

Atalanta felt like they were two boarding school pupils separating after an illegal party in one of their rooms. She had to smile to herself. Angélique was the lively personality she could have befriended, had she made her debut in Paris.

She opened the door wider and stepped in. A strange sensation assailed her. Almost of not being alone. Someone had been in here. Merely to lock her out on the balcony or also to do something else?

She waited a moment, inhaling the scent. Perhaps Yvette had used more horse dung to leave a message? But there was no strange scent on the air at all.

Gooseflesh skittered across her arms as she tried to define what was wrong about the room. With trembling fingers she turned on the light and looked at her bed. Nothing. On the night table the usual items stood: a glass of water, a book and a small jar with cream she rubbed on her hands before turning in to bed at night.

She looked under the bed and inspected her closets. Nothing out of the ordinary. Her nervousness grew less and she almost had to laugh that the mere thought of someone having been in here could have unsettled her so.

At last she came to the dressing table and opened all the drawers one by one. Had someone shuffled through the albums with newspaper clippings and postcards of exotic destinations? She had thought it perfectly harmless to bring those as a pianist like her might dream of visiting such locales to perform.

Her heart almost stopped.

Her *Greek Mythology* had been picked up and put back in the wrong place. She lifted it to expose the notes she had made about the case. They had been disturbed, as if someone had gone through them. They had tried to make a neat stack again, but the edge of one of the sheets was crumpled.

Atalanta's breathing went fast. She knew that with her precautions of using Cyrillic letters and a transposition cipher they could hardly have made sense to whoever had been in here, but it was disturbing to know someone had been consciously looking for something. To establish what she was doing here?

Was the killer now on her trail?

Nonsense. You don't know if there even is a killer, she thought, trying to calm herself. *It could have been a curious maid who also locked the doors not realizing you were out there.*

But anyone inside the room could easily have seen her on the balcony. The doors had been locked on purpose. Besides, deep inside her she knew that even if Mathilde's death had been an accident, Marcel DuPont's had been murder.

And he had claimed to know something important about the day on which Mathilde had died.

Chapter Fourteen

The next morning Atalanta woke up with a nervous energy. It was the day before the wedding and the clock was ticking down to the moment of no return. Her client had asked her to establish that her fiancé wasn't involved in the death of his first wife and while Atalanta hadn't found conclusive proof that he had been, she also hadn't found proof that someone else hadn't been, or that it had been an accident.

Dressing, she wondered how one even established something like that without a doubt. Then her hands stalled and she stared into the distance. But of course. Why hadn't she thought of that before? She needed to talk to the doctor who had looked at Mathilde's body after the fall off her horse. He would certainly know what the injuries had looked like and if these had convinced him, she had indeed died because her horse had thrown her.

Atalanta hurried down to breakfast, found no one there

yet, drank a quick cup of coffee and snatched some brioche, and then set out, on foot, to go to the nearby village where she would find the doctor. Used to walking a lot, it wasn't difficult and even gave her a joyous sensation she had missed. Exercise was simply wonderful. It freed the head of too many worrying thoughts and reaffirmed her belief in her own capabilities. She merely had to take things one step at a time and not think too far ahead.

At the edge of the village a man was feeding his pigs, and in the town square the owner of the local inn accepted a basket with fresh eggs from a slender older woman. Atalanta greeted everyone she met with a cheerful '*Bonjour*' and asked the innkeeper for the doctor's house. It turned out to be on the same square, with a small dispensary where medicines were sold. The lettering on the windowpane gleamed golden in the morning light.

The dispensary was already open and Atalanta stepped into an inviting scent of herbs and spices. An elderly woman with large hands was putting pills in glass pots and barely looked up as she entered.

'This is a wonderful place,' Atalanta enthused. 'I've always admired the medicinal properties of nature. Do you make your medicines yourself?'

The woman now gave her an assessing look. 'Some of them,' she confirmed. 'Others we have sent over from the city.'

'Oh, and is the doctor in?'

'No, he has already gone out to do his rounds. A few

cases of the flu and a toddler who might have measles. What would you need a doctor for?'

'You must have something with lavender to sleep better? I'm in such a state of mind. My cousin and best friend is getting married. To the Comte de Surmonne.'

Now the woman's hands stopped fussing with the pills and she was all attention. 'The Comte de Surmonne? You are one of his guests?'

'Yes. I am to play the piano at the wedding feast. I'm very excited about it. Also nervous, I guess. There will be many important people there.'

'I read about it in the paper.' The woman clicked her tongue. 'Poor comte. He was so devastated when his first wife died. You do know she died?'

'Of course.' Atalanta suppressed the excitement she felt that the woman so readily took the bait and forced a solemn expression. 'It must also have been a blow to the village. I heard she was very beloved here.'

'We rarely saw her,' the woman said dispassionately. 'She was busy at the estate, entertaining friends and making lots of changes. Not everyone liked it.'

'I see. What was the objection to the changes then?'

The woman shrugged. 'The house and gardens have been the same for generations. It is the way it is. Tradition. She wanted to make changes and... people don't much like change around here.'

Atalanta nodded. 'The house and gardens are beautiful, especially the shell grotto.'

The woman gave no visible response to this, indicating

the grotto had no special meaning to her. *Why then did Marcel DuPont go there?* Atalanta cheerfully continued, 'And a fall off a horse... So violent. Breaking one's neck.' She shuddered.

'Her head, more accurately.' The woman leaned on the counter with her large hands. 'She broke her head.'

'Her head? I don't follow. I thought her neck was broken upon impact of the fall.' Eugénie had told her this right in the beginning, and both Raoul and Angélique had confirmed it. How could this not be true?

'She hit her head on something. Perhaps a tree? The doctor said her skull was burst. I remember clearly. We don't have such accidents often.'

'I can imagine. Skull burst. That's terrible. Could the horse have kicked her after she fell off?'

'I think so. The doctor said that it had to have happened from impact with a solid object.'

Had someone hit Mathilde while she was on the ground? Atalanta couldn't ask more specific questions in that direction as it would go beyond normal curiosity. She had to make the most of this conversation. 'And now this poacher has died too. What was his name? Marcel DuPont? Wasn't his head bust as well?'

'No, he was stabbed. No wonder if you live like that. Always drinking and looking for trouble. It's not right to say a man deserves to die, but DuPont was asking for it. Just released from prison and into another brawl.' The woman shook her head. 'They locked up Guillaume Sargant yesterday. The comte's gamekeeper. But he claims he didn't do it.'

'Oh, weren't they in some sort of feud?' Atalanta frowned. 'Of course, as guests we don't know the local relationships, but we did see the police on the estate looking for evidence and the comte mentioned that his gamekeeper had been feuding with this particular poacher for a while. I guess I... hadn't expected to find death here in this friendly place.'

'We all have to die some time,' the woman said philosophically. 'Do you want some lavender drops to help you sleep?'

Atalanta nodded and bought some, along with the local specialty: coffee-flavoured sweets to suck on. With one melting on her tongue, she continued from the dispensary to the little church and graveyard. She walked around for a while, looking at tombstones and wondering if Mathilde had been buried here as well. Most graves were neatly tended, decked with small bouquets of flowers. She hadn't seen her parents' graves in many years. She had rather spent her money on paying off her father's debts than traveling to England. But now that she could afford it, she would go to London soon and visit the quiet graveyard where they rested, united again in death.

Where would Mathilde have been buried?

Could the grave tell her anything? The words on the stone? The loving tokens of remembrance left on the site?

But most of the graves seemed to be of common people,

not members of the gentry. *Perhaps her grave is inside the church?*

Just as Atalanta was about to leave, she saw an elderly caretaker entering, all in black, with a rake in his hand to start cleaning the path. She went over and asked him for the grave of Mathilde, Comtesse de Surmonne.

'She is not buried here,' the caretaker said. 'The comte's family has a tomb on the estate.' He looked her over. 'Are you related to her?'

'No, I'm staying at the estate for the wedding tomorrow.'

'We all guessed he would marry again. He has to. He needs an heir for the estate.'

'Would he marry solely for an heir? Don't you think he loves his new bride?'

The man burst into a cackling laugh and then checked himself, glancing almost guiltily at the graves all around. 'I doubt a man like him loves anyone but himself. He has power and money; he doesn't need to win people's favour. We here, simple villagers, have to stay in his good graces but he himself...'

'It doesn't sound as if you like him.' Atalanta tried to make it sound factual and not judgmental.

The caretaker huffed. 'In the old days the comte owned the village and we all had to dance to his tune. These days he feels he is above us and barely shows his face here. He's always on his trips to Italy to buy those paintings he then sells to art galleries in Paris, they say.'

The *they say* drew Atalanta's attention. 'Don't you think that is exactly how he makes his living?'

'I wouldn't know, mademoiselle, but we have never seen any of these paintings.'

'The comte has a very nice art collection at his house.'

The caretaker straightened as if chastened. 'I wouldn't know, mademoiselle. I'm hardly likely to get invited there. If you will excuse me, I have work to do.' And he walked off, dragging his rake behind him.

Atalanta stared after him thoughtfully. He had raised an interesting point. Of all the art she had seen at the house, nothing was Renaissance. The comte could of course sell it straight away but...

She left the graveyard, bought two apples at the grocer's, and headed back to Bellevue. The apples were juicy and sweet, the sun warmed her face, and the tension of having to solve the case eased a little. For the first time since coming here she truly allowed herself to enjoy her new situation. The freedom of it, the joy of finally having travelled somewhere and seeing all the new sights. Surely, being on a case here didn't prevent her from also passing the time in an agreeable fashion? In fact, she might have overdone it, allowing herself no moments of relaxation at all. Of course her client depended on her, but she would be no good to said client if she didn't keep up her strength.

Hoofbeats came up from behind her and she looked over her shoulder to see Raoul closing in on her riding a gorgeous chestnut. The horse's muscles flowed under his shiny skin and his long mane wafted on the breeze.

Thinking of when she had last seen Raoul—almost in the arms of Angélique Broneur—she flushed and looked for a way to avoid him. Why did his appearance have to spoil the pleasure of this solitary walk?

But as she was on a straight road, with lavender fields on both sides, she couldn't turn anywhere.

'Good morning,' Raoul called. 'Aren't you a horse rider?'

'I've never had a chance to learn,' Atalanta admitted. She had vague memories of sitting on a pony with her mother by her side, but that was it. Her father had never been able to afford horses nor shown an interest in teaching his daughter how to ride.

'It must be bothersome doing everything on foot. It takes forever.' Raoul let the horse walk beside her. The animal snorted and pulled at the reins wanting to go faster.

'I think it is the best way to get to know your surroundings. You have time to look at everything in detail and enjoy what you see. I bet you rush by and don't notice what is there right under your nose.'

'Such as?' Raoul asked, amusement flickering in his dark eyes.

'Such as this stone.' Atalanta pointed at a weathered stone in the grass. It was grey, about two palms high and had numbers engraved in it. 'What can it mean?'

'It is probably part of an old system of boundary stones,' Raoul said. 'It must communicate something about the distances between places or about landowners.' He added ironically, 'Gilbert must dislike it that he doesn't own everything around here.'

The horse whinnied and stretched his neck, ready to break into a gallop again. But Raoul patted his neck and calmed him down. Then he slipped off his back and came to walk beside Atalanta, leading the horse by the bridle.

Nerves flickered in her stomach. He had just professed to hate walking as it was so slow. He had to have some ulterior motive in joining her.

He asked, 'Why did you go into the village? Is the tension at the house getting to you?'

'Why are you horse riding?' she countered.

'I wanted to escape the questions of Madame Frontenac.'

Remembering how the matron had turned her this way and that to assess if she was a true Frontenac, Atalanta flushed. 'I don't assume she is up already.'

'Oh, she likes to get up early whenever it suits her. I didn't feel like having breakfast in her company. Or in the company of the decidedly sullen Françoise.'

'Is Eugénie's other sister here, too?' Atalanta asked. 'I didn't meet her last night.'

'She was probably tired from the journey. She is always tired.' Raoul rolled his eyes. 'I can't imagine how a young woman can have so little energy. Then again, her mother has stamina for two.'

'I saw her briefly. She brought a gorgeous necklace for Eugénie.'

'Bribes,' Raoul said in a dramatic tone.

'Excuse me?'

'Bribes. To get her to marry Gilbert. She doesn't love him.'

The quiet conviction in the statement gave Atalanta pause. 'Does she love Victor?'

Raoul laughed softly. 'Victor would like that. He plays with women as if they are toys. Disposable. But no, I don't think Eugénie ever loved Victor. I doubt she knows what love is.'

'What do you think love is?' She put it half as a philosophical question, not fully expecting him to respond. And if he did, the answer would probably not be anything she wanted to hear.

Raoul walked slowly, kicking against a pebble here and there. 'I think it is selfless and unassuming. It makes the other one more important.'

Atalanta's jaw slackened. Did he truly feel that way?

But Raoul already continued, 'Not everyone is capable of having such noble feelings.' He laughed shortly. 'Don't think I'm blaming Eugénie for not being capable of it. I myself am the same.'

Her heart sank. He denied himself the most beautiful thing in the world: love, connection. Being a part of something. Having family.

But then perhaps he thought it wasn't possible with his lifestyle, risking his neck every time he got into his Maserati?

'I didn't realize,' Atalanta said, 'that you were a race car driver until I heard it last night.'

'From whom?' he pounced.

'Angélique Broneur.' She glanced at him as she said the name. Would his expression betray regret that it had ended between them?

He stared ahead. His profile seemed hewn from marble, tight and cold, giving nothing away. 'You spoke with her last night? Angélique always was a busy little bee.' It sounded rueful.

'I was surprised that you wager your life like that.'

'Excuse me?'

'I can't imagine how you can sit in such a car, driving at high speed, and hoping not to die.' As she said it, her stomach contracted thinking of the risks he took. Why? What for?

Raoul exhaled in disbelief. 'When I am in that car, racing, the last thing on my mind is death. I think of life. I feel alive.' His expression was warm now, his eyes sparkling with fervour. 'I never feel quite like I do in the heat of a race, when the car obeys my every wish and it's almost as if I can fly.'

His words were so passionate they struck a chord inside her. 'But what about the danger?' she asked.

Raoul shrugged. 'That makes it even better. What is life when you never take chances?' His expression became serious. 'Think of Mathilde. She made a choice for security. Living a simple life in the country. Still she died. Because of a stupid accident. A horse going wild.' He shook his head. 'No. I'm not sitting back, afraid of what might go wrong. I won't be forced into believing I can in any way lengthen my life span if I am careful. I believe in fate. If it is your time to go, you go. Wherever you are.'

Was it that simple? 'But is it always fate? Can't it be another's doing?' Atalanta mused.

Raoul turned his head to her in a jerk. 'What are you saying? That Mathilde didn't die of an accident?'

'You understand my meaning right away.' She held his gaze. 'You must have wondered about it yourself.'

Raoul was silent. His jaw tensed as if he was getting angry. For a moment Atalanta believed he was going to swing himself into the saddle and take off, leaving her in a cloud of dust. Then he said, 'A year ago, when she died, it never crossed my mind. Even when I arrived here a few days ago for the wedding, it never occurred to me that it hadn't been an accident. But when that poacher was stabbed...'

'Yes?' Atalanta's lips tightened as she waited to hear if he would say the same things she thought.

'I know the local police think it was just a fight between DuPont and that gamekeeper who had been at his throat before, or between two rival poachers. That the one who had the area to himself while DuPont was in prison wanted to make sure it stayed that way. But why be so stupid as to kill someone when you are the first to attract attention? Now Sargant is locked up and might never get out again. It doesn't make sense.'

'People act under emotion. That need not make sense.'

'Perhaps not. But I heard that DuPont claimed to have known something about the day Mathilde died.' Raoul thought a moment and added, 'Let me rephrase that. When he was arrested, he asked to see the comte. People assumed he wanted to plead his innocence or claim he had been allowed to hunt on his land. But what if he wanted to reveal to Gilbert what he knew about Mathilde's accident, in exchange for his freedom?'

'I've considered that,' Atalanta admitted. 'What does it mean, do you think?'

'Mean?' Raoul echoed.

'Yes. Does it mean she wasn't alone when she died? You said earlier she was with a friend. I now know it was Angélique Broneur. Did Angélique somehow cause the accident?'

She kept her eyes on him to see how he responded to this suggestion. Was the suggestion of murder bothering him so much because he feared his former lover was involved?

'Angélique declared at the time she had gone back to the house because the riding became too rough for her.'

Where he had spoken with passion before, here his words seemed carefully chosen. *Because he was trying to hide something?* 'Yes, that is what she said.' Atalanta waited for his reaction.

Raoul said pensively, 'I was surprised at the time. Angélique isn't someone who turns back at the first hurdle. And she is a very good rider.'

'She told me that she's not.'

Raoul raised an eyebrow. 'Really? Well, let me put it

more carefully then. She used to be a very good rider years ago.'

'When you were in Italy together?'

'She also shared that? She has been very talkative.' He sounded wry. 'Yes, in Italy we were often out riding through the vineyards together. She was usually ahead of me and laughing when she jumped across low walls. I don't see why a ride through a forest would have daunted her.'

'So you think she lied about what happened that day?' Atalanta shrank under her own choice of the word *lied* but she had to probe deeper and discover what lay beneath it all.

'I don't know.' Raoul looked pained. 'I haven't really considered it before.'

'But now that DuPont has been murdered, we must consider it.'

'We?' he queried, his eyes searching her features. 'Why would *we*, mademoiselle? What is it to you?'

For a moment she wished she could simply tell him that she was here on a case and ask him to help her. He seemed to know so many things that could be helpful to her.

But honesty was too risky. She shouldn't forget Raoul could be a suspect. That he might be testing her to see how much she knew.

She said, 'I'm related to Eugénie. I wish her well. I hope her marriage will make her happy. But it doesn't seem to be easy to find happiness here. Mathilde didn't.'

'She found it but it was cut short. I thought by fate. Later...'

'You wondered if it was something more human?'

Raoul laughed softly. 'You're putting words in my mouth. I've drawn no conclusion whatsoever. It's none of my business. Eugénie will marry him anyway. Her mind has been made up from the start. And even if she has doubts, perhaps because of Yvette, her mother will pressure her into continuing with the wedding. She wants a daughter who is a comtesse, nothing less.'

Yes, Madame Frontenac was a force to be reckoned with.

Atalanta walked in silence. She could not reveal to him that Eugénie had received a threatening letter and had become afraid. Her client had confided in her and she wasn't about to break that bond. But on the other hand, she needed to get more out of Raoul. He was a friend of the family and might know relevant things. She simply had to try and hope he would take her alleged family tie with Eugénie as enough of an explanation for her concern.

'Have you ever seen the paintings Gilbert sells? The Renaissance paintings he buys in Italy?' she asked.

Raoul seemed overtaken by the sudden change of topic. 'Why do you ask? Are you interested in one?'

'I know people who might be,' she lied quickly.

'I've never seen one in person. But Gilbert is very busy with them. He travels to Italy every few weeks and spends days in cities like Rome or Verona searching for new gems to pass on to the Parisian galleries. He's a real treasure hunter.'

Treasure hunting... Mathilde had mentioned that to

Yvette. Atalanta asked, 'Where does the comte keep his paintings before he sells them? Are they at the house?'

'I imagine not. He has them sent straight to Paris. He has a bank vault there. It would not be safe to keep them here. They might get stolen. After all, he's away for weeks on end. The staff are here of course but... that is not the same.'

'I see.'

Raoul glanced at her. 'If you know people who are interested, you must tell Gilbert. He's always grateful for new contacts.' He halted the horse and mounted. 'I'll give him the exercise he wants. Good day.' And with that he pushed his heels into the horse's sides and spurred it into motion. Man and rider soon disappeared from view.

Atalanta chewed her lip. Raoul Lemont surprised her every time they were together. There was much more to him than met the eye. That he had also thought about Marcel DuPont's death was exciting as it suggested they might work together to solve it. But she couldn't forget he himself was entangled in the case. She couldn't accept anything he said as truth. Her grandfather had warned her to verify things, always.

For instance: had Raoul told her that Angélique was a far better rider than she had admitted in order to incriminate her?

If he had no interest in rekindling their love affair, he might be spiteful enough to want to hurt her.

With a heavy heart Atalanta continued to the house.

Chapter Fifteen

I n the library Atalanta took some time walking around and looking at all the book titles. There were leatherbound volumes from top to bottom, creating an inviting but totally overwhelming whole. And did she really expect to find something important in a book about local history?

Still, there had been a shell in the pocket of the dead man. The shell grotto could hold the key to his murder. To Mathilde's death as well?

She went to the corner and opened the writing desk that stood there. The lid now formed a surface for her to write on while inside many small drawers and openings for letters showed themselves. She ran her fingertips across the inlaid ivory. This was a delicate masterpiece. Quite feminine. Had it been Mathilde's?

She opened the drawers. There were writing materials in

them: pens, bottles of ink, blotting paper, and a pen knife. Also scraps of paper that had been used to write on, to try different styles of lettering, it seemed.

Then at the bottom of a drawer, beneath some blank paper, she found an overview of the gardens with little notes at various points. At a pond it said: *move elsewhere*. Some places were marked with crosses and names: Persephone, Hera, Minerva.

Atalanta recalled she had found Yvette huddling at the foot of a statue of Minerva. *Do all these crosses indicate statues? One way to find out.*

She took the paper into the garden and walked around. She found the statues where the crosses were and also concluded that Mathilde had not had time to put her plans for changes into motion. The pond was still at the same place where she had marked it ready for removal. And the rose beds hadn't been changed into an arboretum either.

There was just one thing on the paper Atalanta couldn't quite place. A name. Croesus.

Croesus had been a mythological figure, a wealthy king. One could even use the name Croesus to refer to riches.

Treasures also? Why else was the name followed by a question mark? None of the other names were.

The most interesting detail was that 'Croesus' was scribbled in that area of the garden where the shell grotto was.

Atalanta stared in that direction. The police had looked at it and closed it off for the time being. No one was allowed to go there. She could hardly do something illegal.

Folding the piece of paper, she put it in her pocket and returned to the house. She had to talk to her client to see how she was feeling the day before her wedding to the comte.

Atalanta's footsteps were heavy as she realized she had nothing conclusive to report. How could she assure her client that all was well? Or worry her further by saying it was doubtful that Mathilde had died in an accident? The woman at the dispensary had mentioned her head had been hurt, her skull damaged. A blow to the head while she had been down on the ground after a fall off her horse? Administered by a human hand?

It was speculation, not fact.

Did she have a right to disturb the wedding while the comte might not have been involved at all, no matter what had happened on that fateful day?

All he wanted was to introduce some happiness back into his house and heart.

Also for his niece's sake.

But Yvette disliked Eugénie and might never be happy in her company. Whatever Atalanta told Eugénie might have the power to sway her in one direction or the other, impacting both her life and that of many others. How could Atalanta ever handle such influence wisely?

Grandfather, if only you were here to tell me what to do.

When she arrived at Eugénie's room, she realized that she had chosen the worst possible moment. Eugénie was fitting her wedding dress and her mother and both her sisters were rushing around her, fiddling with the sleeves and headdress.

Atalanta excused herself at once and said she'd come back later, but Eugénie called her in and asked anxiously, 'How does it look?'

'We just told you it's *merveilleuse*,' Françoise said, with an exaggerated trill in her voice but Eugénie waved her off. 'I want an impartial opinion. You'd say it was lovely if I were dressed in a jute bag.'

Françoise's expression fell and she looked at her mother. 'Maman, did you hear that? Why must Eugénie always abuse me?'

Madame Frontenac didn't seem to notice her eldest daughter. She was studying her youngest with a delighted look, her hands clasped in front of her chest. 'My baby,' she whispered. Eugénie waved to Atalanta to come closer. 'What do you think?' She turned in a full circle, the skirt of her dress fluttering. 'Is it beautiful enough for a comtesse?'

'It's very impressive,' Atalanta said, admiring the embroidery on the bodice that formed birds and flowers. 'Many hours of hand stitching must have gone into it.'

'Yes, and that is why we're not going to discuss postponing the wedding.' Madame Frontenac wagged a finger at Eugénie. 'Your temple is not so bad that you can't walk down the aisle.'

'But Maman,' Louise said, 'if she doesn't feel well...' Her eyes were eager. 'We could wait another week.'

'The guests are arriving and we'll celebrate tomorrow.'

At her mother's confident words Eugénie's happy look

dimmed and she sank onto her bed. 'I do wonder...' She looked at Atalanta, pleading.

Atalanta's throat was tight. She had failed in her assignment. She could say nothing with certainty, either way.

Madame Frontenac said, 'Don't be silly, girl. You are about to be married to a very eligible man.' She walked up to her daughter and touched the diamond necklace she was wearing, the one she had brought with her the other day. 'Your father and I are very pleased.'

Louise said, 'Papa is not coming.' It sounded triumphant.

Again, Atalanta was reminded of the suit fitting. Martin Frontenac had planned to attend and now he wasn't coming. What did that mean? And what about the claim of the tailor's assistant that the engagement ring Eugénie wore held a fake stone?

'He has business to attend to.' Her mother glared at Louise. 'If you have nothing useful to contribute, you may leave.'

'But *Maman*...'

'Now.'

Louise stood her ground. 'I'm one of the bridesmaids. I need to be here when the bride is fitted for the dress.'

'You're just jealous,' Eugénie spat. 'You wanted to marry Gilbert.'

Louise's cheeks turned deep red. 'I didn't,' she spluttered in a weak voice. 'I matched him with Mathilde.'

'Yes, but you realized your mistake afterwards. You

were happy when she died; you thought your chance had come at last.'

Louise's face was on fire now. 'I did not!' It sounded unconvincing. Eugénie sat up. 'Did you send that letter to me? Did you put it in the basket between the leeks?'

Louise's mouth opened and shut again.

Madame Frontenac asked, 'What letter? What leeks?'

Atalanta said, 'The letter could have been placed in the basket after the cook came home. The maids were busy upstairs. The butler had an afternoon off.'

'How do you know that?' Louise objected and then fell silent.

Eugénie ran to her and slapped at her. 'You did it. You miserable jealous little—'

Louise stepped back to avoid her sister's blows. 'Maman! Say something!'

Madame Frontenac waved her arms in the air. 'Be careful with the dress, girls. It cost us a fortune. What letter does she mean?' She turned to Atalanta. 'What letter are you speaking of?'

Eugénie took the lead. 'I was nervous on my way over here, Maman, and I told Atalanta about a letter I received claiming Mathilde's death had not been an accident and I might be next.'

Madame Frontenac stared at her.

Atalanta expected a gasp, a stagger, perhaps even a half-faint. But the woman said, 'Are you mad, girl? Such letters are always sent in spite and… they mean nothing. Have you got so little courage?'

Then she swirled to Louise. 'Did you write it? You'd better not lie to me now and I find out later it was you.'

Louise looked as if she would have liked to melt into the floorboards. 'I, uh...'

'I want to know the truth, right now,' her mother snapped, underlining the words with impatient taps of her foot.

'Yes, I did send it.' Louise hung her head. 'I was just so angry at her for the way she kept showing off to me that she was marrying and I was not. It was very hurtful.'

'You wrote the letter?' Madame Frontenac demanded.

'Yes. I said so, didn't I?'

'What did it say?' Atalanta asked. 'How was it written?'

Louise looked at her. 'Why do I need to tell you?'

'It is very important that we know for certain it was indeed you. Then there is no threat to Eugénie's happiness and she can wed tomorrow.'

Madame Frontenac's expression cleared. 'Of course. You are wise, girl.' She said to Louise, 'Tell her what she wants to know.'

Louise still looked reluctant but as her mother came over and actually prodded her in the ribs, she said, 'It was written in bright-red ink. It said: *His first wife didn't die in an accident. Be careful. Be afraid.*'

The exact wording. Who could have known it besides the writer?

Madame Frontenac stared at her daughter and then snorted. 'Can you believe something so silly? You read too many cheap novels, girl. I will have to think of a suitable

way to punish you for this. Giving your sister such a fright.'
She turned to Eugénie and cooed, 'But everything is fine
now, my sweet. The letter was just a trick. It meant nothing.
You can marry tomorrow and be happy.' She pinched her
cheek. 'Smile, girl, smile.' Eugénie smiled hesitantly, her
eyes seeking Atalanta.

Her client obviously wanted confirmation of her
mother's conclusion that all was solved now. But deep
inside, Atalanta wasn't so sure. Louise's knowledge of the
letter, without Eugénie having shared it with her, proved
that she had written it. But the big question remained, why
would she do such a thing if she didn't believe something
was wrong?

Atalanta asked Louise quietly, 'Can we talk in the
corridor?'

Louise eyed her with disbelief. 'Why would I want that?'

'Please come and hear me out.'

Louise cast a look at her mother, who was fussing with
the dress again, sighed, and followed Atalanta out of the
room. Atalanta said, 'Do you believe Gilbert, Comte de
Surmonne, killed his first wife, Mathilde?'

Louise looked appalled. 'Of course not. I respect Gilbert;
he's one of my dearest friends.'

'Then why would you risk writing a letter that
incriminates him? To hurt your sister? That doesn't make
sense. It's not worth it.'

'I didn't think Eugénie would share it with anyone. If
only she knew, how would it hurt Gilbert?'

'It would have hurt him if Eugénie had broken off the engagement because of the letter.'

'She wouldn't have done that. She's too vain for that. She wants to become comtesse.'

'Then what was the purpose of the letter? Merely to make her afraid?'

'I didn't think it through that far.' Louise crossed her arms over her chest. 'I only wanted to have a little fun at her expense. The butler had an afternoon off; the occasion was perfect for it.'

'Of course...' Atalanta spoke almost casually. 'The letter didn't say Gilbert killed his wife. It could have been someone else you were warning Eugénie against. Who did you have in mind?'

Louise's eyes flickered. Atalanta wasn't sure if she was genuinely thinking of someone now or was working on a quick way to attribute blame. She said, 'To be honest, I was thinking of Yvette. She has always been an unstable girl.' She took a deep breath and added, 'There was a time when I believed I was in love with Gilbert. I believed he might also fall in love with me. But I tried not to let that happen because of Yvette. I knew he had taken responsibility for her upbringing and... well, frankly, I didn't see myself living in the same house with her. You've seen what she is capable of. She's constantly throwing things into turmoil. With her around, no one can be at peace. So I introduced Gilbert to Mathilde. She didn't mind chaos. In fact, she was very much like Yvette. I felt they suited each other.'

'Yes, I heard Yvette took to her and they spent a lot of time together. Why would she have hurt Mathilde?'

'Because you can never know what is going through her head. She's decidedly unbalanced. Especially when she feels like someone has hurt her feelings.'

Atalanta stared at the wall. Every time she believed she had worked it out, someone took pieces of the puzzle away and added new ones. The picture was never completed. She turned her eyes back to Louise. 'Did you pour mud over Eugénie at the shell grotto?'

'I'm above such childish tricks. Yvette must have done it. Or Victor.'

'Victor?' Atalanta queried.

'Yes. He was quite angry when Eugénie decided to accept Gilbert's offer of marriage. He had hoped to secure her for himself. For money, of course, as his father has disinherited him.'

'And now he's courting you?'

'We are just friends.' Louise stepped back. 'You are very curious. Perhaps too curious for your own good?' She gestured at the room. 'May I go back in?' It sounded challenging.

'Of course.' Atalanta smiled. 'You've done the right thing confessing about the letter. Now Eugénie will feel much better.'

'Still, she will regret marrying him.' Louise sounded satisfied. 'Gilbert is a good man and that goodness induces him to put up with Yvette when he should have abandoned her long ago. She'll be his undoing one day.'

She entered the room and shut the door in Atalanta's face.

Just as well. She had no reason to be present as the dress was fitted. The matter of the warning letter had been cleared up, but other issues were far from obvious. Who had attacked Eugénie at the shell grotto?

Victor? She hadn't really had a chance to talk to him.

A maid came down the corridor in a rush and her expression lit as she saw Atalanta. 'A call for you, mademoiselle. The telephone is in the hallway.'

Atalanta went down and picked up the receiver. 'Hello?'

'This is Renard. I have some information for you. Do not say anything that can give something away. There might be ears listening.'

'Very well, thank you.' Atalanta glanced about her. But she acknowledged that even if she saw no one near, it was possible to listen in, clearly hear every word she said. For instance, if the eavesdropper was positioned above.

'You asked about Yvette, the comte's ward. She is the daughter of his late brother. Upon her parents' death an amount of money was settled on her, in bearer bonds, to be handed over to her when she turns eighteen, to compensate for the fact that all of her family's wealth goes to her brother. He was recently expelled from boarding school for pulling a gun on a fellow student he didn't like.'

Atalanta gasped.

Renard continued, 'There was a prior incident when he shot an arrow at his music teacher. The man was injured in the shoulder and couldn't play the violin anymore.'

VIVIAN CONROY

Imagine that. Not being able to play the instrument you loved and on which your livelihood depended.

Renard said, 'The family bought him off. Seems like this young man has a propensity for violence.'

And he might not be the only one. Was Yvette the same, eager to punish the people who had slighted her, or even remove them completely from her life? Where her brother seemed rather blunt in his methods, with his actions immediately leading back to him, Yvette had been cleverer... if she had indeed been involved in Mathilde's death. It had been ruled an accident without question.

It hurt to close the net on Yvette, but she owed it to her client to establish how dangerous the girl really was.

Renard continued. 'You also asked about Raoul Lemont. Son of a French father and a Spanish mother. Studied at various universities, then started racing. Is currently one of the most lauded drivers in the races held in Italy and Germany. Doesn't seem to care whether he lives or dies.'

Renard paused and added, 'He has been named in connection with various women, even a married baroness, but I haven't been able to establish that he had an affair with Mathilde Lanier.'

Atalanta wanted to ask about Angélique Broneur but mentioning names might draw attention. 'Very well,' she said again.

Renard said, 'I've also heard something very interesting about Mathilde's family. Her father died when she was just ten years old and she was always very close with her mother. Madame Lanier was broken after her daughter's

236

death and her health suffered as a result. She spent a lot of time abroad, to visit springs and other places promising healing, but she has returned recently, having heard she has only a few more months to live.'

A woman with nothing to lose.

Atalanta clutched the receiver. Why had she appeared to attend the wedding of her daughter's widower? *Does she have some plan she wants to execute here?*

Or was she merely intending to close the book before she died? Make peace with her daughter's death before her own time came?

Renard said, 'You be very careful as you navigate these deep waters.'

'I will, *merci*. Call again if you know any more.' She hung up the receiver. Looking up, she saw Gilbert standing on the stairs. Knowing that she had been discussing his affairs, investigating whether he was guilty of murder, blood rushed into her cheeks. 'I'm trying to arrange for a concert,' she lied. 'A friend is trying to find a venue and other musicians.' Her voice shook and she feared he'd see through her ruse at once.

'I see.' He ran down agilely. 'You must let us know when the details are known. I'm sure Eugénie and I would love to attend.'

Atalanta felt like she was now certainly crimson with embarrassment but kept smiling. 'I will. You are too kind.'

'On the contrary, I've been caught up in too many affairs, not paying proper attention to my guests. But I intend to make up for that. You must allow me to show you the chapel where the wedding will take place tomorrow. My servants are currently decorating it.'

'I would love to see it.' Relieved by the distraction, Atalanta followed him through a corridor and a small wooden door into a back part of the house. Another door gave access to a chapel with wooden benches on either side of the aisle and a platform in front where the priest could stand.

Tapestries decorated the walls and the saints depicted on the altarpiece were dressed in rich blues and reds with gold-leaf embellishment. Servants were busy decorating the heads of the benches with snow-white roses.

'Won't they die before the wedding starts tomorrow?' Atalanta asked.

'They stand in vases with water, which are then attached to the benches with white linen and lace. All very well thought out.' Gilbert smiled. 'I hope you approve.'

Atalanta answered his smile. 'Indeed, I do. The windows are beautiful.' She pointed up at the stained glass forming a scene of a man and woman joining hands.

'All my ancestors wed here,' Gilbert said.

'Are they also buried here?' Atalanta asked. 'I heard something about a family tomb?'

'The vault, yes.' He pointed at a gaping square opening beside the platform where steps led down. 'I don't set foot there often. It's dark and damp; a desolate place.'

As he spoke, something moved in the shadows of the opening. A figure arose, dressed all in black.

Gilbert stepped back with a gasp, colour draining from his face.

Atalanta's heart also skipped a beat, but the slender frame seemed familiar. 'Madame Lanier,' she whispered to Gilbert.

He controlled himself with a visible effort and stepped forward. 'Madame Lanier, are you not well?'

'I've visited Mathilde.' Madame Lanier's eyes were red-rimmed. 'I've told her you are marrying again.'

There was a silence and Atalanta half expected the elderly woman to continue to tell them what Mathilde had thought of that. She spoke of her daughter as if she were still alive.

Gilbert said, 'She told me that I should remarry, should something happen to her before we had children. She understood very well that a comte has an obligation to his estate and his people.'

Madame Lanier gave him a sharp look. 'Why would Mathilde have thought something should happen to her?'

'Come, come, you know what she was like. She had been injured before. She told me she wasn't going to change her ways, wasn't going to be careful just because she was a married woman, and a countess at that.' He smiled softly. 'I said I would never ask her to change, because I loved her just the way she was.' His eyes turned dark with pain. 'We could have been so happy.'

Madame Lanier put her hand on his arm. 'You need not worry. She was happy as well. She wrote to me how happy she was. She said she couldn't wish for more. That she knew where your heart lay, with your true treasure. Oh that we could cling to the things we love, and keep them close to our hearts. But they fall away from us, like dust.'

A tear trickled down her cheek and she hurried down the aisle, a sober breakable figure, the black of her clothes in sharp contrast with the bright-white roses.

Gilbert said, 'She should not have come here. She's asking too much of herself.'

They stood in silence, the light atmosphere having evaporated. Even the sweet scent of flowers on the air seemed inappropriate.

Gilbert focused on Atalanta and asked, with a catch in his voice, 'Do you think I'm doing the wrong thing in remarrying?' He seemed desperate for denial, but at the same time resigned to condemnation.

'No, you cannot pine for someone who will never return.' After a moment she added, 'But you've made a choice that might cause trouble. Eugénie doesn't get along with Yvette. I understand she is your responsibility until she turns eighteen. That's two more years.' *Having been here for a few days, experiencing the constant tension, I can't imagine how long two years will feel.*

'You think I should have waited until she was of age before I found myself a new wife? I did intend to, but I met Eugénie and... she brought light back to my life. Is it selfish to wish for happiness? Perhaps.' He turned away from her and walked off, ignoring a servant who wanted to ask something about the decorations.

Atalanta smiled at the overtaken girl and told her it all

looked stunning and the bride would be very pleased. This brought a hesitant smile to her face.

But Atalanta's own mood wasn't so easily restored. Unease whirled inside of her and she needed to get away.

I need to breathe fresh air and think.

Chapter Sixteen

Although the police had said that access to the area of the shell grotto was prohibited, Atalanta was inevitably lured to it. The map Mathilde had made of the gardens had marked the shell grotto, and with the tantalizing clue 'Croesus'. Did it refer to some hidden riches? Loot?

Louise had said so disparagingly that Mathilde and Yvette had been treasure hunting, and that it was a fantasy they had indulged in. But what if it had referred to some sort of reality? Something Mathilde had discovered as she made plans to change the gardens?

Atalanta ignored the pricking of her conscience as she bent down under the coarse rope that was strung from yew to yew to barricade the path to the shell grotto. She entered it and breathed the damp air.

A cold sensation wriggled up her neck. What if someone was lurking to strike at her? To hurt her?

She stood with her back against the wall, watching the light, to determine if there was a sudden shadow, but nothing stirred. Her heartbeat grew steadier and she willed herself to do this systematically. How could she best determine if the grotto contained a secret?

Something worth killing for?

She directed her attention to the shell wall with all those elements like parts of a mosaic depicting the happy nymphs and deer with hunting dogs. Marcel DuPont had a shell in his pocket.

Taken off the wall? Picked up from the ground?

What had he been doing here?

Meeting with Sargant? To try and tell him of the thing he knew about Mathilde's death and ask for money to stay silent?

But Sargant was his sworn enemy.

That doesn't make sense.

Had DuPont known something about this grotto? When he had been arrested for poaching and had asked for the comte, had he meant to tell Gilbert about a find here?

Or about something Mathilde had been up to before she died?

The woman in the dispensary had mentioned her head been damaged, her skull broken. Had she been investigating this cave and had someone thrown something through the opening? Or approached stealthily and bashed her over the head? Had the murderer then put her body on a path and spurred the horse on its way to make it look like an accident?

The idea that something deadly had transpired in this cave increased her heart rate. But she had to stay calm. She listened carefully for the sounds filtering through the opening. Then she took a deep breath and stepped up to the shell wall. She touched the shells, big ones first, and tried to push them inwards or turn them. Was there a lever? A way to open a secret compartment? A hiding place Mathilde had found here?

Croesus…

She sat on her haunches trying lower shells, looking for a rhyme or reason to their patterns, but nothing moved under her exploring fingers. Was it madness to think there could be a hiding place in the rock face? Wouldn't it be solid?

But still, why had Mathilde marked this spot? What had Marcel DuPont been doing here?

'Lost an earring?' an ironic voice asked.

Atalanta shot to her feet and scraped her shoulder on the rock wall. 'Ouch!' She raised her hand to rub the hurt shoulder.

'The police said not to come here,' Raoul said as he studied her with a cynical expression.

'Then what are you doing here?' she asked.

'I followed you.'

She blinked. Plain admission was the last thing she had expected. 'You followed me? Why?'

'Because I have nothing better to do? Because you seem to be getting into scrapes all the time?'

'Scrapes?' Atalanta repeated with disdain. 'I'm a grown woman, not a schoolgirl you have to rescue.'

Something flickered in his eyes. Annoyance? 'I wonder what you are really up to, here at Bellevue, Mademoiselle Frontenac.' He looked her over. 'You can fool others with your story of playing the piano at the wedding feast, but not me.'

Atalanta's heart hammered. 'Go and ask Eugénie. She invited me to come along.'

'Yes, she invited you to come along, I do believe that. But what is your ulterior motive?'

'I have no idea what you are talking about.'

'Then what are you doing here?'

'I'm interested in mythology.'

'Oh, yes. Atalanta.' He said the name slowly. 'Your parents, I suppose, instilled this interest in Greek myths in you by naming you after a fabled woman.'

'Indeed they did. My mother gave me a book of Greek mythology when I was just a child.'

'Hardly stories suitable for a little girl.'

'My mother loved those stories and read to me from the book. She left out those passages that were too shocking.' Atalanta smiled. Her fondest memories were of those afternoons when her mama had read to her.

Raoul said, 'Atalanta. Able to keep up with any man. And a huntress at that. I wonder...' He leaned closer. 'What are you hunting here?'

His nearness increased her heart rate. He was dangerous to her mission in several ways. She laughed nervously. 'I

246

wanted to see the shell pattern up close, to ascertain how it was created.'

'And you conveniently ignored the police's orders to stay away from here? Or the fact that Eugénie got attacked here? Come, come, you have more common sense than that. You're looking for a pattern indeed, but not one made up of shells. A pattern between events.'

He was getting too close for comfort. 'It was probably Yvette attacking her, pulling a childish prank. No mystery in that. They are not the best of friends.' Atalanta took a deep breath. Her chafed shoulder burned, but she was determined not to show it to him. She should distract him from his interest in her actions. *At once.* 'You can better spend your time with Angélique Broneur. She seems eager to rebuild what you had in Italy.'

'How would you know?'

'She told me so.' It was a half-truth but she would never admit to him that she had observed the near kiss he had refused.

'Our time in Italy was ages ago. I was a different man then. She was an innocent girl, not full of her diva allure as she is now.' It sounded wistful. 'Why would she tell you something personal like that?'

'I don't know. She seems open, exuberant. A lively personality.'

He smiled an indulgent little smile that suggested Angélique still had a bit of a hold on him. 'She certainly is. It's good that she came.'

'See. All is well.' Atalanta turned to the shell pattern

again and let her gaze roam it. Her eye fell to a place where a shell seemed to be missing. She leaned down and put her little finger in the cavity. Was this where Marcel DuPont had removed his shell? Why?

She tried to poke her finger in deeper but it seemed to hit on solid wall.

'Don't damage it,' Raoul warned her. 'It's old and Gilbert is terribly protective of his possessions.'

Atalanta wondered if the comte had written the note luring Eugénie to the cave under the impression it would be Victor waiting for her there and he had poured the mud over her to punish her. If he was so possessive, it had to displease him that the blond man still seemed to attract Eugénie's attention.

But the chauffeur had said the comte had been in the café all morning, meeting with someone. He couldn't have returned to the estate.

A sound rang out through the cave, a quiet scraping as of someone was moving above.

Atalanta lifted her head and looked up at the opening. Did she see a shadow there?

Raoul had also perked up. 'Someone is watching us,' he said under his breath. Then he rushed outside. Atalanta followed him to where he stood staring up at the rock. A blackbird flew up and sat on the branch of a nearby tree, calling indignantly.

Raoul shook his head. 'We're growing paranoid. It was just a bird looking for insects amongst the moss that covers the stone.' He reached out his hand and grabbed hers.

'Enough of this morose hiding inside. We must enjoy the sun-filled day.' He pulled her arm through his and marched her off. 'I won't tell Gilbert about your little outing.'

'I doubt he would mind,' Atalanta said, more confidently than she felt.

Raoul slowed his pace and gestured with his free hand. 'Look at the view. The lavender fields, the land in the distance. And listen.'

Atalanta strained her ears. 'I don't hear anything. Just birdsong.'

'Exactly. It is quiet. Something that those country lovers find so charming.'

'But not you?'

Raoul laughed. 'I'm a city person. I can't wait to get away from here and go back to Rome.'

'For another race?' Atalanta's heart sank as she thought of him wagering his life. But he didn't feel that way. It made him happy. Made him feel alive. 'If you don't like the peace of the country, why come here? I understand you were friends with the comte years ago, but... it would have been easy to make up an excuse not to come. Even Monsieur Martin Frontenac, the father of the bride, is not present.'

'I was worried it would be seen as exactly that, an excuse not to come. And who needs an excuse? People who have something to hide.' Raoul walked even slower, his eyes on the view. 'It is no secret that there are rumours I was in love with Mathilde. People seem to think I fall in love with every woman I meet.'

'Perhaps every other woman you meet?' Atalanta teased him.

Raoul looked her in the eye. 'And in what category do you fall, Mademoiselle Atalanta? The one I did fall in love with or the one my affections skipped?'

It felt like an insult, almost. Atalanta replied, 'It doesn't really matter, monsieur, as I have no wish to get involved in any kind of personal relationship. So if you do not care for me, all the better. We can just be friends.'

'Friends?' he repeated. 'Friends trust and appreciate each other. I'm afraid you don't like me, let alone trust me. Or am I mistaken?'

Caught. If she said she liked him, he would smirk. If she said she didn't like him, she would sound prim and proper but not be expressing her real feelings.

On the other hand, he had also mentioned trust. And she didn't trust him, at all. That was the worst of it.

'Have I finally dumbfounded you?' he asked with a grin.

'I don't start to trust people as soon as I know them. That takes time.'

'But you know, instinctively, whether they are trustworthy or not. How about me?' He seemed determined to press the point.

'I never know whether you are serious or not. That makes it all harder.'

Raoul threw his head back and laughed. 'Serious? Why do women always want to make everything so serious?'

'Because we are in a vulnerable position compared to

men. Our reputation is ruined sooner. If you flirt, you are thought charming. If I flirt, I am thought...'

'Wanton?' He wriggled his eyebrows. 'I wonder how you would flirt, Mademoiselle Atalanta. Would you look deep into a man's eyes? Would you manipulate your cigarette? Oh, pardon me, you probably don't smoke. I think you would consider spending money on tobacco a waste.'

'You're teasing me.'

'A little. You are so prim and proper that I can't resist.' He thought a moment and said, 'No, the word *proper* is not quite applicable. I don't think you are entirely proper. I do think you entertain wild fantasies of what your life could be, if you had money and opportunity.'

Caught again. Atalanta flushed. He seemed to know things about her he definitely could—and should—not know.

Had he been in her room? Had he looked through her drawers, leafed through her albums with their travel plans?

And through my case notes? If he has, what did he make of those? Can he read the Cyrillic alphabet?

Perhaps his races had taken him to Russia?

'Why would you think so?' she asked in a shaky voice.

Raoul ignored the question and continued. 'You are not proper, perhaps, but sensible. Yes, that is a much better word to describe it. You're not carried away by your fantasies, but you keep them in check by your sense of reality. You remember who you are and what you are here for.'

Atalanta tried not to betray her nerves as he came so close to the truth. Even if he had recognized the Cyrillic letters, the transposition cipher ensured he wouldn't have been able to read the notes. He couldn't mean the case. He thought of her position as a distant cousin, someone not quite in the same league. Someone who should be conscious of her station and not... indulge in the attention of this handsome man.

It was no genuine interest anyway, on his part. Just a game.

A battle of wills perhaps, even? He was testing her to see if she'd give anything away.

'Am I insulting you by applying the word sensible?' Raoul asked. 'I know ladies who would vehemently object to the term.'

'I don't see why. Sensible means to have common sense. I should hope I have some. But you're right. I also have dreams. I would like to see all the major cities.'

'You believe your music can take you there? First a concert in Paris, then Nice, Monaco. Rome, perhaps?'

Atalanta wanted to ask him if he'd come and hear her play if she ever did get to Rome, but she was no concert pianist and they would never meet again after this case had ended.

Unfortunately.

'If you'd ever visit, I would be honoured to be your guide.' He made a mock bow with his head.

Atalanta huffed. 'You promise it easily now, but what if

it takes me two years to make it to the eternal city? Would you even remember my name?'

'It's not a name one easily forgets.' He looked into her eyes.

It seemed the world around them blurred a bit and there was nothing but the sincerity in those golden-brown depths. But Atalanta's senses were on alert, whispering to her not to let herself fall into the atmosphere of confidence he was trying to create between them.

'I'll make a note then to contact you if I ever do visit Rome,' she said lightly. 'Have you got a permanent residence there?'

'No, but if you address your letter to the Hotel Benvenuto, they will forward it to me. I don't believe in tying myself to places.'

'But one has to have a place to call home,' Atalanta objected.

'Does one? Who says so?' He studied her closer. 'And where is your home, mademoiselle? What address in Paris could I write to if I were so inclined?'

Atalanta scrambled for an answer. She couldn't give her real address. She didn't know where her supposed parents lived. How unfortunate that he showed this interest. Still, she was also fluttery with happiness inside.

Raoul said, 'You are a woman of mystery, Mademoiselle Atalanta. A sensible woman of mystery. A contradiction in terms. Something I'd like to unravel.'

'You can always write to me care of the Frontenacs. I'm sure they would pass on any letters.'

'Having first opened and read them? Madame Frontenac is insatiably curious. I would rather not feed her interest in my affairs, or yours. She might not think a… friendship altogether appropriate.'

Atalanta flushed again as her own suggestion of them being only friends was flung back at her in this manner.

'But Gilbert mentioned to me that you talked to a friend on the phone about a concert you are going to arrange. I might write to you at the concert hall where you perform. Send you flowers?' He let go of her, stepped up to a flowerbed, and picked a purple dahlia. He held it out to her with a flourish. 'This is a down payment to assure you I will make good on my promise.'

Atalanta accepted the flower from his hand. Her heart beat so fast she could scarcely draw breath.

Raoul bowed to her and walked away, quickly. He passed Françoise, who was headed in their direction. She cast curious looks at Atalanta and the flower in her hand. 'I'm so sorry if I disturbed a… personal moment?'

Her smile was obviously feigned, her eyes openly inquisitive. 'I wasn't aware Raoul had transferred his attentions so easily. Just last week when he was in Paris with us, he only had eyes for a German princess who was holidaying there. He couldn't stop staring at her diamond earrings. He will have to marry well if he's to keep up his extravagant lifestyle. They say he earns money from racing, and has a deposit box at the bank full of his late mother's jewellery he can pawn, but banks don't have access to the deposit boxes and their employees can't see inside them.

Only the owner is allowed to access them and Raoul can go to that bank pretending he is getting his funds there all he likes, not that anyone really believes that.' She started upright. 'Oh, I mustn't gossip so. Maman would slap my arm for it. May I invite you back to the house for tea? We have finished fitting the dress. Eugénie is all in a flurry.'

Atalanta smiled at the poor acting of the woman who had of course shared all she wanted Atalanta to know on purpose. She had conveyed clearly that Raoul had no money and would have to look to a wealthy spouse to support him. Such alliances were not unheard of, and if both parties agreed to it, they could be quite comfortable.

Atalanta's instinct refused to accept that Raoul, who seemed fiercely independent, would ever ally himself with a woman merely for her fortune, but perhaps she misread him. He had said marriage meant nothing to him, but he might consider it a respectable way to get access to money.

She followed Françoise, rehearsing some questions to ask the bride about her dress and other preparations for the big day tomorrow. It seemed unlikely anything would yet occur that could stop the wedding now that Louise had admitted to having written the letter and Atalanta's search of the shell grotto had delivered nothing but a sense of defeat. She knew she was somehow looking at it the wrong way.

But she had no idea how to change her perspective.

Chapter Seventeen

T he day of the wedding broke upon Bellevue in the full glory of a gorgeous orange and golden sunrise. Atalanta stood at her open balcony doors surveying it with mixed feelings. With Madame Frontenac having arrived and taken matters vigorously into her hands, the course to the vows was firmly set, but the murder of the poacher preyed on her mind. Why, upon his release, had he rushed to Bellevue, to the shell grotto of all places?

Croesus, it whispered in her mind. *Croesus is the key.*

A knock at the door announced the arrival of the maid with hot water to freshen herself. The bathroom in her wing had been allotted to the close relatives of the bride, while the bathroom in the other was Eugénie's to use as she pleased.

The maid curtseyed. 'It's such a beautiful day, mademoiselle. I can't wait to see the bride in her dress. Her mother said it is very stunning. Have you seen it already?

You must have. And the flowers... The master sent the gardener out for the bouquet. The other flowers are already at the chapel. I saw how they got picked. All white roses. He's been growing them since spring. He must love her very much. Isn't it romantic?' The girl flushed. 'Pardon me, I'm talking too much.'

'No, I'm quite grateful to have the conversation. Everyone else is busy. Have you worked here long?'

'Since last December, mademoiselle. The maid who served the master's first wife left right after her accident to return to her family and, after a while, they felt more hands were needed.'

'Even though the master is often away?' Atalanta queried.

'It is a big house and he doesn't like dust to settle on his art objects. He's so particular about them. I'm afraid to go near them. The best pieces he keeps in his study and tidies himself. I'm glad for that. I would be worried I'd drop them. They are so precious I'd spend a lifetime trying to repay him.'

The girl considered a moment how long that would be and shuddered. 'I'm not staying here forever. Just long enough to earn money for a wedding dress of my own and to put towards the little house Giles wants to buy us.'

'Giles is your fiancé?'

'Yes. He works in the stables.'

'Will you buy a little house here on the estate?'

'No, mademoiselle. In a nearby village. Giles can join the

blacksmith there. We need to work here for a few more months and then we can move away.'

'I see. I wish you every happiness.'

'I won't have a big wedding like today, but it will still be very special.'

'I'm sure it will.' Atalanta waved in farewell as the girl retreated to the door. She washed and dressed herself, put on her jewellery, and checked her appearance from all sides before leaving her room.

There was a wedding breakfast below with local specialties and champagne, before they went down to the chapel for the ceremony. Raoul toasted her with his glass as soon as she entered. 'Can I say how ravishing you look?' He gestured to a footman, picked up a glass from the tray he carried, and handed it to her. 'To a memorable day.'

She touched her glass to his. 'Cheers.'

'Have one for me?' Angélique appeared beside them in striking blue with golden peacock motifs on her sleeves. 'My throat is parched.'

'I can't imagine why. I thought you drank cocktails straight out of bed,' Raoul said lightly but with a hint of disapproval. Angélique laughed. Atalanta thought she smelled some alcohol on her breath. Angélique said, 'It will be hot again; one has to drink enough.'

'Water then, not champagne,' Raoul said. His slight frown betrayed concern, as if he feared she would drink too much and make a scene.

Atalanta stepped away to greet the bride, her mother and sisters, and others present. There was a hum of voices as everyone shared tales of other wedding days to pass the time until the priest arrived.

As soon as he was said to be in the chapel, the guests filed out of the room to move there.

Atalanta realized that she had not seen the slender figure of Madame Lanier anywhere this morning. She leaned over to Françoise who walked close to her and inquired where the former mother-in-law was.

Françoise shrugged and started a conversation with a local matron. All the guests had entered the chapel. Only Atalanta lingered, waiting for Madame Lanier to appear. Perhaps she was in need of some support on this day which was no doubt very difficult for her?

A shriek from upstairs drew Atalanta's attention to the staircase with a jerk. Eugénie came rushing down, with a furious expression. 'Where is Yvette? She has taken my veil. I want it returned *now*. I have had enough of her little tricks. If anything has happened to it, if the merest smudge is on it, I'll strangle her. With my own two hands.'

'Calm down,' Atalanta hushed her. 'Is the veil not in your bedroom?'

'No, else I would not be looking for it, would I?' Eugénie gave her a disgusted look. 'The little witch must have taken it while I was in the bathroom. She knew I would return after breakfast to put on the veil. She's upset because I convinced Gilbert that a dog need not be present at a wedding. He ordered the servants to keep the dirty rag in the kitchens for the day so it can't ruin anything.'

Oh, no. Pom-pom meant the world to Yvette.

'To get even with me, she took my veil. I want to know where it is. Now!'

Madame Frontenac appeared from the direction of the kitchens, dragging Yvette along by her elbow. The girl shrieked, either in real or exaggerated pain.

'Don't hurt her,' Atalanta said.

'I will really hurt her if she doesn't return my veil right now.' Eugénie glared at the girl. 'Where is it?'

Yvette sighed and stared up at the ceiling. Eugénie snapped. 'Ruining my veil won't entice me or Gilbert to let your ugly snapping monster of a dog attend the wedding. Tell me where it is. Now!'

'If you really want to know, I put it on another bride.'

'Another bride?' Eugénie stammered. She glanced at her mother and Atalanta, not understanding. 'Who? Where?'

Yvette pointed at the entrance to the chapel. 'The veil is in there. In the subterranean burial chamber. I put it on Mathilde.'

'Mathilde?' Eugénie looked pale. 'How do you mean?'

'She has a tomb with her likeness cut out in the marble. Like she is lying there sleeping. I put the veil on her.'

'You are evil!' Eugénie slapped at her. 'I hate you. You monster. Go and fetch it. Fetch it right away.'

Yvette seemed startled by her fury and pulled free from Madame Frontenac's grasp. 'I'm not getting it for you. Why would I? I don't want you here. You ruin everything.' She rushed off upstairs. Eugénie wailed. 'I'm not getting into some dark burial chamber to get my veil back.' Her features contorted and Atalanta feared that a flood of tears would ruin her makeup. 'I'll get it,' she offered quickly. 'You only have to wait.'

She dashed into the chapel and down the aisle. The guests were taking their places, laughing and talking, not paying her any heed.

At the top of the steep steps leading into the burial chamber she took a deep breath and started to descend. It was so dark in there. *I should have brought a light.*

The sole of her shoe slipped in something. She sucked in air and balanced herself carefully. Should she go back for a light or feel her way around?

Better hurry. Eugénie was cracking and any delay would disturb her more.

Determined, Atalanta pushed on. Her foot hit against something solid, blocking her path. She leaned down to feel what it was. A shoulder. Hair. Not cold marble, but soft, smooth human hair.

Atalanta shrieked. She had always imagined that if she ever made a gruesome discovery she would be composed about it, but her brain didn't have time to work. The scream came from within before she could check it. She turned away and rushed up the steps, where curious faces appeared asking what was wrong.

The priest stood there alongside Raoul and Gilbert. She stammered, 'T-there's a-a dead body in there.'

Gilbert said, 'Several actually, all ancestors. They've been dead for quite some time.'

His attempt at humour wasn't appreciated by anyone.

Raoul caught Atalanta's arm. 'Can't you see that she means it? Someone light a candle!'

The priest didn't hesitate to reach for the already lit candles on his lectern and Raoul walked down the steps. After a few breathtaking moments of silence he called, 'Someone fell down the steps and died. It's Madame Lanier.'

Atalanta lifted a hand to her mouth. The grieving mother who had wanted to spend more time with her dead daughter ahead of the wedding?

Unsteady on her legs from exhaustion or emotion?

Perhaps blinded by tears?

An unfortunate misstep, a fall, the hard impact against the unforgiving marble floor?

Had she had time to realize what was happening, or had it been over right away?

'I can't believe this,' Gilbert muttered. 'Not another accident. Not on my wedding day.'

'There will be no wedding today,' Raoul said. 'We need a doctor here and we might as well inform Monsieur Joubert so he can officially establish how she died. We wouldn't want anyone to say nasty things about it later on.'

Gilbert stammered, 'Joubert? Police? Why?'

Raoul touched his arm. 'Just to protect your reputation, *mon ami*. Have no fear. It will all be settled soon.' He looked at Atalanta. 'Why did you go down there?'

'Eugénie wanted her veil,' she replied automatically.

'Her veil?' He looked confused. 'And it is in there? In a burial chamber?'

'Yvette put it there. To get even with Eugénie for persuading Gilbert her dog can't attend the wedding.'

Gilbert raised a hand and shaded his eyes. 'I can't believe she can never be sensible about anything.'

Raoul's eyes flashed with anger. 'She should really stop doing that. She...' He fell silent, his jaw tensing. 'Perhaps Madame Lanier caught her while she was at it? Perhaps...'

Atalanta could finish his thoughts: the older and infirm woman had called out to her, Yvette had been startled, and had rushed up the steps, pushing past Madame Lanier. The woman had taken a tumble and died.

'We must protect her,' Gilbert whispered. 'We must tell another story to the police. Something, anything.' His eyes were wide with shock.

Raoul put his arm around him. 'We had better go to the library. You need a stiff drink.' He said to Atalanta, 'Go and tell the bride there will be no wedding. Do it gently.'

Atalanta nodded automatically, but inside everything was screaming. Her hand had touched a dead body. And how could she tell this to Eugénie in a gentle fashion? There was no way to soften the blow. Her wedding day was ruined.

The bride was still waiting in the hallway with her mother and two sisters. 'Well?' they demanded in unison.

Madame Frontenac surveyed Atalanta's empty hands. 'Could you not find it?'

'I bet Yvette tore it or smudged it,' Eugénie wailed. 'I will kill her.'

'There's something else amiss.' Atalanta tried to sound

calm. Raoul depended on her to help him keep order. 'Madame Lanier went to see Mathilde's grave and she fell down the steps into the burial chamber. I'm sorry to have to tell you she is dead.'

There was a stunned silence. Eugénie blinked as if she didn't follow and Louise bit her lip. To bite back a cry of dismay? Or to hide a smile?

Then Madame Frontenac said, 'And? She should not have been here in the first place. She has nothing to do with Bellevue anymore or with Gilbert. He's marrying Eugénie now—'

'Maman, how can you say that?' Françoise interrupted. 'That poor woman died. That is terrible.' She kneaded her hands, pressing her rings deep into her flesh.

'How has the veil fared?' Madame Frontenac inquired. 'Did you get it?'

She wants to carry on with the wedding as if nothing happened. 'I've not looked for it yet. But we don't need it now. The doctor has to come.' She didn't want to mention Monsieur Joubert in his capacity as police officer just yet.

'Why if she's dead? We might as well leave her there. It is a burial chamber after all.' Madame Frontenac puffed up her chest. 'She should be pleased she has the chance to be buried in such a beautiful room. Her daughter didn't deserve it either. Mathilde had no title; she was nobody really.'

'Maman,' Françoise said again, looking askance at Atalanta. 'You cannot say such things. If there has been a death, the doctor must come and take care of things. The wedding can take place another time.'

It was sound advice, but the insistence in her eyes also suggested she was eager for any kind of delay. Didn't Louise say the other day that the wedding could be postponed for another week? Why were both sisters so keen on that?

'No, it must take place now.' Madame Frontenac looked frantic. 'I have come over especially. As have all the guests. We cannot let the death of some insignificant woman ruin it.'

'The doctor will be called,' Atalanta insisted. 'The wedding won't take place today. You had better return to your rooms and have some rest.'

All the while Eugénie had said nothing. She looked dazed, struck dumb by this turn of events.

Françoise and Louise put arms around her and led her away.

Madame Frontenac seemed to want to argue again, but as she caught Atalanta's eye, she huffed and followed her daughters upstairs.

Chapter Eighteen

A talanta went to the library door and knocked. It took a moment, then the door opened a crack. Raoul peered out, looking grim. His expression relaxed a little when he recognized her. 'Oh, it's you.' He surveyed her and said in a low voice, 'How are you? It can't have been pleasant to stumble upon Madame Lanier's body.'

'I'm fine. We must keep the situation under control. Madame Frontenac is very angry that the wedding can't take place. And does the comte really think Yvette is involved in Madame Lanier's death?'

Raoul held her gaze. 'Ever efficient and full of questions.'

Her cheeks turned hot. He had asked her how she felt and instead of taking that chance to share something personal she had ruined it by being businesslike. But that was just it. She didn't want to dig into her feelings now or she'd burst into tears.

He looked away and waved her along. 'Do come in.'

Gilbert sat in a chair, his face buried in his hands. 'It's over now,' he muttered. 'Over now.'

Raoul nodded in his direction and then shook his head as if to say the comte was in no condition for serious conversation.

Atalanta said, 'Eugénie didn't take it too badly.' It sounded quite poor, but she hoped he would not despair of ever marrying her.

Gilbert stirred and looked at her, his eyes red-rimmed. 'Who?'

'Eugénie. She didn't seem to fully understand it and—'

'But I do.' Gilbert sounded desperate. 'It's all over now. The doctor, the police. How could you mention the police?' He glared at Raoul.

His friend made a helpless gesture. 'We cannot keep this death under wraps. All your guests were there and witnessed the discovery of the body. We must act as if we are confident it will have no serious consequences.'

'No serious…' Gilbert raked his hands through his hair. 'But it's disastrous, man, can't you see?'

Raoul exhaled. 'Of course, a death at a wedding is unfortunate and—'

'What can we tell Joubert?' Gilbert threw himself back and stared at the ceiling. 'Can we convince him that someone snuck into the chapel to steal the silver? That he was caught by Madame Lanier and he pushed her down the steps? Something like that. Anything to prevent…' He sat up again and looked at Atalanta. 'Have you removed the veil from the burial chamber?'

'Not yet.'

'But you must. Joubert will want to know how it got there. Yvette's name can't be mentioned.'

'But Yvette was there and...' Raoul added slowly, 'She might be an important witness.'

Gilbert shook his head. 'She must be kept out of it entirely. Oh, that veil. How can we—?'

Raoul walked over to him. 'We're not going to lie and twist the facts. Joubert will no doubt establish that she slipped and fell. I saw that there was water on the steps.'

'Water on the steps?' Gilbert echoed.

'Yes. Probably from the flower arrangements.'

'It's true,' Atalanta said. 'My sole also slipped on something when I walked down.' She could again feel her heart skip a beat as she had almost lost her footing. Those steps were too steep to be safe.

'She slipped and fell and died, poor woman.' Raoul sounded compassionate but not overly emotional. He seemed to be in charge of the entire situation. 'The doctor will establish that her injuries are consistent with a fall. That will be the end of it.'

'If it hadn't been for the veil. It proves Yvette was there and... Oh, *non, non.*' Gilbert hid his face in his hands again.

Raoul looked at Atalanta as if asking for her help. She asked softly, 'Why is that so bad, comte? Raoul said there was water on the steps. Water makes marble slippery. It's perfectly logical—'

'Oh, yes, of course. If you don't consider...' He fell silent.

Raoul exchanged another worried look with Atalanta. 'If there is something you wish to tell us before Joubert arrives, now would be the time to do it,' he said.

Gilbert looked up. His eyes were frantic, showing white, as with a spooked horse. 'Tell you?'

'Yes, you can rely on us to help you.' Atalanta came to stand by Raoul's side. 'We will not lie, of course, but—'

'If you won't lie, you're of no use to me.' Gilbert turned away from them. 'Leave me.'

Raoul said, 'Tell us what is bothering you. We want to help.'

'But you cannot help me unless you are prepared to lie to Joubert.'

'Do you know more about Madame Lanier's death? Did you...'

'Me?' Gilbert stared at him, his jaw slack. Then his expression changed. 'Yes, that is the answer. Of course. Why couldn't I think of that myself? I will confess to it. I was sick and tired of her constant whimpering about Mathilde and I pushed her down the steps. She fell and died. *I* did it. That is it. *I* did it.'

Atalanta stared at him in disbelief. What was he suddenly raving about?

He jumped to his feet and paced the room. 'I must think this through. They will believe me when I say I pushed her. I'm strong enough for it, for certain. But the veil. How can I explain the veil? Yes. I will tell them Madame Lanier took the veil. She took it from Eugénie's room and put it on her dead daughter. It drove me mad and I pushed her. It can work, it can actually work.' He clapped his hands together as if he was overjoyed.

Raoul stared at his friend. 'Are you contemplating confessing to murder?'

Atalanta's stomach clenched. 'You can't seriously mean that?'

'Yes. I killed Madame Lanier. I also killed Marcel DuPont. I did it. They can take me along right away.' The comte reached out both his arms as if to offer his wrists for the handcuffs. 'I did it.'

Raoul's expression was one big question mark. 'What does Marcel DuPont have to do with it? I don't follow. You?' He glanced at Atalanta.

She nodded slowly. Blood pounded in her ears. Things clicked into place in a terrible way like when a chess player, confident in his strategy, suddenly sees the opponent's end game. Sees where all those earlier seemingly random moves led. 'You want to confess to two murders to protect someone who you think is guilty. Yvette,' she added in a hoarse whisper.

'Guilty?' Raoul echoed. 'Of shoving Madame Lanier down the steps and stabbing DuPont? You must be mad. The whole strain of marrying again got to you and now with this dead body you have snapped. Yes, you have brain fever. Once the doctor is here, he must attend to you first.

He can't do anything for Madame Lanier anymore, but he can prescribe you a sedative.'

'I don't need a sedative or a doctor. I don't have brain fever. I want to confess two murders to Joubert so he can take me along and lock me up. Stop talking about Yvette. She was never in the burial chamber. She didn't put the veil there. Madame Lanier did. Eugénie was mistaken when she assumed it was Yvette.'

Atalanta said, 'But when Eugénie accused Yvette of taking the veil, she admitted to it. She said she had done it because Eugénie wouldn't allow Pom-pom to be present at the wedding. He had to stay with the servants all day.'

'Be silent.' Gilbert glared at Atalanta. 'If you mention any of that to Joubert, all is lost.'

Raoul sucked in air. 'You don't seriously believe her guilty? You're not in earnest sacrificing yourself for her?'

'I should never have stayed silent. I made it all worse. So much worse.' Gilbert rubbed his face. 'I am to blame. I'm the adult. She was just a child at the time. She still is. A vulnerable, excitable child.'

'What should you not have stayed silent about?' Raoul asked.

'You know something about Mathilde's death,' Atalanta said. The cold feeling inside intensified until she was almost shivering. 'You had your suspicions it was Yvette all along.'

Gilbert shook his head but the truth was written plainly across his ashen face.

Raoul cried, 'Why did you not speak up? I can't imagine

Yvette hurting Mathilde on purpose. She loved her. It must have been a prank gone wrong.'

'Of course it was. But Joubert would never have seen it that way. He takes his duties very seriously. Not to mention he only feigns his respect for the gentry. He's a socialist at heart. If he had lived during the revolution, he would have been the first to stick those aristocratic heads under the guillotine. Joubert would have taken her along and locked her up. My little girl. I love her like my own daughter. I would do anything to protect her.'

'Even face the hangman's noose?' Atalanta asked softly. 'If you confess to two murders, that is your prospect for the future. And you will also be blamed for the death of Mathilde. After all, why kill DuPont but because he knew something?'

'I never thought of that wretched poacher again,' the comte groaned. 'He said he wanted to see me but I had no idea about what. When he came back however... He must have seen how Yvette put an obstruction in the forest path Mathilde would take. He must have known it was she who caused the accident and wanted to use it as leverage to get me to release him. I never thought...'

'He was stabbed to death,' Raoul said softly. 'I can see Yvette pulling a prank that goes horribly wrong, but I can't see her stabbing an old man in cold blood. You must think logically, *mon ami*. Forget about your fears for a moment and envision the scene. Yvette and DuPont? He was an older man, yes, but still a man. He was much stronger than her. He wouldn't have been stabbed by a sixteen-year-old girl.'

'It's possible if she caught him unawares. Because, like you, he believed her incapable of it. But her brother... Perhaps it runs in the family?'

Atalanta swallowed hard. Renard had told her about the gun the brother had pulled on a fellow student and the arrow shot at his violin teacher. Was it not logical to assume Yvette had similar impulses to her brother's and had grabbed a knife when she felt threatened?

'He asked her for money to keep his mouth shut about her guilty secret. She knew blackmail never ends and...' Gilbert gasped for air. 'When she met Madame Lanier, who kept talking about Mathilde, she couldn't take it anymore and had to kill her as well.'

Atalanta's brain scrambled to find a defence. But what he said seemed eerily, chillingly plausible.

Raoul pursed his lips. 'I don't believe Yvette did any of that. Are you even certain she played a prank on Mathilde that caused her fall off the horse?'

'Of course I don't know for certain but I've had my suspicions. Yvette was so silent that day. Not at all like her. She seemed afraid. It was only after it was ruled an accident that she became her old self again. But she did have mood swings, moments where it was like... she didn't care whether she hurt others or herself. I attributed this to...'

'A sense of guilt,' Atalanta supplied.

'Yes. I despised myself for thinking this of my own niece, a girl I care for and love, but... I couldn't dismiss the feeling that something was wrong with Mathilde's death. Perhaps only because I couldn't accept she was truly gone. Would never return to me.' He drew breath with a sharp intake. 'Why did DuPont have to rush here from prison? Why couldn't he have gone someplace else to start a new life?'

Raoul went over and leaned down to him. 'You cannot honestly believe Yvette is guilty of murder. See sense, man. This is unfortunate on your wedding day, but there is no need to be dramatic about it and turn yourself in to the police.' He looked at Atalanta again. 'I'm sure Mademoiselle Atalanta and I can figure out what happened. We will prove that Yvette had nothing to do with it. Then you can set your mind at ease.'

Gilbert stared into nothing. 'I have never had an easy moment since Mathilde died and I started to believe Yvette was responsible. I was always afraid for her. Every time she did something unreliable, it seemed like further proof of her instability. Her guilt.' His voice cracked. 'I can't bear to lose her as well.' He pushed his hands against his face.

Atalanta's eyes pricked. This man was only trying to cling to some of the last family he had left. Even though he saw what she was capable of at the worst of times, he loved her for what she was at the best of times. That was so familiar.

'We will find out what happened. To Mathilde, to Marcel DuPont and to Madame Lanier. You stay here and calm down.' Raoul gestured to Atalanta to come into the corridor with him. 'Poor man,' he said. 'He is completely out of his wits.'

'Do you realize you promised him you'd solve three murders?' Atalanta asked him. Her breathing was shallow. She understood the need he felt to help his friend, but he really had no idea how enormous the task was he had taken upon himself. There was so little time before Joubert would be here.

'What do you say?' Raoul pressed. 'Will you help me?'

'Why would you ask me to help you?'

She expected him to say he had earlier already called her sensible and someone sensible was just what he needed for this task. But right now she wasn't herself. Her brain was a muddle and her legs were filled with jelly. The life of a girl might depend on them.

But his answer was completely different and surprised her when he said, 'Because of all the people here, you're the only one who has honestly tried to like and befriend Yvette.'

She bit her lip. She could not tell him she had recognized herself in the orphaned girl. Her parents were supposed to be alive and well, in Switzerland. *Don't forget the part you play.* 'Befriending her didn't work out at all.' Atalanta sighed. Yvette hadn't confided in her and she could give Raoul nothing he needed to prove her innocence. 'Besides, how can I honestly investigate whether she's guilty of anything if I care so much?'

Raoul held her gaze. 'If you care, you must help me to find the truth. We will clear her name and set her free. Or else... find help for her. But we won't abandon her. We won't.'

The passion in his voice touched Atalanta deep inside. She had come here to help Eugénie, she believed, but the case had taken her in another direction. But then, hadn't her grandfather mentioned that? The need to follow where it led you.

Was this it?

Helping Yvette, no matter what?

'We won't abandon her,' she repeated and straightened up. 'Where is Yvette now? We must find her and get her to talk to us before Joubert arrives. I can't judge whether he likes the gentry or not, but he might not be too gentle with a girl he starts to suspect.'

'Good thinking. Come along.'

Raoul led the way to Yvette's room. The girl was not there.

'Would have been too easy,' he muttered. 'Where can she have run off to?'

'The stables? She does love the horses.'

They went to the stables and found Yvette patting a brown horse with a white patch on his nose. She whispered sweet words to him, with a blank expression on her face, as if she was far away with her thoughts.

Atalanta said, 'Did Madame Frontenac hurt your arm?' Nice and easy. It would serve no purpose to pounce right away with questions about Madame Lanier.

'Not that anyone cares.' Yvette spun to her. 'Did you find the veil for the queen of Bellevue? She acts as if she is high above us all. You all do her bidding, simpering like idiots. Especially you. As if you're her lapdog or something.'

Atalanta didn't blink. 'Yvette, we need to know something. It's very important. When you took the veil to the burial chamber, what did you find there?'

'Find there? Nothing. It was the dead of night. It was dark and I hurried.' Yvette shivered a moment.

Atalanta asked, 'You didn't do it while Eugénie was at breakfast?'

'No. I took the veil last night before she went to her room. I kept it with me and then when everyone was fast asleep, I went to the burial chamber.'

'Were the steps slippery?' Raoul asked.

'The steps?' Yvette's forehead furrowed. 'No, they weren't slippery. Why?'

'You put the veil on the tomb's sculpted head and then you went back? You didn't see or hear anyone nearby? Hiding in the chapel?'

'No. I don't think so. I didn't look closely.'

'Was Madame Lanier there? Praying for her daughter?'

'No. I didn't see her. I think she was in bed. What would she be doing in a cold chapel at that hour?'

'So you placed the veil there in the night?' Atalanta wanted to make absolutely certain as time was crucial in this case. 'Not while the guests were at breakfast? Eugénie said—'

'The veil was in a box in her room. I took it when she was downstairs with you around ten last night. Gilbert had just told me Pom-pom had to stay with the servants all day during the wedding. That I had to bring him there as soon as I got out of bed the next morning. I was so angry that I wanted to get even with her. I thought she would look in the box before she went to bed and would make a fuss. I was only going to give the veil back to her if she allowed Pom-pom to be there at the wedding. But nothing happened. She didn't notice.'

Yvette hung her head as if she was recalling her dejection over her plan gone awry. 'Then I had the veil and didn't really know what to do with it. Set it on fire? Cover it in horse poo? It didn't feel very imaginative. I thought about wrapping it around the Minerva statue in the garden after I had used red paint from that ugly red room of hers to draw tears of blood on her face. It would have been fun if Eugénie had seen it hanging there from her window, had run out to collect it, and then got a bad scare with the bloody tears and all.'

'That *is* imaginative,' Raoul said dryly.

Ignoring his comment, Yvette continued. 'I didn't think I could get out at night with the front door locked so I thought about the chapel and the tomb and putting it on Mathilde's likeness. It would be even more shocking. As if she had claimed the veil for herself, not wanting Eugénie to take her place. So I went down and put it there.'

'What time was that?'

'About three? I don't know for certain.'

'Madame Lanier was not there?'

'Why do you keep going on about Madame Lanier?'

'Because she lies dead in the burial chamber.'

Yvette snapped her head round to look at Raoul. 'You are making that up,' she said in a hoarse voice.

'No. I'm not. She is dead and with you having put the veil on the tomb...'

'They think I killed her.' Yvette didn't look stunned or appalled, just incredulous. 'What a joke. Why would I kill a woman who never did me any harm? She even liked me.'

Raoul shot Atalanta a glance. 'Monsieur Joubert will want to question you. Just tell him what you told us and it will be fine.'

'Joubert is a stupid ass. He thinks his uniform makes him special. But I won't answer questions as if I am some suspect. This is my home. He's an intruder.' Yvette stroked the horse again.

'This isn't the time to throw a tantrum,' Raoul warned her. 'It's very serious. If you get accused, Monsieur Joubert could take you along to jail. You know where suspects get locked up in the village?'

Yvette looked at him, still disbelieving, then slowly her expression changed. She ran to him and hugged his neck. 'You wouldn't let that happen to me. You would protect me.'

Over her head Raoul looked at Atalanta. She had never seen him so serious before. Almost sad, too. Did he realize that they might not be able to save her?

Atalanta blinked against the burn behind her eyes.

Raoul put his hand on Yvette's shoulder and said, 'I can't protect you if you don't work with me. Tell Joubert what you told us and it will be fine. Don't add fancy details, or make up stories. And you'd better not tell him at all about Minerva with the bloody tears. Just that you wanted to play a little prank with the veil. A schoolgirl joke. That sort of thing.'

Yvette stood back, her cheeks reddening. 'I'm not a schoolgirl.' She seemed heavily disappointed that Raoul had used this word to refer to her.

Was she a bit enamoured with the handsome race car driver, as Eugénie had suggested?

If she is, I can't blame her.

Yvette wanted to run off, but Raoul grabbed her arm. 'You're staying at the house. I won't let you hurt your own interests by running off. Your uncle is terribly worried about you. You have to start growing up and thinking of others once in a while.'

Yvette opened her mouth to retort, then dropped her gaze, nodded, and let herself be brought back to the house. After they had delivered her to her room, telling her to stay there until she was called for, Raoul said to Atalanta, 'What can we do now?'

Atalanta took a deep breath. 'If Yvette told us the truth, we know that Madame Lanier went to the burial chamber after three and met her death there. She could have slipped and fallen. She could also have been pushed.'

'Yvette said the steps were not slippery.'

'But there was something on the steps when I went down. Yvette might have missed the puddle of water Madame Lanier trod on. She is a girl, agile and fast. She'd walk differently from a woman of Madame Lanier's age.'

'Yes, of course.' Raoul rubbed his forehead.

Outside, hoofbeats could be heard. It was the local doctor carrying his large leather bag. He disappeared into the chapel. Not much later, a car arrived and two men alighted—Joubert and another uniformed policeman.

Raoul and Atalanta watched them go into the chapel as well. Her heart hammered. What would they think?

Clearing her throat, Atalanta asked, 'Do you think Joubert brought someone of higher rank?'

Raoul shrugged. 'Possibly. A small village usually has but one officer of the law, but this could be a local chief of police. Contrary to what Gilbert suggested, they are not averse to the gentry, but eager to please them. As long as the doctor establishes that the injuries are consistent with a fall.'

'After Mathilde's accident a year ago?' Atalanta shook her head. 'The doctor will look closer now than he did then. And even then, he said it was a broken skull and not a broken neck. She could have been hit with something.'

'You think she was deliberately killed?' He stared at her. 'How do you even know what the doctor said at the time?'

Atalanta thought that some kind of admission would help their cooperation and said, 'Eugénie received a letter that claimed Mathilde did not die in an accident. This spiteful accusation cast a shadow on her happy wedding preparations. Therefore, she asked me to come with her and determine what I thought.'

Raoul slapped his fist into the palm of his other hand. 'I knew you weren't what you pretended to be.'

Atalanta flushed. 'I only lied to help Eugénie, to establish if someone had written the note to spoil her big day for her, instead of actually wanting to warn her. I... managed to find out it was Louise. It all seemed solved then.'

'Louise wrote a letter like that?' Raoul whistled. 'I would never have guessed. Yes, she hates Eugénie for marrying before she does, but why incriminate the man she cares for?'

'You think she cares for the comte?'

'I've thought so for quite a while. But she could have snared him herself, I suppose, instead of introducing him to her sister. I don't understand women.'

'Louise wrote the letter. She recounted the exact contents to me, and Eugénie never shared it with anyone but me. That fit. But Marcel DuPont really knew something, else he wouldn't have been killed.'

'Joubert assumes Sargant killed him over the old feud.'

'Yes, but what was the shell from the grotto doing in his pocket?'

Raoul pointed a finger at her. 'You were at the grotto investigating the circumstances of Marcel DuPont's death?'

'I felt I owed it to Eugénie. She took me into her confidence and asked me to help her.'

'Hmm. Did you discover anything?'

'Nothing.' Atalanta felt bad admitting it, but Raoul seemed to brighten. 'There. Nothing to find. No leads for the police. They can't tie it to the grotto, to Yvette, or anyone else here. We need not worry.'

He repeated as he paced, 'We need not worry. We

shouldn't be carried away by emotion. That leads to bad decisions. Racing is like that. Life is like that.'

'I agree that we must first know what the doctor says.' Atalanta made an inviting gesture. 'Shall we see if we can overhear something?'

In the chapel the doctor had disappeared into the burial chamber. One of the policemen was lighting his actions while Joubert stood staring down the steps.

Atalanta and Raoul could approach without being noticed.

The doctor's voice sounded hollow from the depth. 'She has a substantial head wound. She must have hit her head on the floor here when she fell. Perhaps the shock of the fall, the fear, also caused a heart attack. That I can't establish. She has been dead for about… seven hours.'

Raoul checked his watch and whispered to Atalanta, 'Means she died around four in the morning. That would fit with what Yvette said.'

'Any signs of foul play?' Joubert asked. 'Was she pushed?'

'Hard to tell. A fall causes bruising and… Hey! That is remarkable. There's no bruising that I can see. How odd.' The doctor hummed to himself. 'I'd say you would expect to have bruising. Looks like merely the head wound.'

Raoul grabbed Atalanta's arm and exerted pressure. 'This is *not* good,' he whispered.

'Does that mean someone clubbed her,' Joubert asked, 'and then put her at the foot of the steps to make it look like a fall?'

'Possibly.' The doctor seemed to straighten up as his voice became louder. 'I dare say it is odd. Mathilde, the late Comtesse de Surmonne, died of a fall, in which she hurt her head. I always thought it was the consequence of the horse throwing her, but now that I think of it... she might have been hit over the head and then it was made to look like a fall off a horse.'

Joubert swore. 'Are you now telling us that the accidental death of the comtesse last year was murder?'

'I'm not saying anything of the kind. I'm merely observing a possibility. You have to do the sleuthing, not me.'

'But you have to provide us with the information we need. If you had told us last year that someone bashed in her head...'

Atalanta held her breath. Raoul was still clutching her arm as these revelations tumbled over one another, leading them further and further away from an easy outcome.

'With such trauma it is often hard to tell how it came about.' The doctor sounded reproachful. 'I had no reason to doubt that she had fallen off her horse. It was a very wild horse and it was captured on the run. All the circumstances made it look like—'

'Circumstances are not facts.' Joubert swore again, but his colleague said, 'We can't be sure about what happened a year ago. We're not going to look at that again. This one murder is enough. Did the woman die here, you think? Or was she moved?'

'I can't tell for certain,' the doctor said. 'She didn't bleed much.' His voice became louder, and his head appeared out of the vault. He spotted Atalanta and Raoul. 'I dare say we have company.'

The policemen looked angry. 'We're not yet ready to question witnesses. You must stay around the house. Nobody can leave.'

'We'll make sure everyone understands that,' Raoul assured them and led Atalanta away. As soon as they were out of earshot, he said, 'So it was murder. Not a fall down the steps, but murder. I can't see Yvette having done it. And why? Because she didn't like Madame Lanier? If she killed everyone she doesn't like, Eugénie would be dead as a doornail.'

Atalanta shook her head. 'It's not a topic to make fun of.'

'But motive must be most important in a murder case. People must have a reason to take action. They don't bash other people's heads in for fun.'

Her grandfather's advice had told her to go back to the beginning. To the motive that puts everything into motion. The first death: Mathilde's. Why did she have to die?

Raoul frowned. 'We must tell Gilbert that it looks like murder. He must not be caught unawares.'

Atalanta hated to face the comte with this bad news, but nodded her assent. With heavy steps she followed Raoul up the stairs. Her first case was taking a terrible turn. A more experienced detective might have known what to do.

But I have no idea.

They went to the library and found it empty.

'I told him to stay here,' Raoul said with a grim expression. 'Where can he have disappeared to?'

They heard voices and went to the door of the study that stood open. Gilbert sat behind his desk smoking and Victor stood in front of it. 'I'm telling you it was this chap DuPont.' He turned when he heard their footfalls.

Gilbert said, 'Victor is just telling me about the day he and Louise arrived here. DuPont addressed her at the inn where they had coffee.'

'I clearly saw him talking to her. I think she also gave him something. Money perhaps?' Victor shrugged. 'I didn't think about it at all until now. I overheard the police as they came into the house. One of them said to the other that it was remarkable there had been another death on the Bellevue estate. That they hadn't cleared up DuPont's yet as it was an odd thing with the money. There seems to have been the remainder of a bank note left in his clutched hand. Someone paid him money before he died.'

'And now Victor thinks it was Louise,' Gilbert said, rubbing his forehead with a weary gesture. 'But I don't believe it. Why would she feel the need to pay a poacher? And why would she then stab him? It makes no sense at all.'

Victor wanted to protest, but Gilbert waved at him with the cigarette in his hand. Smoke curled to the ceiling. 'Please leave. It's difficult enough as it is.'

Victor said, 'You want to save Yvette, and you can, but only by casting suspicion on another.'

Gilbert stared at his retreating back.

Raoul said, 'Why on earth would Victor point the finger at Louise? I thought he was in love with her.'

Gilbert laughed. 'Victor wanted Eugénie and after she accepted my proposal, he turned to Louise as a second choice. I think she knows it but indulges it to make Eugénie feel bad.' He added after a moment, 'After all, Eugénie still cares for him.'

So the comte knows about that.

'Why would you think that?' Raoul asked. He stood with his arms crossed, staring at the comte. 'She is marrying you.'

'Not after all this.' Gilbert stubbed out his cigarette. 'There will be no wedding. No honeymoon, no happiness. All gone now. Because of some water on the steps.'

'I'm afraid it is more complicated than that.' Raoul explained what the doctor had found. 'He thinks Madame Lanier received a blow to the head.'

'So Yvette will be suspect anyway.' Gilbert paled again. 'She hit Eugénie with the bath brush. That bruise is still visible. It proves she is violent. She lashes out at people without thinking.' He gestured wildly. 'She must run away. Escape arrest.'

Atalanta flinched at this suggestion. 'No. That will only confirm her guilt. There will be a manhunt for her. She could…' She fell silent before putting the worst scenario into words.

Raoul said quickly, 'Atalanta is right. We mustn't lose our heads and—'

'Man, you race cars and you call that sport. You know no

fear. But I do. I would rather die than see anything happen to her.' Gilbert closed his eyes. He looked very old and tired.

'We promised we would help you,' Atalanta said, 'and we will. You and Yvette.' She looked at Raoul. She saw the despair raging inside her mirrored in his eyes. But there had to be something they could do?

Chapter Nineteen

When Atalanta's turn came to be questioned by the police, she was calmer than she had anticipated. She had promised herself she would not lie but would also not be offering information that wasn't asked for. *Say as little as possible.*

Joubert introduced his colleague, who had something of royal bearing, as the local police chief, Monsieur Chauvac.

'You are a cousin of the Frontenac family?' Chauvac asked. He pronounced the distinguished name without the usual awe.

Perhaps he himself came from a wealthy family and looked down on those who had acquired their riches recently, not by inheritance of lands and valuables but by business endeavours.

'Yes, I accompanied Eugénie to play the piano at her wedding. I'm a music teacher.'

'I see. And you've been here with her since her arrival? You met Madame Lanier, the deceased?'

'I did.'

'You were also the one who found the body?'

'I stumbled upon it when I wanted to fetch something from the burial chamber.'

'What was that?'

'The bridal veil.'

'And why was the bridal veil in the burial chamber?'

Atalanta was tempted to make up an old tradition, but she said in a neutral tone, 'Mademoiselle Yvette, the comte's niece, had placed it there. It was a schoolgirl's joke. A prank because she doesn't like Eugénie, while she did like Mathilde, the comte's first wife.'

'I'm asking for facts, mademoiselle, not for your personal opinion.'

'But I know for a fact that she doesn't like Eugénie. She said so herself, in the presence of others. Several times.' Atalanta thought it could not hurt to stress this, as Eugénie was still alive and well. 'Yvette also placed a wet broom in a guest's bed on a prior occasion. She is like that.'

'You went to fetch the veil and then?'

Atalanta described the event as best she could. 'When I heard it was Madame Lanier, I thought she had slipped and fallen down the steps because she had been to the burial chamber before and—'

Chauvac stopped her with a hand gesture. 'I'm not interested in what you thought.'

'But it does matter that she had been there before, visiting the burial chamber.'

'*I* will determine what matters.' The police chief smoothed his neatly trimmed black moustache. 'When the body was discovered, where was the girl, Yvette?'

'Outside the chapel. The others were angry with her because she had put the veil in the chamber.'

'And when she heard about the death, what did she do?'

'She ran off, but she's always running off when she's angry or emotional so it doesn't mean—'

'I will determine what it means. Did you go and see where she was?'

'Yes.'

'And where was she?'

'In the stables.'

'Getting a horse ready to flee.' Joubert looked excitedly at his chief.

Chauvac acted as if he hadn't even heard him and asked Atalanta, 'What did Mademoiselle Yvette say when you found her?'

'I asked her to come back to the house and she did. She was merely patting the horse, not saddling it.' Atalanta threw Joubert a scorching look. He didn't seem impressed.

Chauvac cleared his throat as if to draw her attention back to him and continued questioning. 'While you have been here at the estate, have there been other incidents with Mademoiselle Yvette? Has she shown violent tendencies?'

Atalanta hesitated. 'She is a young girl. In my experience—'

293

'I'm not asking about your experience, or about other girls. I'm asking about this girl, Mademoiselle Yvette, the comte's niece. Did she show violent tendencies?'

'I can't really answer that question.'

'Refuses to answer the question,' the police chief said to the other man. 'They are all trying to shield the girl.'

'I'm not a psychiatrist,' Atalanta protested. 'I can't judge whether—'

'I'm merely asking for what you saw and heard. Others have given their testimony without hesitancy.'

I bet Eugénie has. But then the incongruity struck her. 'If others gave testimony to Yvette's behaviour freely, why then do you say we are all trying to shield the girl?' Had Eugénie been reticent? No, she refused to believe that.

The police chief gestured with a hand. 'I put the questions; you answer them. Has the girl struck anyone in your presence?'

'Yes.' *I'm so sorry, Yvette, but I vowed I wouldn't lie.*

'Has the girl behaved in an inexplicable way in your presence? Trying to cause herself harm?'

Atalanta took a deep breath. Again, she was sorely tempted to lie, or at least evade an honest answer. 'Do you mean the incident at the lake, during the picnic? She was only making a fuss for attention.'

'I'm not asking you to evaluate what happened or speculate about her emotions. I ask if she tried to harm herself. If she was wild and unpredictable.'

'Yes.'

'Thank you. You see, that wasn't so hard.'

Anger bubbled inside her but she bit it down.

The police chief studied his notes. 'Did you arrive on the day Marcel DuPont was found dead?'

'Yes. They removed his dead body as our car passed. We didn't realize at the time he was dead. Our chauffeur remarked about drunken tramps and—'

'When you came to the house, was Mademoiselle Yvette there?'

'Yes, she was. She came out with the servants to greet us.'

'Did you notice anything odd about her? Were her clothes dishevelled? Her shoes muddy? Her mood downcast?'

'No, she seemed to be her usual, obstinate self.'

'I see. And while you were here, have you heard mention of Mademoiselle Yvette having to be entrusted to the care of a psychiatrist?'

'I've heard mention of it, but I'm not sure—'

'Thank you, that is all I need to know.'

Atalanta sat up straight. 'If someone mentions to another that I should be entrusted to a psychiatrist, does that mean I am truly unbalanced, or only that the other person thinks so? It could be said out of spite.'

'You mention the word unbalanced. Interesting.' Chauvac looked her over. 'Did Mademoiselle Yvette quarrel with Madame Lanier, as far as you know?'

'No. I didn't see or hear them quarrel and I doubt that Yvette had anything against—'

He raised a hand. 'I won't repeat what I already said.'

Atalanta sighed and sagged against the back of her chair. 'I understand that you are looking for facts, but what are facts? If neither of us heard them quarrel, does it prove they did not quarrel? If there was a quarrel, does it prove it became lethal later? It proves absolutely nothing and you know it.'

'We're searching the girl's room for evidence. If we find something conclusive…' The police chief made an eloquent hand gesture. 'Now, is there anything else you can tell us? Facts, please, not speculations.'

'I wouldn't know.'

'Thank you. You may go.'

Atalanta rose and at that moment the door was thrown open and another policeman stormed in. Apparently he had arrived at some later time, without Atalanta seeing him.

'Look what we found in the girl's room!' he shouted excitedly. He held up Yvette's painting kit, the one she took into the forest with her whenever she wanted to work on some artistic creation. It was full of paint brushes, tubes of paint, and scraps of paper. But at the bottom was something that caught the light: a small knife. The blade was stained with something like dry rust.

But Atalanta realized with a shudder what it was. Dried blood.

The blood of Marcel DuPont?

The police chief rose to his feet. 'We can take her to the town hall. There we will see how much we can get her to confess, and also about Madame Lanier.'

Atalanta protested, 'Anyone could have placed the knife in her painting kit.'

'Oh, of course. A killer walks about with a knife and then places it in a young girl's painting kit. Would it not have been more logical to throw it away? Sink it in water? Bury it? There are many options when you're outside. Why bring it inside?'

'I wager Yvette's fingerprints are not on it,' Atalanta said firmly. She had to fight their conclusion, cast doubt in their minds any way she could.

'I don't take such wagers,' Chauvac scoffed. 'Get the girl.'

The policeman who had found the kit left the room, followed by Joubert, who seemed eager for some action.

Atalanta said, 'Are you not rushing this? Have you collected all the evidence?'

The police chief looked at her. 'Madame Lanier was a respectable lady without enemies. Who would want to harm her?'

'Give me one good reason why Yvette would want to harm her,' Atalanta countered. She was determined to stand her ground. She owed it to the comte, to Raoul, and to her own conscience.

The police chief sighed. 'The girl was in the burial chamber overnight to put the veil in place. She met Madame Lanier there. They got into an argument or she pushed her in passing. It need not have been intentional.' He twisted the signet ring on his finger. 'But the discovery of the knife... If she killed DuPont, she must also have killed Madame Lanier in cold blood. A wicked girl. Depraved to her core.'

Atalanta's heart sank. So many people had already expressed doubts about Yvette's state of mind. Was she beyond saving already?

In the corridor there was screaming and the sound of things falling over. Atalanta rushed out of the room and saw Yvette kicking at the unknown policeman who held her, while Joubert tried to pull her arms behind her back to handcuff her. Struggling, they bumped into a sideboard and a tall, dark-red vase with dancing men depicted on it teetered dangerously.

Atalanta rushed over to prevent it from falling, but Joubert shouted, 'If you hinder the arrest, we will take you along as well.'

I have to stay free to investigate and help Yvette.

Atalanta froze.

The vase tipped over and crashed to the floor. Slivers shot in all directions.

Gilbert came running down. 'That is a Greek amphora,' he cried, 'with a scene of Bacchus's followers. Do you have any idea what those cost?' He leaned down to study the broken pieces.

Yvette had stopped fighting. She looked at her uncle. 'You don't care that I'm arrested. You always loved your stupid antiques more than you loved me.'

The comte became pale. 'You know that is not true. I would put myself in your place if I could. But...' He reached out to put his hand to her cheek, but she averted her head.

'Why,' he said in an agonized tone, 'did you have to do it? Why destroy yourself and me and everyone who cares about you?'

Yvette glared at him. 'I didn't kill anyone. They're all lying.'

The policemen pulled her away. Chauvac had come from the room and greeted Gilbert. 'I'll let you know what we discover. *Au revoir.*'

Gilbert stood staring as his niece was taken away. He said in a hoarse tone, 'I can't believe this. Why?'

'They found a bloodied knife amongst her painting things,' Atalanta said softly. 'They probably believe it was the knife used to kill Marcel DuPont.'

'That old poacher? Why would Yvette kill him? I can't see her doing it.' He seemed to have forgotten he had himself assumed she might have done it and had wanted to confess in her stead. 'It's all a misunderstanding. I must telephone for a lawyer. The best there is.'

He turned to the phone.

Atalanta muttered that she was sorry and went upstairs. The energy that had burst through her as she had wanted to save the vase made her legs tremble.

Raoul came to meet her. 'What was that commotion?' he asked with a twinkle in his eye. 'Did you get into a brawl with our dear police chief?'

Atalanta shook her head. 'There's no time for humour. Yvette has been arrested.'

'So soon?' Raoul looked surprised rather than shaken. 'Why? What can they have by way of solid evidence?'

Atalanta told him about the discovery.

'The knife must have been placed there.' Raoul gestured with both hands. 'Everyone knew Madame Lanier's body had been found. People were dashing up and down and all around. Anyone could have slipped into Yvette's room and placed the knife in her painting kit.'

Atalanta nodded. 'I told the police chief I don't believe her fingerprints will be on it. But he seems convinced of her guilt already.'

Raoul sighed. 'Normally in the countryside the gentry have a lot of power. They can twist legal battles to their advantage. Judges rule in their favour when there is a land dispute, for instance. And the police like to please them by arresting peasants for poaching with little to no proof. To end this tragic situation, many newly appointed police chiefs vow to do this differently. They want to show they are not afraid to touch the gentry where it hurts. So arresting the niece of the comte is a good way to prove how devoted Chauvac is to this cause.'

So I read him right. He doesn't care for names or reputations. Atalanta pursed her lips. 'I appreciate his dedication to treating each possible suspect the same and not eliminating people beforehand because of their family name or status, but he could be so devoted to his cause, as you call it, that he's interpreting everything to Yvette's disadvantage.'

'And we could be blinded by our affection for her and interpret everything to clear her name.' Raoul held her gaze.

'At least, I can't deny I feel sorry for Yvette. Not because she's arrested for murder. No, long before that, I felt sorry for her because she's so unhappy. She misses her parents; she can't see her brother often. She does adore Gilbert but she can't really show it in a way that... She's a troubled girl. And I'm worried that will harm her position now.'

Atalanta nodded. 'I understand. I heard rumours her brother is also rather difficult?'

Raoul laughed softly. 'You mean that incident where he shot an arrow at someone he didn't like? I agree it was impulsive and rather dangerous but it happened in an instant. It was not premeditated. I have only briefly met the boy but I don't believe he is evil.'

'Still, people can also harm others in an instant. Get carried away by emotion.' Atalanta felt her courage wane. What if Yvette had done rash things? Without thinking? Would she have to pay the highest price for that? Pay with her life?

Raoul touched her arm. He squeezed a moment as if to encourage her. 'We have to talk to Louise about her encounter with Marcel DuPont.'

'Oh yes, what a good idea.' Doing something always brightened Atalanta's mood, gave her energy. 'Where can she be?'

'I think after her chat with the police she went into the gardens. We must try and find her right away.'

Chapter Twenty

They found Louise sitting on the bench beside the bower, a plucked rose in her hand. She was idly removing all the petals, letting them drift to the floor. Raoul said, 'How are you? Over the shock a little?'

Louise raised an eyebrow. 'You speak about a murder as if it was a mouse running through the chapel. I can get over that, but not over a dead body appearing on my sister's wedding day.'

'Madame Lanier was a broken woman.' Raoul shrugged. 'And close to death.'

Atalanta was surprised by the casual tone he took. *Is it a strategy to provoke Louise into a response?*

'Does that make it right when someone pushes her down the steps?' Louise asked with a raised brow.

'I just wonder why bother?' Raoul said, looking intently at her. 'She was going to die anyway. She had heard from her doctors that her lungs were weak.'

Atalanta struggled not to betray surprise. She had learned this from Renard but how did Raoul know? *Is it common knowledge in certain circles? Gossip at parties?*

Louise looked shocked. 'She was dying?'

'Yes, so why bother to kill her then?' Raoul planted his feet apart. 'Was it a mistake, Louise? Something you could have avoided?'

The words fell like the blow of a door snapping shut. Louise blinked. 'I… What are you implying?'

'Or was it an easy way out,' he continued in a level tone, 'after you had already acquired a taste for murder when you killed DuPont?'

'DuPont?' Louise dropped the entire rose and stood up. 'I need not listen when—'

'Not so fast.' Raoul placed himself in front of her. 'You spoke with DuPont hours before he died, on the day you arrived here. He harassed you for money.'

'He didn't. He didn't even mean to speak to me. He wanted Eugénie.'

'Eugénie?' Atalanta echoed.

'Yes,' Louise nodded wildly. 'DuPont came up to me outside an inn where we had coffee. He had a newspaper clipping with a photo of Eugénie. It was taken at some party and it mentioned that this ravishing socialite was about to marry the Comte de Surmonne.'

Her voice was twisted a moment as if she could barely speak of her sister's good fortune. 'He showed me the clipping and said that if I wanted the wedding to continue, I should pay him money. Else he would come and ruin it all with what he knew about Mathilde.'

'He said that to you?' Raoul asked.

'Yes, believing I was Eugénie. I told him I was her sister. He compared my face to the photo and said we looked so alike. I told him I truly was her sister and if he wanted to talk to Eugénie he had to go to Bellevue where she was staying. He said he would. That was the end of it.'

'Really?' Raoul asked cynically.

Atalanta pounced. 'Victor said you gave him something.'

'Victor told that to you?' Louise's voice was laden with loathing. 'Why on earth would he have?'

'Actually,' Raoul said, 'he told the story to Gilbert. We only came into the room and overheard part of it.'

'To Gilbert? Why?' Louise's eyes shot from Raoul to Atalanta and back.

Raoul shrugged. 'You have to work that out for yourself. I don't think he said it just to make conversation.'

'The brute.' Louise swallowed.

Raoul leaned closer to her. 'You gave DuPont money, Louise. And we want to know why.'

'Yes, I did.' She waved an impatient hand. 'He mentioned not having money to travel to Bellevue. This inn was a few kilometres away and he was an older man so I handed him a few francs to get some farmer to take him along. It wasn't much money.'

'Coins?' Raoul asked. 'Or a bank note?'

'Coins for certain.' Louise wrinkled her nose. 'I abhorred that vile little old man with his insinuations. How could he know anything about Mathilde?'

'DuPont was arrested for poaching on the estate on the day Mathilde had her horse-riding accident.' Raoul held her gaze. 'He may have been a witness.'

Louise looked uncomfortable. 'I see.' Her hands wrung together, as if she was crinkling something. 'I see.'

'DuPont's death is highly significant,' Raoul continued. 'You must tell us everything you know about this meeting at the inn.'

'I just did.'

'Was there any detail that might help?' Atalanta encouraged. 'Did you notice anything particular about him?'

'He was dirty and he stank, as if he had been sleeping in a pigsty. His hands were grubby too. He had smudged the newspaper clipping.'

'Did he put it back in his pocket after he had shown it to you?'

'No, he was holding on to it and to the coins like an avaricious beggar.' Louise snorted. 'Who did he think he was, threatening me?'

'You were angry with him. Angry enough to get even and stab him?'

'You think I carry a knife in my purse?' Louise threw Raoul a disgusted look. 'And why are you asking all of these questions? Are you suddenly with the police?'

'Yvette was arrested,' Atalanta said.

306

Louise's expression turned gleeful. 'Really? How appropriate. A few days behind bars might teach the little monster a lesson.'

'I thought Eugénie called her a little monster. Are you suddenly good friends with Eugénie?' Raoul asked.

Louise widened her eyes at him. 'I've always been good friends with Eugénie. And of course when my little sister is maltreated, I support her. Yvette is unwell in her head. I told the police.'

So it was Louise who had been smearing Yvette. Probably not even thinking through properly what she was doing to the girl. 'I wager they were not interested,' Atalanta said.

Raoul stirred and cast her a short questioning look.

Louise turned to her slowly. 'Why wouldn't they be?'

'Because the police chief told me he only handles facts, not suppositions, theories, ideas, or opinions.'

Louise laughed softly. 'He told you that? He told me no such thing. I shared freely what I had heard about Yvette and what I had myself seen of her erratic behaviour and he didn't stop me once.' She tutted. 'You must not have struck the right chord with him, Mademoiselle Atalanta.' She glanced at Raoul. 'Is that all? Because it is getting hot and I want to go indoors.'

'Naturally. I'm sure your little sister is desperate for your company and support.' Raoul's tone was sarcastic and Louise had the decency to at least flinch a little. She walked off quickly.

Raoul said to Atalanta, 'Do you believe her?'

'It sounds plausible enough that DuPont took her for Eugénie. They do look alike. And newspaper photos can be very grainy and vague. He must have believed he had the right woman.'

Raoul nodded. 'And the rest? That she told him to go to Eugénie and that was it? Would Louise, with her love for the Frontenacs' spotless reputation, have taken the chance that this dirty old man would cast a shadow on the happy wedding proceedings? Is it not far more likely that she would have asked him to meet her again later so she could give him more money and, on that occasion, she killed him? If she arranged for a new meeting, she could then have brought a knife.'

'It's possible,' Atalanta admitted. 'But I'm bothered by the shell he carried in his pocket. If he was killed in the shell grotto, how could Louise have moved him all the way to the ditch? Is she strong enough for that? Wouldn't someone have seen her?'

'In the heat of day, between noon and three, there aren't many people out and about, but I do admit that Louise isn't the person to hoist a dead body onto her shoulder. It must have been someone else. Victor perhaps? He did watch the exchange between Louise and the man. He could have gone after him to find out what it was about.'

'Yes.' Atalanta pointed at him. 'You're so right. We must talk to Victor.'

They found him sitting in a chair on the terrace, reading a book. Raoul leaned over to discern the title. 'Jules Verne. How appropriately escapist on such a grim day.'

Victor tilted his head. 'Have you come to criticize my choice of literature?'

'No. I want to know more about the man Louise met at the inn. Exactly what you saw.'

'It was an old, dirty man. She talked to him and gave him something. That is all I know. I already said so. I told Gilbert.'

'We know.' Atalanta gave him a winning smile. 'But you are an artist. You draw little scenes and you bring out all the details. You must remember more than just that he was an old man. You did see what Louise gave him.'

'No. It could have been money. I thought I heard metal clinking. But I'm not sure. There was a car pulling up and the roar of the engine drowned out other sounds.' Victor rested his hands on the open book on his knee. 'What is this about? Does it matter?'

'DuPont is dead,' Raoul said unceremoniously. 'And we want to know who killed him.'

'Louise?' Victor wasn't laughing. 'She was upset when he had talked to her. I asked her if she was fine and she said she was, but she looked distracted.'

'Where did you go after that? You came to the house later.'

'We parted ways. I wanted to visit a friend who lives nearby so I left Louise in the village to do shopping.'

So either of them could have met DuPont and killed him, Atalanta acknowledged. For Victor it would have been easier as he had the car to move around quickly and even take the body to a different spot—if DuPont had been killed in the shell grotto, that was.

'Come, come,' Raoul said. 'I know you, Victor. You're a gentleman. You protect the women in your life. You know the old man had upset Louise. While you were on your way to this friend, or coming back from him, you saw the man by the roadside. You pulled over and talked to him. You wanted to know what he had been harassing Louise about.'

'I didn't see him again,' Victor said. It sounded rushed and insincere. 'You must ask Louise.'

'Why did you tell Gilbert about the incident at the inn?' Atalanta asked. 'Why this morning after the discovery of Madame Lanier's dead body? Why not sooner? Or why mention it at all?'

'I don't know. I felt compelled to do so.' Victor picked up the book again and turned a page. 'If you will excuse me, I'm reading.'

'Yvette has been arrested,' Raoul said, 'and you're reading?'

Victor glared at him. 'She means nothing to me. You go and encourage her childish infatuation with you by playing her hero.'

Raoul's neck reddened. 'She is in deep trouble. Don't you care?'

'I barely know her. I feel no need to do anything to—'

310

'You barely know her,' Raoul said, 'but you do know her brother. Didn't you teach an art class at the school where he's a student?'

Victor stiffened. 'Possibly. I teach a lot of art classes.'

'What did you think of him?'

'I teach so many classes I couldn't possibly recall the pupils. I'm only there for a day or two.'

'Yes, well...' Raoul frowned. 'Perhaps he wasn't even allowed to take your class. He was always in trouble for some prank he'd played. Getting himself suspended too. Perhaps that gave you the idea? To use Yvette to cover for your crime?'

'Now I've had enough.' Victor stood. 'You seem intent on provoking a fight but I'm not responding. I've committed no crime here...'

'Except for luring Eugénie to the shell grotto with a note pretending you wanted to meet her and then throwing mud all over her,' Atalanta said. It was a bluff but she wanted to gauge his response.

Victor glared at her. 'What? I did no such thing. I don't want to meet her away from the others and I certainly don't hate her enough to throw mud over her like that unknown maniac did.'

'But you must have felt the sting of her rejection when a better party came along,' Raoul said.

'These things happen. And I have Louise now.'

'Louise is in love with Gilbert,' Raoul pointed out as if it was a common fact.

Victor's eyes flashed. 'Not for long.' He shut his book and stalked inside.

'What does he mean by that?' Atalanta asked. 'Is he on some kind of campaign to show Louise that Gilbert is not worth her time?'

'Gilbert is forbidden anyway as he's marrying Louise's sister,' Raoul said. 'I don't see...' He fell silent and stared into the distance. 'Can that be it? Did Victor kill DuPont hoping to incriminate Gilbert? Get him locked up and convicted? If he caught wind of DuPont's claims that he knew more about Mathilde's death...'

'It's possible,' Atalanta said, 'but the knife used wasn't found amongst Gilbert's things. It was put in Yvette's painting kit. Why would Victor incriminate Yvette? He might not particularly like her but he has no reason to hate her either.'

'I agree.' Raoul sighed. 'We're going around in circles, getting nowhere.'

On the one hand, it was good to know he wasn't achieving miracle results where she had struggled so far, but on the other hand they needed a breakthrough to help Yvette.

Fortunately, I have a source I can tap into. Renard had told her, via Mademoiselle Griselle, that she wasn't alone. Perhaps it was time to really let that sink in?

She need not do everything alone; now she had friends to turn to for help.

'Yes, well, I'm going to take a stroll to the village,'

Atalanta said to Raoul. 'Walking always gives me good ideas. I'll talk to you later.'

She walked off, hoping he wouldn't follow her. She wanted to call Renard from a phone in the village and see if he had any useful information for her.

Chapter Twenty-One

R enard was audibly relieved to talk to her. 'I was hoping you would contact me. I'm very curious how things are coming along.'

Atalanta felt a lump in her throat now that she had to admit her failure to solve the case. 'I feel like I have so many strands that I'm quite at a loss to see how they all come together.' She told him what had happened that morning.

Renard said, 'I'm sorry to hear you found the body. That must have been a gruesome experience.'

'I feel sorry for Madame Lanier. Even though I know she was already dying. Do you know who inherits her money? It could be important. I mean, when Mathilde died, her dowry reverted to her family. Is it possible that now that her mother has died, money is coming back to Gilbert?'

'I doubt it, but I can look into it.'

'Yes, and I would also like to know the precise

arrangements for Yvette. What she owns, what happens to it if she dies.'

'Dies?' Renard echoed. 'You think she may be the next victim?'

'I was rather thinking of her being convicted of murder and being given a death sentence.' Atalanta sighed. 'Does her brother benefit from that?'

Victor had denied having met him, knowing him, or even recalling him. But what if the two of them had met and discussed things and the brother had asked Victor…

It seemed so complicated but people did a lot when the reward was right. And Victor had no money. He was snubbed by Eugénie. *Perhaps he thinks he'll never have a chance for a good marriage and happiness unless he has access to funds?*

'Have you heard anything that may help?' she asked Renard.

'Yes, I was just thinking about the best way to contact you, as I knew today was the wedding and calling the house might not be… appropriate.' Renard sounded very proper. 'I learned something about Angélique Broneur.'

Atalanta had to admit she had almost forgotten about the beautiful singer. 'Yes?' she encouraged him.

'She's in financial trouble. She had to sell her house on the outskirts of Paris and the two horses she kept there.'

'Horses?'

'Yes, she's an expert horsewoman and liked to ride every day when she was at her house.'

'She told me she wasn't very good.'

'But she is. She was even training one of the horses as a show jumper.'

'So she's not afraid to jump over dead trees either?' Atalanta said slowly, thinking of Angélique's assertion that on the day of Mathilde's fatal accident she had returned to the house, leaving her friend to a wild ride of which she wanted no part. *Why not, if she's an experienced jumper?*

Renard said, 'She seems to have accrued debts because she had to cancel a concert tour she was going to do. Trouble with her voice. Some say it is because she drinks too much.'

'I see.' Atalanta imagined Angélique, unsettled by her financial troubles, drinking from her private bar. Going to the chapel on a whim to see the tomb of her dead friend, drawn there by a sense of guilt because she had been involved in her death.

Perhaps Madame Lanier appeared and said something to that point, never having believed that Angélique had not been with her daughter, or a comparable remark suggesting she knew it all. Atalanta pictured Angélique striking at her or pushing her so she staggered backwards and hit her head against the stone wall.

It was a possibility they couldn't discount. 'Thank you for telling me. This could be very important. Oh, one more thing. Do you happen to know where Angélique was before she came to Bellevue? Did she have obligations in a city like Nice or Monte Carlo, taking her far away from here?' *And making it impossible that she had killed DuPont.*

'No, she isn't taking engagements at all. I heard that she

was to visit a friend in Saint Piage, close to Bellevue, before she came to you.'

So she had been in the vicinity.

Still, why would she have known about DuPont? Or DuPont about her?

Atalanta was suddenly struck by a very interesting idea. She told Renard, 'I must dash. I'll call again soon to get the information I asked you for.'

'Be careful, Mademoiselle Atalanta. There might still be a killer on the loose.'

Atalanta put down the receiver, so full of her new idea she barely considered the words. She had to talk to Louise again.

Louise wasn't pleased to see her. She sat at the piano, running her fingers idly across the keys, producing a hesitant tune. 'Not again,' she muttered as Atalanta closed in.

'I want to know one more thing. This newspaper clipping DuPont showed you.' Atalanta spoke softly so no one could overhear. 'Was Eugénie alone in the picture or was there someone with her?'

'I think...' Louise frowned hard. 'Yes, now I remember. It was Angélique beside her. The article mentioned the pretty socialite and the talented singer invited to perform at her wedding feast.' It sounded as if she liked Angélique as little as her sister.

Atalanta said, 'And did DuPont also mention her to you?'

'No. He took me for Eugénie.' Louise thought a moment. 'I told him Eugénie was at Bellevue and he asked if the other woman was as well. I said she was at Saint Piage.'

'You knew Angélique was there?'

'Yes, she told all of us before she left Paris.' Louise shrugged. 'Does it matter?'

Atalanta's mind whirled. Had DuPont found out where in Saint Piage Angélique was staying? Had he approached her? Had she killed him to prevent him from telling Gilbert the truth about what had happened that fateful day?

Louise looked up at her. 'Why are you so interested in clearing Yvette's name? First you wanted to help my sister find out about the mysterious letter and now... You are apparently eager to get in someone's good graces. You don't care who it is. Eugénie, Gilbert. As long as they might be grateful and reward you.'

'I have means of my own.'

'Oh, really? A career in music is not exactly a stable existence, as Angélique can tell you. Her voice is going and her career is over. Good thing there is no wedding and no performance at the feast tonight. Everyone would have heard how horrible she sounds these days.' Louise stood up and shut the piano with a bang.

Atalanta thought hard. Had Angélique killed Madame Lanier to prevent the wedding from taking place? And her secret of her deteriorating voice getting out?

But why had she accepted the invitation to perform?

319

Could she not have faked an illness? A cold, a sore throat, anything not to have to sing?

Would she kill someone to avoid a performance that could have been avoided by far simpler means? It seemed unlikely. But the confrontation with Madame Lanier in the burial chamber while Angélique had been half-drunk and full of remorse was plausible.

Atalanta chewed her lip. The trouble was that she had so many possible scenarios she wasn't sure which way to turn, which clues to follow, which leads to dismiss. How to close the net around the killer.

What had her grandfather written in his letter to her? *Always go back to the beginning.* It had sounded like obvious advice. But she saw now that it was easy to get completely distracted by all the information that had been compiled. That she had been so eager to dart in every new direction she had been offered, that she had forgotten where she had begun.

What had been the starting point? The first stone to fall and set all the others in motion?

Mathilde's death. Her so-called accidental death.

If she assumed, having seen its recent repercussions, that it had not been accidental, she had to ask herself the all-important question: why did Mathilde have to die?

She went to her room and extracted a new sheet of paper. On it she wrote the names of all the people involved.

Gilbert, Comte de Surmonne, husband.
Yvette, his niece.

320

Angélique Broneur, a family friend and alluring woman.

Louise Frontenac, a friend of Mathilde's who had matched her to the comte.

Eugénie, her sister, the comte's current fiancée and second wife-to-be.

Victor, a family friend.

Raoul, a family friend.

Of the latter two she wasn't certain they had been in the vicinity when the accident had happened. She would focus on the names higher up the list and discern their motives.

It seemed obvious that if a woman had killed Mathilde, she had wanted to have the comte to herself. Eugénie. Louise. Angélique. But had any of them taken trouble to secure him? Eugénie had been matched to the comte by her sister. Louise hadn't tried to become the new comtesse. Angélique... she seemed happy with her career.

Had the accident been caused by her reckless behaviour and had she been afraid to admit it? Had DuPont known that? Had he approached her at her friend's house in Saint Piage? Had he called her and had she come over to Bellevue? Had he shown her where he had stood, what he had seen? Had she then killed him and hoped it would look like a brawl gone wrong?

No, Atalanta was getting ahead of herself. Mathilde's death was her focal point now, not DuPont's. At the time of Mathilde's accident he had still been very much alive. And a witness.

Of that she was certain. If he had claimed to know something *after* his release from prison, she might have concluded he had thought up a story to get money. But he had asked for the comte to come and see him right after his arrest on the day of the accident.

Why the comte?

Because he wanted a reward for his information? Or because Gilbert himself was involved?

Had DuPont wanted to tell him he knew he was guilty? He could have done so without risk as he was imprisoned and Gilbert could not have harmed him in there.

Still, it seemed very risky that a poacher would dare address a comte in such a manner.

Gilbert... Atalanta's pen hovered over his name. The question was: if he had indeed had a hand in his wife's death, either by contriving her fall or by actually hitting her over the head and making it look like the horse had thrown her, why would he have done so? He had nothing to gain from her death financially. Her dowry went back to her family.

Had he discovered she was unfaithful? Had he been jealous and angry?

Or did it have to do with her actions around his house? Wanting to change things that had been the same for generations? Her plans for the garden. The word 'Croesus'.

The X at the shell grotto.

Those were leads left to her by the dead woman herself. Her voice speaking from beyond the grave, as it were. Atalanta thought her grandfather would surely have attached special meaning to it. But she herself was not sure it meant anything at all. Anything other than a plan for a garden such as women made when they had moved from the city to the countryside and wanted to put their stamp on their new home.

Did the shell grotto hold a treasure? Had Mathilde found it and had her husband killed her to keep it a secret?

Madame Lanier had also mentioned the word treasure. She'd said that Mathilde had written to her that she knew her husband's real treasure. On the surface it seemed those words could refer to herself, her being his beloved treasure. But what if they referred to something far more substantial? Was it possible Gilbert had killed Madame Lanier to prevent her from speaking to anyone about this treasure?

But he had been so devastated by the death and so upset it might be blamed on Yvette. Even if she suspected he could be ruthless enough to kill someone, would he really go so far as to have blame fall on his beloved niece? The one he tried to protect against all odds? He hadn't cared for other people's opinions, for their suggestions he should rid himself of the difficult girl.

So how could she ever make that fit?

No, she had to move on to the others.

Atalanta worked on her list of motives for a long time. It was hard because she had never known Mathilde and couldn't assess whether she had been a woman who inspired strong feelings in others. Had women hated her enough to hurt her?

Yvette had certainly not hated her. On the contrary, the

two of them had been the best of friends, roaming the land together and treasure hunting.

Had Mathilde involved Yvette in the search for what she believed was hidden in the gardens or the shell grotto? Or had it been a harmless game, to keep Yvette occupied?

Croesus. That seemed to be important. Wealth, money, possessions. Gilbert had a beautiful home here, full of art he brought back with him from his travels. Choice pieces, each one more desirable than the other. The best he kept to himself in his own room, where no one was allowed to go. The maid had said she wasn't even supposed to dust there.

Could he have some treasure there? A very special piece? But why would he not share it while other objects were on full display? What could be so extraordinary about it that it warranted total secrecy? Could it be so important he had killed for it?

No, that seemed unlikely. Somehow she felt she was closing in on some truth, but wasn't sure if she was seeing the full picture. His travels, his discoveries, sales made…

She tilted her head. She had the idea she was missing some vital pieces. Perhaps Renard's additional information about Madame Lanier's inheritance and the arrangements for Yvette could provide those?

Chapter Twenty-Two

I t was very quiet at dinner without Yvette to laugh too loud or make an inappropriate remark. Everyone was consumed with their own thoughts. Gilbert barely touched his food and sat staring at the table, while the others did eat but while trying to make as little noise as possible.

'It's like a tomb in here,' Angélique said at last. The high colour in her cheeks suggested she had drunk a cocktail or two before coming down to dinner.

'That's a very unfortunate term to use,' Raoul reproached her without real severity.

'Well, we need not really let our heads hang over the death of a woman who was past her prime.'

Gilbert looked up. 'I wish you wouldn't speak like that about my late mother-in-law.'

Before Angélique could protest, he added, 'And speaking for myself, I'm not so much concerned with the death of a woman who was perhaps close to the grave already but about the future of a girl who should still have her whole life ahead of her.'

'With Yvette's propensity for drama,' Eugénie said, 'it was only a matter of time until she did something to get herself into trouble.' She glanced at Gilbert. 'It couldn't have been prevented.'

'It might have if you had been nicer to her,' he snapped. 'Because you tried to destroy the photographs of Mathilde, you hurt her feelings so much she wanted to get even by taking your veil and putting it—' His voice cracked.

'I wasn't about to destroy photographs of Mathilde. I only wanted to damage the wretched album because she had hurt me first. It was mere retaliation.'

Madame Frontenac tutted. 'You're not sixteen anymore, Eugénie. You should have risen above it.'

Eugénie made a face at her mother and focused on her plate again.

Louise said, 'What did the lawyer you consulted say, Gilbert?'

Atalanta was surprised she wanted to know. Was she uncertain whether Yvette could be detained? Was she worried that if the girl got released, the investigation would focus on other possible suspects?

'He's coming over to see Yvette. He said...' Gilbert waited a moment, fiddling with his napkin. 'That a plea of temporary insanity might save her. It would of course mean she'd have to be treated.'

'Placed in an asylum, you mean,' Eugénie said with barely hidden enjoyment.

Her mother threw her a warning look. 'How dreadful.' She leaned over to Gilbert. 'Are you contemplating it?'

'I don't see I have much choice. I'll certainly not let her die for a crime she didn't commit wilfully.'

'Or she didn't commit at all,' Raoul supplied.

Gilbert didn't seem to hear him. 'I will not let her die,' he repeated slowly, 'so the treatment is the best possible solution. I do understand it will taint our reputation to have it said we have a… patient in the family, but…'

'Better than a convicted murderer,' Victor observed drily.

Gilbert shot him a scorching look. 'I don't want to hear your comments, or you can leave. In fact…' He looked around the table. 'Why don't you all leave? There is no wedding anymore.'

'But certainly you will still marry Eugénie?' Madame Frontenac said. 'If the police agree to release Yvette into the care of a specialized doctor who can see that she is well treated at some secure place where she can't do anyone harm, the wedding can go ahead as planned. I know you have nothing to do with the poor girl's delusions so I'm still happy to have my daughter wed you.'

Eugénie seemed to want to say something—perhaps express doubts, Atalanta wondered—but her mother gestured at her with a hand not to do it. She smiled at Gilbert. 'You are a decent man. How you handled this whole atrocious affair makes me admire you all the more.'

'I have no wish to marry after all of this,' Gilbert said. 'Eugénie might be totally innocent of the… escalation, but to my mind she played a part in aggravating Yvette's condition. It may be unreasonable but after what I've been through, I'm in no mood to listen to reason. I want everyone gone.'

Raoul said, 'But the police will want us to stay until they are certain they have the case solved.'

'We're not staying for some investigation,' Madame Frontenac corrected, 'but because we are here for a wedding. You *will* marry my daughter.' There was a steely ring to her voice.

Gilbert got up and threw his napkin on the table. 'I don't want to hear another word about it.' He left the room.

'Dreadful behaviour,' Madame Frontenac said.

Victor soothed, 'The man is just not in a mood to plan another date for the wedding.'

'Hah, I don't know why you should say so, or why you should be so understanding. You never liked Yvette. No wonder after what her brother did to you,' Louise sneered.

'Her brother?' Atalanta pounced, and Raoul said, 'So you did teach an art class at his school?'

'Yes, he told me that Yvette's brother ruined the class by drawing something extremely unsuitable,' Louise said to them.

Victor turned crimson. 'I should never have told you!'

Madame Frontenac said, 'What was it he drew, Louise?'

Louise said, with a glance at Eugénie, 'I had better not expound, Maman, but it was very shocking.'

'I don't see how or why Victor would blame Yvette for a joke her brother made,' Raoul said.

'If you say so.' Louise sipped her wine.

Raoul said to Madame Frontenac, 'I'm surprised you still want the marriage to take place. Yvette is unbalanced and so is her brother, judging by reports I heard about his actions at school. What if it runs in the family? Do you feel confident letting your daughter marry such a man and bear him an heir?'

'My thoughts exactly,' Eugénie said.

Madame Frontenac hastened to say, 'The comte's brother married a woman below his station. I'm sure the instability comes from her side of the family. She was an *actress*.'

She managed to put a whole world of disdain into the word.

Atalanta said, 'If Eugénie feels uncomfortable about the marriage taking place, she should be allowed to break the engagement.'

Madame Frontenac turned crimson. 'And do you expect any other man to touch her then? I think not. She will have to marry him now. There is no other way.' She rose and quit the room.

Eugénie burst into tears. 'I don't want to marry a man who has murderous relatives.'

'We don't even know if Yvette is guilty,' Raoul said. Eugénie wailed, 'I don't care. The idea of it is enough. And to think Yvette will be committed to an asylum... The glances people will shoot me... I can't live with it. I can't.'

'We can elope,' Victor said. 'I still love you.'

'Victor!' Eugénie and Louise cried at the same time;

Eugénie with disbelieving joy, her sister with incredulous anger.

'Do you mean that?' Eugénie asked.

'He doesn't have a franc to his name,' Louise spat. 'He cannot keep you in a way you are used to.'

'We can travel and he can draw. It would be so adventurous.'

For once Atalanta felt some sympathy for Eugénie even if her plan was ill-thought-out and probably disastrous for both of them. Adventure was a major draw.

'Why don't we run away now?' Eugénie said. She looked at Victor with adoring eyes. 'I'll pack my things quickly.'

'You'd have to return that,' Louise said, pointing at the ostentatious ring on her finger.Eugénie pulled it off and threw it on the table. It rolled and landed against a wine pitcher. 'There, have it if you want it. You always wanted Gilbert for yourself. Now have him and bear his mad children!' Eugénie ran from the room.

Raoul said to Victor, 'You can't mean this.'

Victor gave him a slow, wolfish smile. 'Why not? Eugénie always adored me. I will take her places until she tires of it or I tire of her. She can always come back to her parents. Madame Frontenac may seem stern now but she'll never turn away the apple of her eye.'

Louise looked appalled but her lack of protest confirmed to Atalanta that indeed Eugénie was her mother's favourite, and that she got away with anything.

'I'll tell Maman now.' Louise jumped to her feet. 'She'll stop her. Prevent this disaster.'

Victor said, 'Don't, Louise, hey? Don't be such a spoilsport.' He raced after her.

Raoul stood to collect the ring from the table. Angélique said, 'You can't put it into your pocket.'

Raoul snorted. 'I'm not a thief.' He took the ring to the window and studied it, holding it up to the light. 'I'm not an expert on stones either, but I doubt this stone is real.'

Atalanta recalled the cook at the Frontenacs' Parisian home telling her so. Or at least suggesting it.

'Is it a fake?' Angélique said, 'Gilbert always struck me as rather cheap. He puts his precious money into art sooner than presents for his fiancée. You wonder why he even wanted to remarry. He never seems to care for anything but his precious discoveries.' She emptied her wine glass and held it out to Raoul. 'Be a darling and fill this for me.'

'You've had enough to drink, *darling*,' Raoul said with mocking emphasis. 'You had better go and lie down.'

'I'll do no such thing. I want to be part of the drama that's about to unfold. Do you hear that?' Angélique raised a hand. Upstairs, doors were banging. 'Madame Frontenac will not let her daughter leave with this undesirable. And Gilbert might feel a need to defend his honour by drawing his duelling pistol. I wager that within'—she checked her elegant wristwatch—'ten minutes, blood will flow.'

'Enough blood has flown already,' Raoul said tightly. 'Keep this for me, will you?' With those words he tossed the ring to Atalanta, who caught it with both hands.

He winked at her. 'Excuse me while I go and prevent another murder.' And he quit the room.

Left with Angélique, Atalanta saw her chance. 'Did you meet up with Marcel DuPont?' she asked.

Angélique closed her eyes languidly. 'Who?'

'Marcel DuPont, the poacher who witnessed Mathilde's accident. He contacted you when you were with a friend in Saint Piage.'

Angélique's eyes flew open. The easy confidence in her features died.

Atalanta added, 'I already know you did, so you might as well tell me what happened next.'

'Nothing. He called me on the phone. He said he had information about Mathilde's death. He asked me what it was worth to me. I said absolutely nothing. I never went to meet him.'

The words came out quickly, almost like they had been rehearsed, and Atalanta wasn't convinced. 'You did *not* meet him? You weren't in the least bit curious what he knew?'

'No. Mathilde was dead and gone. What was there left to say about it?' Angélique pulled out a cigarette, put it in her holder and lit it. 'Why are you spying on me?'

'I'm not spying. I want to help Yvette. She didn't kill Marcel DuPont. The knife was put in her painting kit.'

'And you think it was me?' Angélique watched Atalanta through a haze of smoke. 'You think I put it there to make her look guilty.'

'I think you are clever enough for it.'

'Clever enough certainly.' Angélique's tone was light, as if they were again chatting over cocktails, but her eyes were cold and assessing. 'I have nothing to hide. I didn't kill DuPont. Or Madame Lanier, if that was your next question.'

'Or Mathilde?' Atalanta asked.

Angélique's eyes widened a fraction. 'Mathilde? She died falling off her horse. It was an accident.'

'So everyone has been saying. But the doctor said the injury could have been sustained from a blow to the head. Did you argue with her? Did you strike her down and then make it look like she was thrown by her horse?'

'No. We never argued. We only had fun. We were best friends.' Angélique manipulated the cigarette between her fingers. 'I had no reason to wish her harm.'

'You were in love with Gilbert.'

Angélique laughed. 'We can't all be in love with Gilbert. I leave the pining to poor Louise. And you, Mademoiselle Atalanta, do you find the comte attractive as well? Oh, no, you're in love with Raoul. More interesting because he is aloof. Because he does dangerous things.'

Atalanta felt an annoying flush come up. 'I don't—' she spluttered.

Angélique stopped her with a hand gesture. 'I don't blame you. I wish you well. Have him for the time being. He'll never stay with you, but he can be good company while it lasts. I know.'

Atalanta's heart sank at the idea of Raoul casually caring for her and then leaving her. But such a scenario only existed in Angélique's mind. She and Raoul had joined forces to help Yvette. Nothing more. She said, 'You're very cleverly trying to distract me from the topic of our conversation.'

'*Your* conversation. You started it and you may end it speaking to the china on the table. I'm off.' Angélique rose and moved to the door, surprisingly steady on her feet.

Atalanta said, 'We're not all fooled by your don't-care attitude. You do care. About Gilbert and about losing your voice. About having to sell your horses, especially the showjumper you were so enthusiastic about.'

Angélique paled. 'You do know all of my secrets.'

'I'm only trying to help.'

'Help? Then go away and leave us be. You have nothing left to do here. There will be no wedding, no performance.'

Upstairs, something crashed to the floor. *Or someone?*

Atalanta stared at the ceiling, her heart racing. Raoul thought he could prevent a murder but what if he got caught between the eager lover and the irate groom?

'Told you so.' Angélique checked her watch. 'Blood within ten minutes.'

Chapter Twenty-Three

Atalanta ran upstairs and found Victor on the floor in the corridor rubbing his jaw. Gilbert stood over him, saying, 'You're not running away with her. You have no means to keep her. You'll only ruin a decent girl. She'll never have another chance to marry well. I may not want her anymore, but I won't let you do that.'

Raoul stood beside them and said to Atalanta, 'Victor did deserve that one blow.'

Atalanta shook her head at him. 'Where is Eugénie?'

'Locked in her room by me.' Madame Frontenac marched over to them. She spat at Victor, 'If you try to run away with her, I will have you tracked down by the police and charged with abduction.'

'Your daughter is of age and can make her own decisions. She is no longer a minor needing a chaperone.'

'But we still control all of her money,' Madame Frontenac said, 'and she knows it. I am sorry to destroy the

335

pretty image you have of her, dear boy, but Eugénie cares more about her dresses, hats, and earrings than she will ever care for you.'

She walked to her own room and closed the door softly.

Victor sat dazed and Raoul burst out laughing. 'She's got you there, dear boy.' The repetition of Madame Frontenac's mocking endearment made Victor's ears turn red.

Gilbert seemed to come to his senses. He stood upright, rubbing his hand. 'I need a drink...' he muttered and walked off.

Raoul watched him worriedly. 'I'd better keep him company.'

Victor scrambled to his feet. 'I think it's best if I leave before I cause more trouble.' He looked down the corridor and saw Louise coming. 'Oh, no.' He ran in the opposite direction.

'You can't leave,' Louise shrieked. 'You could be a murderer. The police want to talk to you. I'll tell them about Yvette's brother. You hated him, and her, too. You put the knife in her painting kit. They have to take your fingerprints. Hey!'

Atalanta stopped her by placing herself in her path. 'Please, Louise. You are by far the most sensible and intelligent person in this house. Don't let yourself be dragged into this chaos of emotions. Be dignified.'

Louise seemed to want to protest, but then she took a deep breath and said, 'You're of course right. I'm the most sensible and intelligent. I always have been. I'm not prone to hysteria. I shouldn't let this useless con-artist fool me. I never loved Victor. I just pretended because it made Eugénie angry.'

'Do you love Gilbert?' Atalanta asked softly.

Louise looked her straight in the eye. 'I did, once. But I soon realized what he was like. He doesn't care for people. Only for things.' She turned and walked off with her head held high.

Atalanta nodded to herself. Yes. Several people had said it now, phrasing it differently, but it came down to much the same thing. Gilbert, Comte de Surmonne, cared for art, money, and possessions, above all else. That defined him as a human being.

Still, all these jealous women were wrong about one thing. Perhaps he wouldn't fall in love, but he did value family, blood ties. He loved Yvette. He wanted to protect her. He had done everything for her. He had—

'Mademoiselle! Telephone.' A maid came up to her.

Atalanta descended quickly. 'Yes?'

'Renard here. I made haste looking into what you wanted. I have connections who owe me favours and they were very helpful indeed.' Renard sounded self-satisfied. 'Madame Lanier's fortune will go to relatives, not a franc to the comte. And Yvette's money, entrusted to her when her mother died, is only in the comte's care until she turns eighteen. If she dies sooner, he will lose control of it as it will revert to her brother.'

So it had never been in the comte's interest to harm Yvette. It still wasn't. She was sixteen. He still had control of her money for two more years. He wouldn't want her convicted, tried, hanged.

He would...

Atalanta clenched the receiver. She looked about her and spoke softly so as not to be overheard, 'What would happen if Yvette was considered unfit to control her own money?' Her heart beat faster.

'Then the comte would continue to manage it. Her brother has money of his own and their mother wanted Yvette to have something for herself.'

'*Merci*. That's very interesting.' Atalanta stared at the gorgeous view of Paris overhead. Turning on her heel she counted the art objects in the hallway alone. So much he kept and never wanted to part with.

Never... sold for profit.

Money.

The root of all evil. Is it the answer here?

A solution began to unroll in front of her just like the mist rising slowly from the land in early morning, turning vague shapes into distinct outlines. Yes, she saw it now. It all fitted. All the little things that hadn't made sense.

But how to prove it?

Renard spoke in the distance. She said, 'Pardon, what are you saying?'

'Your grandfather had one motto, mademoiselle. If you are hunting a fox, you must have a fox's cunning. If you are hunting a wolf, you must have a wolf's strength. If you are hunting a killer, you must be as ruthless as he is. And determined to complete what you started. At all costs.'

He added, after a moment's silence. 'This is your first case. You must mix determination with caution. You're not dealing with a thief or an impostor but with someone who hasn't hesitated to resort to violence. Several times.'

'I know.' Atalanta said it with a heaviness inside but at the same time with conviction that for that exact reason she had to stop this killer. Such a man couldn't be allowed to stay free. She had to risk everything, even her life, to solve this case. She owed that to the girl who had asked her once why she'd even care.

Because the most terrible thing in life isn't having problems or having to fight to survive. It's the assumption that no one sees you, that no one cares.

Perhaps once she herself had felt that way. But not today. She said to Renard, 'Don't worry about me. I have a secret ally. I'm not alone.'

Chapter Twenty-Four

R aoul had said it was an insane plan and it would never work. But Atalanta had insisted that it was the only way. 'Will you help me or not?'

Raoul had agreed with a sigh and instructed the stable boy, who was asked inside to help. After all, they didn't want to do any real damage.

Atalanta's heart was hammering in her chest. It was so dangerous and yet also exhilarating.

Then the smoke began to curl through the corridor. She banged on doors and cried, 'Fire! The house is on fire!'

People shrieked and soon doors were opened and half-dressed figures raced downstairs. Atalanta hid in a niche and watched the bedroom door of the comte. He appeared in a satin dressing gown and made straight... not for the stairs, but for his study. The room where his most precious things were kept.

Where no one was allowed to enter.

Atalanta followed him softly. He went inside. She waited. The smoke was thinning already. Raoul had taken no risks and asked the stable boy to douse the straw again.

Inside was the metal clinking she had expected.

She pushed the door open. The comte stood on a table against the wall. He had removed an oil painting that hung there and had opened a safe behind it. He was stuffing handfuls of paper into a large leather bag.

'I'm sure Yvette will be pleased you're saving her inheritance from fire,' Atalanta said drily.

The comte dropped the bag. Papers drifted out and scattered across the floor. They were bearer bonds.

'Or should I say, what's left of it?' Atalanta held his gaze. 'You've spent a considerable part of it on art. Art you crave, art you claim to sell to galleries, but often you want it so much that you keep it. And you need more money to buy new pieces. Yvette won't know until she is eighteen. That is still two years off. And… if she were found to be unstable and not capable of handling money, you would remain in charge. She need never know you have spent it.'

The comte watched her with flashing eyes.

'You made a mistake though,' Atalanta continued. 'You married. Your wife, Mathilde, had big plans for this house. She wanted to make changes to the furnishings and the gardens. That would cost money, money you weren't willing to spend on her. She also asked questions about sales you made—or rather didn't make. She was too close to you. You should never have taken her into your home. So one day when Angélique came back early from a ride, and you realized your wife was alone on a dangerous path, you went there. You scared the horse and she fell off. The horse ran and you hit her on the head. She died there, but you hadn't gone unobserved. Marcel DuPont saw you and then he was arrested for poaching on your land. He wanted to meet you, and tell you what he thought he knew. You didn't go; you were distracted, or didn't know it was about Mathilde's death. But when DuPont was freed, he became a problem.

'He came to Bellevue looking for Eugénie; she hadn't yet arrived. You lured him to you, promising him money, and as he was counting it, you killed him and took the money from his hand, but a small snippet stayed in his palm. You also looked through his pockets and found the article about your and Eugénie's wedding. Perhaps you contemplated letting it sit there as it might point at her or Angélique but you didn't dare risk it and removed it. Instead, you put a shell in his pocket to suggest the killing had to do with the grotto, with the rumours of treasure. You knew Mathilde was looking for a treasure in the garden, at the grotto because she wanted to know where her Croesus, her rich husband, got his source of income. She should never discover it was Yvette's inheritance, which is why you killed her. But her interest in the grotto now served your purposes. Let the police look there; there would be nothing to find. I also fell for the idea and spent time at the grotto, pushing and shoving shells to find a lever and open a secret compartment. Only later did I understand that your treasure was here, in your study, where no one was allowed to enter. You even kept Mathilde away by smoking here, the thing she hated so much.'

The comte didn't speak. Only his eyes were alive in his marble features.

Atalanta continued. 'You kept the knife you had used to stab DuPont. Perhaps you were worried about disposing of it or you already had the plan to use it later. To put it on someone and have them take the blame. There would be enough people around for the wedding. Madame Lanier appeared and she mentioned that Mathilde had written to her about where your true treasure was. You were worried Mathilde had spilled to her that you didn't sell much and yet always had funds to buy more art. Perhaps the lady had had time to ponder this and understand what it meant? Why else would she come here for your wedding to a new bride? You were worried and you had seen her come from the burial chamber when you showed me the chapel. You guessed, rightly, that she would return there and you hit her over the head, believing it would look like she had fallen down the steps. But Yvette told me that when she placed the veil in the tomb there had been no slippery patches, no water. You sprinkled it there, from the vases holding the ornamental roses, to complete the illusion of an unfortunate fall. Too bad for you the doctor wasn't convinced and the police started to make a fuss. But then you had already pointed attention where you wanted it. By acting stricken at the idea Yvette had done it, you made us all suspect her. You pretended not to want us to think so but you planted the idea in our heads. It was perfect. All the people who were a threat out of the way and Yvette deemed unstable, committed, would put her money safe in your hands.'

'This is an amusing tale,' the comte said, 'but it will not work. You can never prove these bearer bonds were part of Yvette's inheritance.'

'No, but I can ask for a look inside the safe at the bank that is supposed to hold them and they won't be there. You are the only one with access. As someone told me, the bank can't check on the contents of deposit boxes and vaults, and nobody knows what is actually in there.'

He laughed softly. 'So clever. I assume you also cried fire when there was none. A trap. I should congratulate you, Mademoiselle Frontenac. Or is it not Frontenac? Who are you really?'

Atalanta said, 'My name is Atalanta Ashford and your fiancée hired me to find out if you had killed your first wife.'

The comte blinked. 'Eugénie thought I had killed Mathilde? Why on earth?'

'Because of a letter Louise sent her to hurt her and make her unhappy ahead of the wedding. Louise never meant to incriminate you, just ruin her sister's happiness.'

The comte shook his head. 'So petty.'

'It was an act driven by desire. Her desire for your love or your desire for art, what is the difference?'

'Art is grander than all other matters. It exceeds feelings; it exceeds life.'

'And therefore you may kill for it?'

'I assure you that poor woman Lanier was already

dying. And DuPont was a measly man without a purpose in life. He merely stole and drank too much.'

The way he arrogantly dismissed other people's lives as worthless made her blood boil. 'And Yvette? A lively young girl of sixteen with her life ahead of her committed to an insane asylum. What is your excuse for that?'

He froze a moment. 'It need never have come to that. I would have found a masterpiece and sold it and given her the money she was entitled to. I would have.'

'You may have told yourself this lie, but you know you never would have been able to part with a true masterpiece, had you found one.'

The comte began to collect the bonds from the floor and put them in the bag. He said, 'We are all alone here, Mademoiselle Ashford. The others fled the house in fear of the alleged fire. I'm not about to let myself be intimidated by a mere woman. A hired hand.' He closed the bag and then jumped on the table again to close the safe and put the painting back in front of it.

His assured actions overtook Atalanta and she didn't know what to do next. She had been so proud of herself as she laid it all out for him and he had not denied it.

He said, 'In this bag is a fortune in bearer bonds. You can have a share of it if you agree to keep your mouth shut about this fantastic tale you have spun. How about that?'

Really? He believed she'd accept money in exchange for her silence? 'I won't let Yvette suffer for your greed.'

'That is unfortunate.' He pushed the table back into place as it had moved a little under his weight. Then, in a fast movement, he yanked open the drawer and produced a pistol.

Who had mentioned a duelling pistol? I should have remembered. A fatal error.

The comte pointed it straight at her. 'I was here collecting a few art objects to save from the fire when you came in. You wanted to steal from me. I shot you. I had to. I will place some objects in your room to prove you had been stealing all the while you stayed here, posing as a guest. The police will believe it. They will never think Eugénie hired you. She'll not say so either. She'll be ashamed to have thought this of me. Especially now that Yvette is in custody for the crimes. She hates Yvette and can't wait to see her convicted.'

Atalanta had to admit this might be true. Her heart rate sped up and all of her muscles tensed. She had no idea how good a shot the count was. Could she throw herself to the floor? Roll away and then—

The comte said, 'It was my pleasure to have made your acquaintance, Mademoiselle Atalanta. You were a worthy opponent.'

Despite her precarious position, a warm feeling seeped through Atalanta's chest. She had cracked the case and her grandfather would have been proud of her.

'I wouldn't pull that trigger if I were you,' a voice said.

Atalanta had been expecting him and still she was startled. The comte stood rooted to the floor, staring at Raoul, who had appeared in the doorway. He pointed a pistol at the count.

No! He hadn't told Atalanta he had a weapon with him.

What if an exchange of shots left both of them injured or dead?

Raoul said, 'Stealing to pay for the art you want is one thing, Gilbert, but letting an innocent young girl get locked up with mental patients so you can go on stealing from her is beyond belief. I would like to shoot you on the spot. Or perhaps just hit you in a place where it hurts.'

'Raoul, please,' Atalanta said. His anger reverberated around the room and in her own chest where she was so mad at this callous, greedy comte. But Raoul mustn't take an irrevocable step. 'Don't shoot, Raoul. You will yourself be arrested.'

The comte used the moment that both of them were distracted to dive away. With the bag clutched in his hand, he managed to roll across the floor behind his desk, ending up on his feet again near the window. He threw it open and climbed out of it onto the balcony.

'Come back here!' Raoul lowered his pistol and ran to the window. Atalanta was there a heartbeat ahead of him. They both looked out. The count was climbing agilely from one balcony to the next. 'There is one with latticework against it,' Raoul cried. 'He thinks he can climb down that way.'

They ran from the room, along the corridor, down the stairs, and out of the front door. The other inhabitants were standing closely together, watching the house as if they waited for flames to burst out of the windows or roof. When they saw Atalanta and Raoul rush out and run around the house, they stared with mouths agape.

At the back Raoul pointed. 'The wretched fellow is already on the lawn. He sprints like a greyhound.'

'He is running for his life,' Atalanta said drily.

Raoul and Atalanta ran after Gilbert across narrow paths, ducking under hanging tendrils, rounding statues, and jumping across box hedges.

The comte knew his garden well and turned it into an obstacle course for his pursuers.

Atalanta called to Raoul, 'Left here. A shortcut.'

He heeded her advice at once and they sprinted down the lane. 'There he is,' Atalanta pointed. Raoul dived. He managed to swing his hand with the pistol against the comte's knee. The man yelped in pain and dropped the leather bag. He grabbed for it, but Atalanta had the other edge of it and she pulled. 'Give it up, Gilbert. It's over.'

'I can reward you handsomely if you let me go.'

'Money means nothing to me,' Atalanta said, 'but justice does.' She pulled the bag away.

The comte stood empty-handed, keeping his weight off his injured knee. He made no further attempt to flee.

Raoul pointed the gun at him and said, 'Atalanta, you tie his hands behind his back. Use the belt of his dressing gown.'

'I can think of that myself,' Atalanta said. She approached the comte with caution but he seemed to have given up. She took his belt and tied his hands. As she assured herself that the knots were tight enough, she asked,

'Tell me one thing, count. Was it worth it? Three murders, sentencing a young girl to a terrible future.'

'It was never the plan.' The comte sounded dejected. He lifted his head and looked at his house in the distance. That gorgeous white house Eugénie had once called sheer perfection. It seemed to dawn on him that he would no longer live there, would no longer enjoy his walks and rides amongst the lavender; that this was the last time he would look upon its silent glory and stand here as Gilbert, Comte de Surmonne; that he was soon to be a case in the newspapers, a sensation for journalists to write about.

No longer a human being, but a spectacle.

A convict and, after trial, a dead man.

'It was never the plan,' he repeated. 'But once you get started, you have to go on. There's no way back.'

Raoul put the pistol in his waistband and took the comte by the arm. 'We're going to the house and I'll call the police.' He said to Atalanta, 'We must also tell our befuddled guests there was never a real fire.'

'Eugénie will be so mad she has to stand in the chill without reason,' Atalanta said. Nervous tension released itself in the need to laugh out loud at the whole situation. 'And Madame Frontenac will never believe that her coveted future son-in-law is a murderer.'

'I don't even believe it myself. But you made a compelling case... Mademoiselle Frontenac?' The question mark was more playful than serious as he had probably overheard her words to the comte in which she had revealed her real identity.

Still, Raoul halted and reached out his free hand to her. 'Raoul Lemont.'

Atalanta shook it. 'Atalanta Ashford.'

It felt glorious to claim her real name, which was also her grandfather's name. The man who had spotted her talent for sleuthing and put her on this new course in life.

Chapter Twenty-Five

The police had come with a very sceptical police chief Chauvac in the lead, but after he had checked the bag carried by the comte and heard Raoul's corroboration of what Atalanta revealed, he began to take the matter more seriously. He called Paris to have lawyers look into the exact situation of the inheritance of Yvette Montagne, he ordered the Parisian police to go to the bank and demand a look in the safe where her bearer bonds were supposed to be, and he asked for more details of art transactions to see if the comte had indeed made sales explaining his fortune.

He wanted to interview all the guests about what had transpired after Yvette had been taken into custody, and no one was pleased that they had to stay up and answer questions, except for Louise, who told the police chief what Yvette's brother had done to Victor out of pure spite.

Atalanta and Raoul, their testimonies given, sat in the

library with sherries Raoul had poured for them from the captured comte's liquor cabinet. 'I wonder,' he said, looking around at the books, 'who all of this will belong to now that he's going to be hanged. He has no children and his parents are both deceased. His brother is no longer alive either and...'

'I think it will be Yvette and her brother inheriting,' Atalanta said. 'I would think it a sort of poetic justice if the art objects bought with her inheritance will now be hers.'

'I doubt Yvette will appreciate the irony. In her way she cared for Gilbert and she will be very upset to learn what he did to her.'

'But she'll also be relieved Mathilde's death was not somehow her fault. That little dog of hers is always running around and she may have thought he scared the horse.'

Raoul nodded. 'Poor girl. Never had much of a home anywhere. Now what will she do, with this sensational trial hanging over her.'

'She must travel,' Atalanta said with conviction. 'Travel makes everything better. Other places to see, things to do, people to meet. She needs a sensible companion to watch over her and it will be fine. At least, it will be better than it has been.'

Raoul lifted his glass. 'I'll drink to that.' He studied her. 'Atalanta Ashford. You are not by any chance related to Clarence Ashford?'

'He was my grandfather.'

'I should have known right away. He once solved a little matter at a race where I was competing. A very clever and tactful man. But did you say *was*? Has he passed away?'

'Yes. I inherited this assignment. Eugénie wanted my grandfather, really, but she got me.'

Raoul looked her over. 'How interesting. Are you really a concert pianist?'

'I taught music and French at a Swiss boarding school, but I don't have to anymore.'

He understood the implications but asked no questions, because it would have been rude, she assumed.

'So what will you do next?'

'I have no idea. See some magnificent cities, I suppose.' She wished he would invite her to Rome or Tuscany, to show her the country which was half his heritage so she could discover its beauty through his eyes, but she wasn't about to push herself into his company.

'Moscow perhaps?' Raoul asked. His eyes twinkled. 'You already know the language, judging by that cipher.'

'*You* were in my room searching my things?' Atalanta stared at him. In the commotion of the past hours she had forgotten all about that. 'Why did you lock me out on the balcony?'

'I only wanted to ensure you didn't catch me in the act. I had meant to unlock the doors again before I left, but your notes befuddled me and I heard Angélique's voice in the corridor as the maid took her to her room, next to yours. I wanted to talk to her so I left in a rush. Only later did I realize I hadn't unlocked the doors. I guess an apology is in order?'

Atalanta didn't know whether to be angry that he had actually dared search her belongings, or to laugh at his bold admission. And he hadn't been able to crack her cipher. She was proud of herself.

There was a knock on the door and Eugénie entered. She said, 'Oh, I'm sorry but... could I speak to you a moment?'

Atalanta stepped out with her. Eugénie said, 'You handled the case for me and although it turned out very differently from what I had expected, I'm grateful for what you found. I now don't have to marry this... monster. Even Maman sees that. I cannot, however, pay you any money for it as Maman has taken away my money and jewels so I can't elope with Victor.'

'I don't need money. I have plenty of my own.' Atalanta smiled. 'I'm glad you feel my services were satisfactory.'

'I want to forget about this whole unfortunate affair. I'm going to ask Maman to take me to Vienna or someplace where we won't hear of it. And Françoise and Louise can't come. They have to find their own diversion.' She walked off without saying goodbye. Atalanta could already picture Eugénie and her mother in Vienna bickering about what to see and do and who to meet or avoid.

She re-entered the library and found Raoul standing at one of the bookcases, leafing through a big volume. 'Medieval murder,' he read from the spine. 'A history of the most sensational murder cases. Do you think our comte got his inspiration here?'

'I doubt it. It was simply a matter of an opportunity

offering itself ready-made. Mathilde wanted to ride a horse she couldn't handle. He had thrown her before, so it would not look suspicious. The comte even waited until a guest was staying here to complete his plan. The best possible cover, and a distraction, should any suspicion arise.'

'Still, I don't understand,' Raoul said, 'why Angélique didn't accompany her. She's a good horsewoman.'

'That is exactly why. She takes risks, but she is not willing to risk injuring the horse. Especially when the horse is not hers.'

Raoul nodded. 'That makes sense.' He smiled at her and picked up his glass again. 'To the future, Mademoiselle Ashford. A future in which you can travel as much as you like.'

And in which I will help people to the best of my abilities, Atalanta added to herself.

After all, she had now discovered those abilities to be even better than she had ever hoped. She could follow in the footsteps of her grandfather and get to know him more and more through the passion for puzzles they shared.

A passion for protecting the innocent and bringing the guilty to justice.

An exhilarating game where thinking ahead was as important as trusting her gut feeling to lead her in the right direction.

Raoul stood close to her as he touched his glass to hers. He stared into her eyes. 'Never have I heard a woman talk about murder with such passion, Mademoiselle Ashford.'

Had he really said that?

Or had she imagined it? An echo of her fantasies of old?

She need not fantasize any longer as her life now promised to be full of mystery and adventure.

She couldn't wait to see what lay ahead.

Acknowledgments

As always, I'm grateful to all agents, editors and authors who share online about the writing and publishing process. Special thanks to my fabulous editor Charlotte Ledger, who immediately understood where I wanted to go with this series and whose excellent feedback helped me bring Miss Ashford even more vividly to life. Thanks as well to the entire One More Chapter team for their work on the series and to Lucy Bennett and Gary Redford for the wonderful cover illustration which captures the series feel brilliantly.

The first seed for this series was planted years ago on a vacation in Switzerland where on a walk I passed a sign explaining the beautiful building behind it had once housed an international boarding school. As my writer's brain is always working, wherever I am, I thought it would be wonderful to someday do something with an international boarding school setting, against the glorious Swiss mountains. And when Miss Atalanta Ashford first presented herself to me, she was working at an international boarding school, and her adventure unfolded from there.

Bellevue is a fictional estate, but its beautiful elements are based in real life, for instance the shell grotto with its mythological patterns which could be found at many manor houses and even royal palaces. If you ever have a chance to see one for yourself, do it: it's worth it!

**Don't miss Miss Ashford's next adventure
taking her to glorious Greece
in the gripping**

LAST SEEN IN SANTORINI

**Coming in ebook January 2023 and available to
pre-order now!**

Read on for an exclusive peek at the first chapter…

Chapter One

August 1930

Miss Atalanta Ashford couldn't quite believe she was
casting her eye across the *laguna* of Venice. The water
moved in countless shades of blue and green and the sun
made everything sparkle: the bright colours of the boats
that took tourists across to Murano, the famous glass island;
the spires of Venice's many churches in the distance and
closer to her, the lemons in twined baskets on the dock
waiting to be transported.

There was an air of expectancy, with everyone bustling to do some task, make the best use of this beautiful day. New arrivals discussed where to go first: to a workshop or the museum. A man with a hat askew on his rich dark curls carried a large canvas that he wanted to place in the best possible spot to paint the sights. And local women offered flowers and freshly baked sweet treats. From where she stood, Atalanta could smell the butter and sugar worked into them. It seemed as if she was the only one standing still, not pushing to the nearby café to occupy the table with the best *laguna* view, or going to explore Murano's famous glassware created by true artists with the blowpipe. She was like a statue in the midst of a crowd rushing to and fro, caught in the moment, unable to move away from a sense of disbelief that this could actually be her life now.

It was so hard to grasp that only a few weeks ago her daily routine had consisted of giving lessons to pupils at an exclusive Swiss boarding school. A strict schedule of teaching French and music, having meals and correcting essays and tests, with barely half an hour to herself to take a little walk down into the picturesque village with its wooden houses and decorated balconies, or further up the mountain to the ruins of the old burg overlooking the lush valley where the river wound its way between the snow-capped mountains.

It had been her favourite leisure-time activity: to walk and fantasize that she was elsewhere, in some remote, possibly exotic destination, seeing the wonders of the world. She knew the sights only from books and postcards her students sent her during summer holidays. But they had come alive in her imagination: the Parthenon rising above her in white marble columns or the sleepy sunlit villages of the Italian countryside amongst vineyards and olive groves. She had pretended to hear other languages and bitten into her simple bread-and-cheese sandwich lunch as if it were calzone. But with all the mental power in the world, she had never been able to guess that her dreams were about to come true, far beyond what she had imagined.

All because of her dear grandfather.

His death had left her with a fortune, houses in various places, cars and stocks, more money than she could ever spend. And a rare vocation: to follow in his footsteps and do his life's work: sleuth discreetly for the upper ten. Her very first case had taken her to a lush estate in the glorious lavender fields of Provence where a company of rich and famous people had gathered for the wedding of the Comte de Surmonne. The sights had been breath-taking – the whitewashed house with sleek turrets, the rich gardens full of roses, dahlias and an amazing shell grotto – but she had not been able to fully enjoy them with the strain of unravelling clues and facing a cunning killer who stopped at nothing to keep their secret safe. So after a successful conclusion of the case, she had decided it was time for a little holiday. Some days spent far away from crime and the complicated thought process that came with assessing if perfectly normal-looking people might be cold-blooded murderers.

With her unlimited funds Atalanta could go wherever her heart desired, and she had retrieved her box of cut-out magazine articles and postcards that students had sent her. Her box of places she had wanted to go to, long before she had come into money. The box of her hopes and dreams that had carried her through the most difficult times after her father had died and she had been all alone in the world, with a load of debts on her shoulders. Now that everything was so much better, that box was still like an old friend and opening it made her heart flutter.

She had closed her eyes and rummaged through it and pulled out a postcard. She had waited a few moments, fingering the card, and then opened her eyes to see where she was travelling to for her holiday.

Venice.

The mere name on the card, printed in a dark yellow almost like gold, had taken her breath away. It had to be a magical city with canals instead of streets, with countless elegant bridges across the ever-present water, with so much romantic history attached. A city of gondolas, delicious food, a language that sounded like poetry and memories to be made.

She had asked her butler Renard to book passage and a hotel. Of course he had managed to get her a room in one of the most illustrious hotels which had received famous writers and artists from all over the world. Their photographs hung on the walls of the high lobby with its stuccoed ceiling full of lions, the iconic animal ever present in the floating city.

The very efficient and resourceful Renard was a treasure with global contacts that came in very useful when she was investigating. But the trip to Venice would be about pleasure only, about spending time in a beautiful place, far away from intrigue and murder.

Ah yes. With a sigh of satisfaction Atalanta turned her back on the dazzling *laguna* view and started to walk, slowly, savouring every step, every sight around her. She inhaled the scents of a hot summer day deep into her lungs: citrus fruit, sun-drenched cobbles, flowery perfumes …

Her gaze brushed past ladies in colourful dresses and large sunhats, one with a small white lapdog on her arm that barked ferociously at everyone in sight. The buildings had fronts full of white stone arches and pillars. At first glance they were all alike but when one looked closer, there were details on all of them: some round like beads, others carved like flowers.

On the corner of a tall apricot-coloured house a man stood in a light suit. A panama hat was pulled into his eyes, hiding his face. But for a moment when she caught sight of him, her breathing stopped and she involuntarily started forward.

Raoul!

Raoul Lemont, the race-car driver she had met on Bellevue in Provence, during her first case. He had been a guest at the wedding of Eugénie Frontenac and the Comte de Surmonne, the grand feast where Atalanta had discreetly conducted her investigation into the question whether the Comte had murdered his first wife, Mathilde. Raoul had

365

been an old friend of Mathilde and at one point even a suspect, to her mind. But she had realized later she had never wanted him to be a suspect because ...

Stop it.

She shook her head with an impatient movement. That man wasn't Raoul. He only bore a superficial likeness to him. She had to stop thinking about him. He was far away from here, preparing for some race.

As a driver of fast sports cars in those daring races that had gained popularity all across Europe, he risked his life on a daily basis, something Atalanta couldn't understand or condone. In general, Raoul was impulsive, irreverent, opinionated and proud. Character traits that made him her polar opposite. Atalanta liked to look before she leaped and assess a matter from several sides before coming to a conclusion. Raoul had even blamed her for being too rational and not allowing herself to feel. But feelings were deceptive and led one astray. It was much better to look at the world with a clear analytical mind and judge facts without allowing emotion to overshadow everything.

She smiled at her own inner dialogue with Raoul, as if he was indeed here by her side, and she needed to defend herself, and her opinions, against him. But he was leading his life full of adventure and risk, and she was on Murano enjoying a well-earned holiday.

And if she didn't want to think of murder, she shouldn't think of Raoul as well, as he had been so closely tied to her case and its dangerous resolution. She had to fully focus on the enchanting views and living the dream of actually walking here, instead of merely imagining it and having to return to her duties at the school. She did miss her students, their eagerness when they learned French by listening to *chansons*, their sulks when there was a test forthcoming. Moments where they confided in her and she felt more like an older sister to them than a teacher. But the strict director had made sure she could never get close to any of them. For the better, perhaps, but it had been a lonely life.

"Buy flowers?" An old woman touched her arm and held out a large twined basket holding several single roses in bright colours: red, pink, yellow. Their stems had been wrapped with cloth and a pin was attached so the flower could be worn like a brooch.

Atalanta's gaze travelled the flowers, admiring the silky smoothness of the petals. They had been grown with loving care. But she shook her head at the woman and walked on. It felt odd buying a rose for herself. It was something adoring fiancés or husbands should do. There were plenty of couples around among the tourists, and many more coming later today. The old woman wouldn't have trouble finding takers for her floral offer.

I'm here for glass. Atalanta halted at a table bending under the weight of vases, vessels and jugs. The sun conjured rainbows in the facets and made the pieces look even more magnificent than they were because of the craftsmanship put into them, skills handed down the generations for as long as Murano had existed. She wanted to buy something, but she had to think carefully about what to get. She'd have to take it home with her and it shouldn't get broken on the journey.

Perhaps a large solid piece is better than those smaller delicate champagne glasses?

But the four-piece set did look lovely, and she could see herself drinking from such a glass at home and remembering this beautiful sun-soaked day and tasting the unlimited freedom her grandfather's inheritance had brought her.

She took several items into her hands, turned them over, ran her finger round the perfectly smooth rim. The seller behind the table tried to explain how good it was in broken English, falling back on Italian every third word. Atalanta tried to follow along as best she could. The exclusive school where she had worked had often housed Italian girls from elite families and she knew a fair bit of the language. But it was special to hear it now on soil where it had been spoken for many centuries. At times she had to pinch herself to make sure she wasn't dreaming.

She said she'd be back later and wanted to look around more first. He kept shouting how good his wares were after her while she walked to the next table and the next seller eager to impress upon her that *he* sold the best wares of the entire island.

The tourists that had been on the boat with her had filed out and were standing at various stalls or ducking through low doors into the buildings to see more inside. It had to be deliciously cool in there, away from the summer sun that burned down mercilessly on everything around. Atalanta felt sweat drip across her neck and slip down under her light dress. On the boat she had already put her white lace gloves in her purse. They might be elegant and a lady should aspire to dress her best on any occasion, but under the Mediterranean sun they were a burden sooner. Perhaps she should have sat down for a cool drink? There was no rush to buy anything right away. She could take the entire day to explore, returning to Venice on the last boat.

Again she caught a glimpse of the man in the light suit with the panama hat. He seemed to be alone. Perhaps that wasn't odd, as she herself was here without a companion. But most people had come either as couples or with friends, and his lone figure drew her attention. He wasn't haggling to get a good deal on glass or admiring the architecture. It felt almost as if …

He was watching her?

A cold shiver crept across her spine. Her grandfather had made it clear when he had explained his work to her in a letter written before his death that it was not without risks. That, in the pursuit of justice, one might also make enemies.

And Renard had told her on several occasions to be wary of everyone, not to take things at face value, not to trust even the stories of her own clients. Perhaps all this mention of having to be careful and expect dangers lurking had made her a touch overcautious?

Even paranoid?

She was on holiday here, there was really nothing to fear.

Still, a sense of unease accompanied her as she continued her search for the perfect glass souvenir, and she caught herself looking over her shoulder at various occasions. The man in the light suit was nowhere to be seen. Happy voices rang out around her, laughter and the tinkle of glass exchanging hands. One couple had bought a man-sized mirror and watched as the seller put it in a crate filled with straw for safe transportation. Three boys balanced on the stone railing of a bridge, singing an aria from *The Merchant of Venice* at tourists in a gondola which approached the bridge. The gondolier shouted abuse at them and warnings that they might fall and land on his boat. Some of the tourists laughed at the antics but a lady in a pink dress ducked and covered her head as if to ward off a boy avalanche.

The three suddenly jumped down the railing and fled when a man in a dark suit pursued them for a few yards, then leaned into the wall of a blue house, gasping for breath and pulling out his handkerchief to wipe the sweat off his brow. A disgruntled father? A private teacher landed with the task of guarding these unruly charges on an outing?

Atalanta smiled to herself. Those were the kind of innocent deductions she had to focus on. Why ruin a beautiful day with worries about her safety?

She fell into a conversation with an English lady who explained to her that she had visited Murano every summer when her husband had still been alive, and this was her first time here without him. "It's like he's still here," she confided. "I can hear his voice and I can see him walk beside me. My children were afraid the trip here would make me sad, but it only makes me happy. We've spent so many wonderful years. I cherish those."

"That is good for you." Atalanta adjusted her sun hat. From the corner of her eye she caught sight of a woman in black with a veil over her face. Her dark clothes stood out among the colourfully dressed tourists and Atalanta wondered if she was a local widow. But her dress looked too expensive and the veil was attached to an elegant little hat that could have come straight from a Parisian boutique. Who was she, what was she doing here?

Questions you will most likely never get an answer to, she chided herself.

"There's a special place here," the English woman by her side explained, "a little courtyard down that street. You can freely enter it, no one will stop you. You can walk over to a waist-high white fence and you have a lovely view of the water with Venice in the distance. My husband and I used to stand there for quite some time and admire it. There's always something new to see. It's a perfect day for it too, sunny and bright. We have also been here when it rained and it's not quite so cheery then." She touched Atalanta's arm a moment. "Enjoy your stay here, my dear."

Atalanta thanked her and walked down the street. The voices of the people died down behind her back. It was much quieter here, without the bustle of sellers. Scents drifting from open windows suggested lunches were being prepared with fresh herbs and garlic. *Lots of garlic.*

Atalanta drew a relieved breath, realizing she wasn't

really a person who enjoyed crowds. Suddenly, in the silence, she could hear herself think again.

She laughed softly and entered the courtyard the English lady had directed her to. It had uneven greyish cobbles that led to a white wooden fence on the other side.

An olive tree threw meagre shade, and from a wire cage against the wall small songbirds chirped at her, flying nervously from one perch to another. She leaned her hands on the fence. The wood had become warm in the sun and the cracked paint felt comfortingly real under her fingertips. Sometimes this new wealthy life was like an elaborate dream, carrying her from one day of wonder into the next, but always with the realization it had to end somehow. She wasn't truly rich, she wasn't really able to do anything she wanted. She would wake up in her small room at the school and then the stern housekeeper would be pounding on her door to tell her she was late for class.

A shadow fell over her. She noticed it in the last instant, caught in her thoughts and turned sharply, her hand up to push away whoever was so close to her.

She gasped, staring up into the deep brown eyes of the man she had thought about half an hour ago. "Raoul," she whispered, her eyes taking in the frown over his eyes, the lines around his mouth, the tightness in his lips. "I thought I saw you earlier, but ... surely you wouldn't be here? What ...?" She barely had breath to continue. Perhaps it was the fact that they had conquered evil together that made her heart race and her mouth go dry.

He said, "You shouldn't wander away from the crowd, Miss Ashford. It may not be safe."

That he called her Miss Ashford cleared her mind. She flushed at her own mistake, using his first name as if they were that familiar. They may have stopped a murderer together, but they had never become actual friends.

At least, she didn't think so.

Her doubts as to what their relationship amounted to annoyed her. She prided herself on her ability to work out difficult problems, but she couldn't qualify what it was that connected this infuriating man and herself. She forced a smile, gesturing around her. "I think it's perfectly safe here. I'm on holiday."

"I know." He kept looking at her, his eyes searching her expression as if he was trying to find something there. Had she changed that much? She had her hair done before she had left for Venice, thinking she needed to have a little polish for the grand hotel's revered rooms, but she had kept makeup to a minimum this morning, and while her dress was fashionable enough, her shoes were chosen to allow for comfortable wandering rather than elegance. He still had to recognize the rather unconventional woman he had met at Bellevue.

His insistence in studying her face had to do with something else.

Suddenly it clicked into place. Him being here, seeking her out away from others. "Has something happened?" she asked. "Do you need my help?" She knew with a breath-taking intensity that she would do anything, travel anywhere, if Raoul asked her to. Perhaps he had a sister who was in trouble? She knew so little of his personal life. Only that he had a French father and a Spanish mother. Nothing about siblings, personal ties. There were so many blanks she wanted to fill in, to get to understand him better.

Raoul smiled, that slow smile she knew so well. The smile he used to keep people at a distance, because it was a little haughty and always made her feel like he was enjoying himself at her expense. Had she drawn a wrong conclusion? Or jumped at a bait he had consciously laid out for her?

"I don't need your help," he said in a low voice, "but you might need mine. You're being watched."

Don't forget to order your copy of *Last Seen in Santorini* to find out what happens next...

YOUR NUMBER ONE STOP

ONE MORE CHAPTER

FOR PAGETURNING BOOKS

One More Chapter is an
award-winning global
division of HarperCollins.

Sign up to our newsletter to get our
latest eBook deals and stay up to date
with our weekly Book Club!
<u>Subscribe here.</u>

Meet the team at
<u>www.onemorechapter.com</u>

Follow us!

 <u>@OneMoreChapter_</u>
 <u>@OneMoreChapter</u>
 <u>@onemorechapterhc</u>

Do you write unputdownable fiction?
We love to hear from new voices.
Find out how to submit your novel at
<u>www.onemorechapter.com/submissions</u>

CPSIA information can be obtained
at www.ICGtesting.com
Printed in the USA
BVHW031655120623
665830BV00023B/1035